She of Strangeness

J. Sheldon Jones

This book is a work of fiction. All names, places and events are fictional and are products of the author's imagination, No part of this book may be reproduced without permission from the publisher except by a reviewer who may quote brief passages in a review.

Published in the United States by FutureEcho Press
Colorado Springs, Colorado

Copyright © 2024 by J. Sheldon Jones

Library of Congress Control Number: 2024902229

J. Sheldon Jones

DEDICATION

To my wife, Eileen, and some friends from Socrates Café who encouraged me to keep writing.

She of Strangeness

1 CHAPTER 1	1
2 CHAPTER 2	12
3 CHAPTER 3	20
4 CHAPTER 4	26
5 CHAPTER 5	33
6 CHAPTER 6	39
7 CHAPTER 7	49
8 CHAPTER 8	58
9 CHAPTER 9	76
10 CHAPTER 10	80
11 CHAPTER 11	84
12 CHAPTER 12	91
13 CHAPTER 13	95
14 CHAPTER 14	103
15 CHAPTER 15	106
16 CHAPTER 16	119
17 CHAPTER 17	125
18 CHAPTER 18	137
19 CHAPTER 19	143
20 CHAPTER 20	146
21 CHAPTER 21	159
22 CHAPTER 22	161
23 CHAPTER 23	164
24 CHAPTER 24	172
25 CHAPTER 25	180
26 CHAPTER 26	192

27 CHAPTER 27	197
28 CHAPTER 28	203
29 CHAPTER 29	210
30 CHAPTER 30	219

1 CHAPTER 1

The tiny Scout ship popped out of hyperspace, and Karel felt a thrill of excitement. This time would be different, this time they would find a world that was home to Intelligent Life.

"This is gonna be the one, Mik, I can feel it."

"I remember that feeling," her partner didn't try to hide his amusement, "it goes away after six or eight disappointments." This was the thirteenth star system Mik had visited.

"I'm immune to wet blankets, you old sourpuss. This is the one."

"It would be nice if you're right," he said, "but it'll take the ship an hour to scan the space around this star, spot all the objects large enough to be worth investigating, identify the best candidates, and ask if we want to approach the planet with the highest probability of being able to support life."

"Which we do." She couldn't imagine not doing it.

"We do," he agreed, "therefore, you will respond in the positive. Then we'll have several hours travel ahead of us. Meanwhile, I'm going to take a nap. When I wake up, I'm going to beat you at cards."

"In your dreams." He usually won, but she was getting better with practice.

"I need to be well rested for the challenge ahead." He went off to his bunk.

When a bell demanded her attention, Karel didn't bother to look at the data. She instructed the ship to approach, orbit and scan the world it had selected for further study.

Karel fixed herself a sandwich to munch on while she studied a course in language theory from the ship's library. When Mik woke up, their perpetual card game resumed as if it had never been interrupted.

The second sounding of the bell brought them both to the console to study the list of figures the ship was displaying on the screen. The planet had abundant vegetation, a substantial animal population, and an artificial satellite!

"If they have the technology to build that thing and launch it into orbit," Karel couldn't keep the excitement out of her voice, "I was right! We've found IL!"

"We've orbited twice," Mik pointed out, "and the ship has only identified two ground patterns that appear to be other than natural. One of them has only a 34.232 percent probability of indicating IL."

"The other one," Karel was not to be discouraged, "has a 92.35 percent probability."

"Ah, the enthusiasm of youth," Mik nudged her with his elbow, "how I miss it."

"Two patterns is better than no patterns, old man."

"Let's look at the lower probability pattern first." He zoomed in on that area. "It's all vegetation, no structures, but it is in straight rows."

"It's been cultivated," Karel said.

"Probably. But who cultivated it? Where do they live? There's nothing nearby that would answer those questions."

The other pattern was about thirty kilometers distant from the first, but it was not likely the answer to Mik's question about where the People lived. There was no road connecting the two, and it seemed unlikely that People would travel that far to tend their fields without one.

"Here," Karel zoomed in on the other pattern, "we have eighty rectangular buildings, in two rows, enclosed by a bigger rectangle."

"With a round structure central to everything else," Mik added.

"Straight lines, right angles, greater than ninety-two percent probability of having been constructed. *We've found IL, Mik!*"

"If those are dwellings," he said, "there's a very small population. Guessing an average of three or four Persons per dwelling, that's only about three hundred Persons."

"We don't know what they look like." *I'm prepared for any possible physical appearance, I hope.* "We don't know how big they are. We know the size of those structures, but we have no idea how many of them could occupy each dwelling. We're not even sure those are dwellings."

"You're right, Karel, we should land and go take a look."

They chose a natural clearing about a kilometer from the place they intended to visit. Mik took the controls. Karel could have done it, she had the training, but he was a better pilot. The landing was smooth, they felt only the tiniest of bumps when they touched down.

Once on the ground, the ship began testing the environment. This took about an hour, but the result was that they could leave the ship without any protective gear. The air was breathable, the gravity was neither too heavy nor too light. It would be uncomfortably warm outside the ship, but this world was safe for humans.

The walk was difficult for Mik. Karel had been exercising regularly, but her partner called it a waste of time. They took their time, stopping frequently so Mik could rest. It took almost two hours to reach their destination.

"Is that a wall made out of logs, Mik?"

"I think it's called a stockade," he said, "but it's for keeping something out."

"Or someone," it could be for protection against animals, or against other IL, "but that's a gate, and it's open."

There was no one in sight when they passed through the gate.

"They could be hiding inside the structures," Mik said.

"Look," Karel pointed to the dusty ground, "footprints." There were four sets, one larger than the others, one a little smaller, and two very small.

"They're bipedal," Mik placed his foot next to the largest set, "this one's feet are about the same size as mine, but it's stride is longer."

"Which way were they going?" They could be leading away from the nearest building, or toward it. Karel couldn't tell from their shape.

"These small dots look like toes," Mik stooped to examine them closely. "no claws unless they're retracted. If they are toes, and at the front of the foot, they went that way." He pointed toward the gazebo in the center of the enclosure. "So, if that's where the tracks lead, this structure is where they came from, and they're not there. Shall we have a look inside?"

"They might not like it. We might be violating their space." This world belonged to the Persons who had evolved on it. Having located IL, their mission was to establish a *friendly* first contact. Giving offense, however unintentionally, would make that difficult.

"They're not here," Mik repeated, "they'll never know."

"The entrances are open," Karel's curiosity overcame other

concerns, "if they didn't want us to see inside, they'd have doors they could shut. It should be all right to look, but we shouldn't go inside."

"Right," Mik stepped onto the porch of the closest building, Karel followed.

"It is a dwelling," Karel's first glimpse of the inside confirmed that.

"The only furniture," Mik said, "is that thing that looks like a chair." It had a seat, a back, a pair of armrests, and a horizontal beam sticking out about a meter on either side. "I wonder what that crossbar is for?"

"Maybe they hang things on it," Karel said, "when they're here. It looks like they took everything with them when they left." The floor was clear. There were shelves, but they were empty. There were things that looked like drawers, but no way to see inside them.

"Nothing more we can learn from the dwelling," Mik said, "shall we see where those tracks lead?"

They left that building and followed the tracks to the gazebo. When they got close, they could see more tracks leading there from other dwellings. It was as if the Persons had exited every single dwelling and walked to the gazebo. There were no tracks leading back the other way, and none leading out the gates. The Persons had stepped onto the gazebo and vanished.

"Do you suppose they have wings?" It occurred to Karel that the crossbars might be for resting such appendages.

"If they did, why would they walk over here, step up under this roof, and then take flight? Wouldn't they take off from in front of their dwellings? Let's look for a trapdoor, some way to leave this structure without making tracks."

They stepped up onto the platform and searched everywhere for something that could have been used as an exit. Finding nothing, they stepped back down and circled the structure, Mik going clockwise, Karel counterclockwise.

"Karel, come look at this!" Mik's voice held excitement. She hurried around to where he stood pointing to one of the pillars that held up the roof of the gazebo. Carved into the wood were letters.

WM. TERVIL
1026-1078 S.Y.

"That's our writing," Karel stared at it in shock, "our number system! How is that possible?"

"I believe," Mik said, "we have discovered what happened to one of the Lost Starships."

"Lost Starships! I thought they were just stories."

"No, they were real." Mik was a history enthusiast. "There were twenty-five ships, carrying five or six thousand men and women. Adults only. Children were expected to come later. They took off from Earth, traveling below light speed, hoping to find a world they could colonize. These folks found one."

"So, that artificial satellite is their starship?"

"Probably."

"What does 'S.Y.' mean?"

"Ship's Year," Mik guessed, "it would be the same as an Earth year, but they'd have started counting from the beginning of the trip."

"So, they'd been gone over a thousand ship's years when this Wum Tervil died?"

"Judging from the faded condition of this memorial, quite a bit of time has passed since then, as well."

"But, if they started with five or six thousand people, and expected to have children, why are there only about three hundred of them left?"

"Possibly because something on this planet kills them. That would explain why they live inside a stockade, and why they have a method of disappearing without a trace. Today, it was the landing of our ship that frightened them, but the disappearing act was in place long before we arrived."

"And we look like them," Karel said, "if there's something on this world, an animal or a hostile IL, that's dangerous to them, we could be in just as much danger."

"If we believe we're in danger," Mik said, "the protocol is to cut our mission short, go back to headquarters, and report what we've found."

"Do you want to do that?"

"I've been to twelve disappointing star systems, this is the first time I've found *anything*! I'm not about to throw away this opportunity."

"Neither am I," Karel was relieved, she'd been afraid he'd want to follow protocol, "and we should acquire more data, anyway. We know these people are human, we are guessing that something native to this planet, possibly IL, is hostile to them. We don't know what that something is, and we don't know anything about the human Persons here. We don't have much to report."

"I agree, we should try to learn more."

"What can we tell from their houses?" That they were dwellings was no longer in doubt.

"There are no nails, screws, or metal fastenings anywhere," Mik's hobby was working with wood when he was at home, "everything is held together by joinery."

"But people who knew how to build spaceships shouldn't be living at this technological level."

"We can't tell what they know, or don't know, without meeting them," Mik said, "we should try to make contact."

"How can we do that? They're hiding from us. They're afraid."

"They won't hide forever," Mik said, "they can't. Sooner or later some brave individual will come out of hiding and approach one of us."

"Or one of the native IL will attack us."

"We could break into the arms locker," Mik said, "we do have a duty to protect ourselves."

"Oh, God, no!" Using a weapon against a Person was not something Karel wanted to think about.

"We should go back to the ship, anyway," Mik said, "we need to get to a safe place and discuss what to do next."

"Let's take a peek into all the houses first," Karel said, "maybe someone left something that could give us more information."

Every house was as empty as the first. The strange looking chairs were the only furniture, but every house had one.

"Now that we know they're human," Mik said during a rest stop on the way back to the ship, "maybe we should dress more, uh, modestly." They were both wearing shorts and sleeveless shirts, showing more skin than some human cultures would tolerate.

"Dress more modestly, in this heat?" She was already sweating.

"Better to be uncomfortable than take a chance on giving offense during a first contact."

He's right. First contacts were tricky. There were many mistakes a Scout could make unintentionally.

"We should split up," Mik said when they had eaten and changed into their cold weather uniforms, "one of us should walk away from the ship, the other should stay here. One of us, alone, will be less threatening, I hope."

"Flip for it?" She pulled out the coin they used for such things. "Winner takes a walk."

Mik won. Karel was sorry it had turned out that way. He had tired easily during their earlier walk. Now she'd have to worry about him. *Well, he can't go out of communicator range.*

She sat down with her back against the side of the ship and looked up at trees so tall she had to crane her neck to see their tops. Sunlight filtered down through the branches, providing enough shade to keep her from roasting. Tiny, fearless, furry creatures bounded across the clearing, stopped, stared at her briefly, and moved on.

Could they be the hostile IL? I hope not!

Watching their random scampering was entertaining. They never approached her, never spent more than a few seconds watching her, didn't gather in large numbers. It was hard to think of them as a possible threat.

The man startled her.

She'd been distracted by the tiny creatures, looking the wrong way, and hadn't heard him coming.

He was tall and muscular, naked except for a leather belt the purpose of which seemed to be for carrying things. He stood looking down at her with a pair of hard, grey eyes behind which she sensed anger.

He had chopped off his hair to keep it out of the way. The rope coiled across one shoulder and the bow on the other left his hands free. A knife and a quiver had been shoved to the back of the belt. All the weapons were accessible.

He carries weapons! They had been right about the planet harboring something dangerous.

He took her in, absorbed her with his eyes, and she sat quietly, daring to make no move that could be misinterpreted.

This was a first contact, and she was nervous. There were so many mistakes she could make. A gesture that seemed natural to her might be offensive to him. The first move had to be his. She would take her cues from him and hope she got it right.

"Yours is womanhood?" His voice was deep and surprisingly

pleasant.

Mine is womanhood? She had been expecting to have to learn a whole new language. After a separation of more than a thousand Earth years, they shouldn't be able to understand each other. Surprisingly, though, he had used words she recognized, asked a question she thought she understood. It was a strange thing for him to ask, but she had an answer.

"Yes," she said, "I am a woman."

Damn, Sang thought. *Now there must be a doing for which I have no wish.*

Perhaps it was not needful. There were she-whisperings that this thing from the sky was a Coming of The Mother, to work vengeance on him and his people. He doubted it, but many feared it might be so.

"Speak truth," he demanded, "yours is womanhood, of sameness to that of any other?"

She had answered his question and didn't understand why he was repeating it. "I am no different," she answered carefully, "from any other woman."

"Your coming," he pointed with his chin away to the south, "is of Term?"

Of Term? Was Term a place, as his actions suggested, or was he asking how long she planned to stay?

"I came," if this were the wrong answer, he would repeat the question, possibly wording it differently, "from another sun." She was sitting in front of the ship she came in.

He gave an emphatic nod, as if this were the answer he had expected. "To my thinking," he said, "you are not The Mother, nor of Her sending?"

The Mother? Me? If that's what they thought, no wonder they ran and hid. "Your thinking is correct," she said, "I am neither of those things."

A Terman she would know me for what I am. A Terman she would try to make running from him. In speaking of Term, he had named a city, and a people, that was not in her knowing. Had he named Poly, instead of Term, its absence from her knowing would have had sameness. This of coming from another sun was truth.

"But you are a she," he repeated for the third time, "of no

differentness to any other!"

Am I a 'she'? Well, if that's your word for it, that's what I am.

Karel allowed herself to nod because she had seen him use the gesture.

"There is," he snapped, "wearing of cloth."

She was, indeed, wearing cloth. A great deal more than she would have chosen in this heat. He, on the other hand, was wearing nothing, certainly not cloth.

"I don't understand."

"It is of not-things," he growled, "that a she make such wearings."

Not-things! Were they taboos or customs? Was her transgression forgivable? Could she recover from the mistake?

She rose carefully to her feet.

"I didn't know." her voice was filled with anxiety, "should I take my clothes off?"

"Heyn."

She felt a flood of relief at his grunt of acceptance. Maybe it was not too late, maybe the thing could still be remedied by removing the cause. She stripped as quickly as she could. So much for offending them by showing *too much* skin.

She placed her clothing on the ground and turned to face him, hoping that she had, at least partially, corrected the mistake.

Damn it! Why did it have to be a she!

Not The Mother, nor of Her sending, else he might have walked away claiming fear of her. From her ordinariness, there could be no walking away. He must make the doing that was not of his wishing.

His hand shot out and grabbed her wrist, spinning her around and twisting her arm behind her back. His leg wrapped itself around her ankles and his shoulder slammed into her back so that she fell on her stomach with a force that knocked the wind out of her. By the time she realized what was happening and tried to struggle, he had her wrists locked behind her and had already taken several turns around them with his rope.

When he finished tying her hands, he leaped to his feet and planted a foot on her back.

"You," he grunted, "and that other, are the allness?"

It took her a minute to understand the question, and another minute to recover enough of her breath to answer it.

"There are only two of us," she said. There was no point in lying. Mik was due to call her any time now. When she failed to answer he would come hurrying back.

The man must not have believed her. He was watching the ship, perhaps expecting someone to come to her rescue from inside it. Mik would be back eventually, but Mik was also wearing clothing. They had both done a 'not-thing', and the contact was a disaster.

Just how serious her transgression was, what it represented in this man's mind, was something she would have to discover. Hopefully she could plead ignorance and be forgiven, but not until she was given an opportunity to speak in her defense. All she could do now was wait and see what came next.

Karel had landed on a rock. It was pressing painfully into her ribcage, and she was beginning to resent the foot that held her there.

It is difficult, she remembered from the textbook, t*o remain objective in painful situations, but a Scout must try."*

What this man was doing to her was, indeed, making objectivity difficult. He had his reasons, and those reasons made sense to him. Her first priority should be to learn what those reasons were.

But she was hurt, and she was losing her temper.

There are none inside her spacecraft, Sang decided.

He made a loop in the long end of his rope and slid it over one of his arms. He bent and grasped the hair of the she with that hand, raised her head from the ground, slid the loop over her head and tightened about her neck.

He held the rope, slid his hand along it to a place beneath her chin and used it to bring her to her feet. When she stood she looked on him with curiousness where there should have been fear. He thought, again, on the need for a doing that was not of his wishing. Did he fail in the doing, another would make it, but there would be criticism of his failure.

He turned and started away. The rope jerked tight. Karel was off balance and was yanked so violently that she pitched forward onto her stomach. He stopped, looked back disgustedly, and came to lift her to her feet. She came up glaring balefully, but when he started off again, she followed.

She of Strangeness

He didn't look back, not once. If the rope grew taut, he gave it a yank that pulled her along. Other than that, he ignored her. That was the special, humiliating cruelty of the thing. If he had hit her, screamed at her, shouted his anger at the thing she had done, it would have been recognition of her existence. She had lost her freedom, and she could have tolerated the loss, but she had, apparently, lost her right to occupy even a small portion of his attention.

Think of me as a person. Think of me as a bad person, if you want. Think of me as a criminal but think of me. Act like you know I'm here!

Sang thought on the she, on this thing of her eyes that was not of shes. This fiery anger as it might have been in the eyes of a man.

Shes showed fear at a taking. They made whinings and beggings and cryings. They asked of a man that he end their taking and send them again to their homes. They howled to The Mother for help. They turned their tongues to threats, naming the doings of the she-whipped when they came to make rescuing.

This she had a differentness, a strangeness. Not once had she made the yelpings that were the things of shes. Not once had she quaked with the fear that had been in Mari at her taking.

How will be my saying to Mari? He had said that he would make no second going to Term or to Poly. He had made no such going. He had made his going to the thing that had come from the sky, because no other had the courage of it.

How could he have known that the thing of his finding would be a she? Even if he had known of it, he could not have avoided this doing. It was a thing of healing. Fear that sends the people into hiding for a longnesss of time brings hunger. Huntings are ended, shes starve, small ones starve. Such fear must be ended quickly.

Of what, then, was this thing that caused a hurting in him when he thought on the saying he must make to Mari? Had she been of men, he would have known the name of the thing that hurt. Promise, and the notness of its keeping, but there is no promising to a she!

Damn it, the rope came to tightness and he gave hardness to its pulling, *one wife is enough. I had no wish for a second!*

2 CHAPTER 2

Karel stumbled. He had been setting a rapid pace, much too rapid. She had fallen behind. She had seen the rope growing tight, had tried to regain her balance and catch up to him before he jerked it again, but she tripped.

She was already off balance when a violent tug sent her lurching forward. She was determined to stay on her feet. She had been flat on her face twice, and she was not going to let it happen again. She managed to get her feet under her, but in the process she stepped on a patch of thorns.

She had been avoiding these patches because she had seen the man in front of her avoiding them. Now she discovered his reason for sidestepping them.

Twenty-five needle-like thorns stabbed into the ball of her foot and stuck there. Her leg felt as if it was on fire. She yelped with the pain of it and hopped after him. For the first time, she was reduced to pleading with him.

"Wait! Stop! I …"

The pain was so great that she could barely keep her wits about her long enough to realize the rope was drawing tight again.

No! If he jerked it again she would be thrown forward again. She would have to drive her feet hard and fast. The foot, with the thorns still in it, would be pounded into the ground, the spines would be driven deeper. The pain was already unbearable.

She experimented desperately. She had to find a way to keep up with him. He would not stop, he would not turn, he would not take notice of her. She had to match his pace or be dragged through the brush, possibly through another patch of those same thorns.

She took several hops and then put the foot down cautiously. One of the spines forced its way in a little deeper, but she missed most of them. She discovered that, by keeping her weight on the heel, she could manage

She of Strangeness

a hobbling gate.

She concentrated on keeping the pace, on getting her leg to swing forward fast enough, on planting the foot correctly.

The remainder of the trip blotted itself from her mind. The pain was spreading rapidly, working its way up her leg, into her abdomen, and into her chest. She seemed to be on fire.

She was barely aware of the boy who slipped out from behind a tree, conferred for a moment with her captor, and then dashed off toward the village. Her mind was slipping away from her. She wanted to sit. She wanted to lie down and rest. *She wanted to get off that foot.*

She was oblivious to the fact that the village had come to life by the time they arrived. From whatever place they had gone, the people had returned. They were busily engaged in the thousand and one details of re-establishing the village.

She wondered why she aroused only minimal curiosity. A captive stranger, one who had come from the thing that had frightened them into hiding, should bring swarms of people to stare, to wonder, to ask questions.

Instead, they ignored her. None of the men so much as glanced in her direction. Some of the women flashed her a brief, timid look of sympathy, then looked away.

Her captor led her to a house halfway up the street. He entered and she followed. Negotiating the step up to the porch was a challenge, but she managed.

The boy who had met them in the forest was seated on the floor on one side of the room. He looked up with an anticipatory grin as they entered. The man addressed himself to a woman who sat cross-legged on the opposite side, nursing a baby.

"The deed was needful," he said. "not of my choosing."

The boy gasped and the man's eyes shot fire at him.

"I have understanding," the woman kept her eyes on a spot on the floor in front of his feet.

"How is it, uncle," the boy said derisively, "that you make apologizing to a she?"

"I have made no apologizing," the man's voice was filled with anger, "I have said the thing was not of my choosing."

He slipped the loop from around Karel's neck, and gave a sharp tug to the cord, freeing her hands. He shoved her across the room, into the chair, and held her there with one hand. He flipped a thong over her head and under her chin, passed the ends through a pair of holes in the back of the chair, caught them on the other side, pulled the loop tight and fastened her in place. He tied each of her arms to the crossbar and stepped in front of her.

"How is your naming?"

Now that she was able to sit, with the weight off her injured foot, she regained a little of her ability to think.

"My name is Karel."

"I am Sang," he tapped his chest, pointed to the boy and then to the woman. "He is Tami, not yet of an age to be called Tami-ser. Her naming is Mari."

Ser? A respect syllable to be added to a male name when its owner reached maturity. Important enough to be included—forbidden—in an introduction. He named himself first, the boy second, the woman third, the baby not at all. *In the order of their importance?*

"You make sitting in my chair."

Karel nodded. She was, indeed, sitting in his chair.

"Is it yours to know the meaning of such sitting?"

Meaning? "How would I know that? I'm a stranger here."

He addressed himself to Mari? "It is needful that I go to a speaking with Elders. Your speaking will be with Karel. The meaning of the chair will be in her knowing before my return."

He stalked out the door. Tami left more slowly, disappointed about something.

Mari took the baby to the back of the room. She spent some time getting him settled before coming to squat on the floor in front of Karel. Her expression was friendly, but she was unhappy about something.

This is an opportunity to learn, I mustn't waste it.

"Your sinning had smallness," Mari said, "that your taking was by Sang. For a brute, his stupidness is small, and he is of less cruelty than most."

My sin was small? Less cruel? I'm a 'she', he's a 'brute'? "Why was I taken?" This seemed to be the most urgent data she needed.

Mari smiled sadly. "When The Mother wishes our punishing, She gives no reason into our knowing."

Punishing? By The Mother? But a 'brute' is going to do it? "I think you'd better tell me what it means that I'm sitting in his chair."

Mari was reluctant to answer the question, but she had her orders.

"There must be no jealousness between us, Karel," she said, "I am first-wife to Sang. It will ever be thus."

We mustn't be jealous of each other? But you are! "You are his first wife, are you saying I am his second?"

"When he finishes the doings of the chair, it will be so."

"So, this is a marriage ceremony. Is that the custom?"

"It is the custom among these brutes."

"And I have no choice?"

"In Term, dames make choosing of once-husbands, here there is no choosing, we are taken."

Once-husbands? But there was a more urgent question. "What are the 'doings of the chair'?"

"There will be a giving of hurt."

Hurt! There goes objectivity. "But," she asked hopefully, "you said he's less cruel than most?"

"Truth," Mari agreed, "but he will have obedience, and there will be pain to warn of punishments to come if it is not given."

"If obedience is customary, I'll follow the local custom. There's no need for..."

"In the way of rightness, as it is with us in Term, dames rule, brutes obey. These brutes give change to the way of rightness, but we are Terman. It needs a muchness of hurt to force us into the way of wrongness."

There's been a muchness of hurting, that's for sure. Through the open doorway, Karel could see people moving about in the street. Most of the women were badly scarred. There was one who had only one breast. Mari's body was free of such marks, allowing Karel to hope Sang was, indeed, less cruel than most.

"I am not Terman. I'm a Federation Scout. To me, the way of rightness is the way things are done where I am. If I was in Term, I'd follow their way of rightness."

"You are of dames, Karel, he cares not that where you are from."

"Do any of you," she caught a ray of hope, "ever run away?" *There was a place to go, Term, where they followed 'the way of rightness'.*

"There are some who try for a running," Mari said with a shudder, "but it is ever that they are caught and punished. The going to Term is a farness, to Poly a greater farness, and these brutes can make tracking of a bird through the air."

But some of you try, and that's also a custom. Karel smiled. "My ship is a lot closer than Term, I think."

Mari's face lighted with pleasure. She preferred being the only wife. "So, it is a ship of space, I had thought it might be so."

"You know about space travel?" Then why had the whole village gone into hiding when the ship landed?

"I was to have been of officers," Mari announced proudly, "and my mother was next to be Captain. It was needful that I have this knowing."

"You needed to know," Karel repeated, "but not everyone does?"

"Officers," Mari answered, "and a few petty officers."

Shipboard ranks had been retained, then, but their duties had probably changed.

"Does Sang know?"

"A brute!" Mari was shocked at the idea. "Where would a brute get a brain to hold such knowings? Of Sang, it is true that his stupidness is less than most, but..." She sniffed indignantly.

I'll decide, for myself, how stupid he is.

Mari's attitude changed. She seemed to be trying to crawl inside herself, to become invisible. Karel caught the significance of the shift before she heard footsteps on the porch. Sang had returned.

He had brought another man with him, a man whose demeanor declared his authority. Sang was treating the newcomer with respect, but not deference.

"You have your seeing, Elder," he pointed at Karel, but did not look himself.

The Elder peered at her in a way that suggested near-sightedness. "There is redness to the hair," he said.

"Of what is that?"

"Of strangeness."

Of genetics, Sang thought, *a thing of simplicity in its explaining.* But was it? It had needed much study before the thing had come to his own knowing.

"She speaks," Sang said, "of coming from another of suns. Perhaps in that place there are many with hair of this color."

She of Strangeness

The Elder seemed to be trying to reach some sort of decision. "There are she-whisperings."

"Fah!" Sang snorted in disgust. "Only fools make listening to such."

"When the whisperings are of The Mother," the Elder replied, "or of magics, such fools are easily found."

"There are no magics, Elder," Sang said. "There are things in the knowing and things yet needful of learning."

"Sang-ser," the Elder put his hand on the younger man's shoulder, "I must think on the allness of the people, on the fear that is in those with belief in magics."

"Would you say, then," Sang's voice was angry, "that I gave no thought to the allness when I made my going to the thing from the sky? Have you made forgetting of our speaking together before my going?"

"Calm yourself, Sang-ser," the Elder was not afraid, but he had no wish for fighting. "I remember our speaking together. It was in you then to know of the fear, and the harm that comes to the people because of it. But that fear is yet to be ended."

"My going was only to make end to the fear, Elder, but the thing of my finding was a she. A she who *asked* to be taken. She stood there, Elder, and waited to be taken.

"A threeness of times," he went on, "I asked of her if she had difference to other shes, and a threeness of times she named her sameness to them." He made a gesture of helplessness. "How else could have been my doing?"

"Sang-ser," the Elder said, "I know that you wished to keep to a oneness of wives. I have no understanding it, but a healer may have strangeness to his doings, and you are the best among the healers."

They were slipping away from her. Karel's mind was beginning to fill itself with things that were not of the here and now. She knew she was dreaming, and she tried to stop it. She tried to thrust the image of her father, long since dead, out of her mind and replace it with Sang and the Elder, to understand what they were saying.

"Elder," Sang insisted, "I know of the she that hers is no differentness."

"I will give you her sameness, Sang-ser, but we need a saying that will speak that sameness to believers in magics."

"Look on her, Elder." He looked himself—and leaped forward.

Sang was on his knees examining Karel's foot before they realized what was happening. His attitude had undergone a change when he looked directly at her for the first time since leaving the ship. He had been angry, argumentative, hostile. Now he was gentle—and concerned.

"There was no speaking of this."

"I tried to tell you," her tongue would not cooperate with her, and the words were slurred, "when it happened, but..."

He had memory of it. But it was ever that shes whined and begged for stopping. How, then, should he know that this whimpering had differentness?

"Karel," he said, "you have made stepping in stakur. There is poison to the thorns of stakur, and it has made working in you a long time. This is understood?"

It was, but not clearly. The dream images kept getting in the way. She tried to answer him, but her tongue had given up.

"You will make no doing, Karel," he said. "The allness of doing will be mine. I am of healers. I can cure you, but you must *make no doing*."

She heard him. There was a freak moment when her mind cleared, and she heard what he said. She nodded.

"Make relaxing," he ordered.

He rose and cut her loose. Then he lifted her gently from the chair. She tried to put her arms around his neck, to help him, but he shook his head.

"There must be limpness, Karel. Make no doing."

Instinctively, she obeyed him. His attitude had changed, his relationship to her had changed. He was focused on saving her life.

He carried her to a matt on the floor and laid her on it. "Limpness," he repeated firmly. "Mari, I will have three jugs. Two with clear water, the third empty. Bring also a rag of cleanliness."

"What has come to be, healer?" The Elder was curious.

"There was stepping in stakur, and she sickens," Sang replied, "speak that to the listeners of she-whisperings."

The Elder smiled to himself and left.

The jugs arrived and Sang set to work. He carefully cleaned the area where the thorns had imbedded themselves. Then he looked up at Karel.

"There will be cutting," he said, "and small pain. Remember of limpness."

"I'll try," she said.

The pain was nothing, a series of pinpricks. The knife flicked, a thorn came out, and he was already working on the next one. She concentrated on lying still. Movement stirred circulation, and she could tell from his actions that the poison was a potent one.

He finished removing the thorns and rose to stand over her.

"How is the seeing," he asked.

"It isn't," she managed to say, and, fortunately for her, that was true. She did not see the worry that came into his eyes.

He reached down gently and turned her head to one side. She would soon come to sleeping, and much salivating. There must be no drowning in it.

"The poison of the stakur seldom kills, Karel," he said. "You will sicken, but there will be no dying."

She had passed into unconsciousness without hearing the lie.

3 CHAPTER 3

There is no hating of more greatness to my hating of death.

A hundred times he had seen it, and a hundred of times he had made fighting with it.

Had he never made meeting of this she, it would have been a goodness. But he had met her, the she was now his. No sooner had she come to be his than death had come to make fighting with him.

There were ways in his knowing in which death could be fought. He sat with the she, to watch for the coming of death.

He saw the slowness of her breathing, and his teeth ground on themselves. He kept his hand her throat, fearing the stopping of her heart. Death came.

Now it could be that there was work of his doing. Now death had meeting with one who knew the ways of fighting against death.

He made a cry of challenge at the stopping of the heart. His fist made poundings against her ribcage, and the other of his hands touched her throat hoping to feel a starting of the pulse. One hand struck at death, the other grasped at life.

It was not enough.

He straddled her and drove, with the heel of his hand and all of his strength, down, as if it could be that he pushed death out from beneath the body of the she.

Her heart had stopped working. Be it needful, he would enter the chest to make squeezings of the heart, but this doing was not yet needful. It was enough that he made pumping without entering.

Again, he drove at her chest, and again. He made a steady rhythmic pumping, stopping only for blowing of air into the lungs. The she made puking into his mouth. He spat these pukings and placed his mouth again on hers. The taste was a vileness, but it was a thing of drawing death from her that he might make spitting of it to a place where it did no harm.

He won.

He joyed that there had been no cutting, no entering, that he had made winning without it.

He held his hand to the throat for a long time, felt the pulse, knew of its strengthening. Betime, it could be that the hand moved from the throat to the wrist.

Color came again to her face, and betime it could be, even, that the hand was taken away from the wrist. The she changed from the sleep of sickness to the sleep of resting, but it was yet needful to make watching of her.

A twoness of days that he had done no sleeping, and a moreness to pass before the thing was ended. He kept watch on the she.

It was early morning of the third day when Karel open her eyes to see Sang standing above her. He was relaxed, no longer worried.

He was also exhausted.

She had no memory of what had happened. She did not know that, during the night, he had carefully cleaned her and slid a dry cloth beneath her head. She knew she stank, a sick, unnatural stench that meant her body was throwing off the poison. She gave him a weak smile and started to speak, but he shook his head.

"There is yet another day to your resting," he told her. "You have your life, but you must come again to your strength."

And which Sang will you be tomorrow, she wondered vaguely, *the healer or the husband who is less cruel than most?*

She was too weak to allow herself to think about that. There would be time to fight that battle within herself when she was at full strength. She closed her eyes and let herself drift back to sleep.

When she woke the second time, it was Mari who was watching over her, and Karel judged herself to be out of danger. Sang would not have left her if...

"He sleeps," Mari said in answer to the unspoken question. "There is hunger in you?"

Karel took stock of herself. Yes, she was hungry. There was also an ache in her chest, and she guessed at its cause. Small wonder that Sang had looked so haggard.

She nodded in answer to Mari's question.

"He has named this the first of my askings," Mari said, "and also a goodness if it is so. He has spoken that you may make a smallness of eating."

She brought a small bowl of soup and helped Karel sit up and drink it. When she had finished, Mari instructed her to lie down and stay quiet, a suggestion that Karel found very appealing.

"This is the allness," Mari said, "of which he will have your eating. He fears…"

Karel knew very well what he feared. The broth and her stomach were barely cooperating with each other, anything else would probably not stay down.

"How long have I…"

"A twoness of days," Mari answered, "and a threeness of nights."

"And he stayed with me the whole time?"

"He is of healers," Mari shrugged.

The shrug impressed Karel more than the words. The fact that he had stayed with *her* meant nothing. *I'm his wife, at least for now.* But to Mari it was normal, the kind of thing he did it for all his patients.

"He saved my life," Karel said.

"He does well for a brute," was the answer.

Oh, yes. Brutes are stupid, even though you're sneaky-secret proud of yours—ours.

"Will he still tie me to the chair, when I'm strong enough?"

Mari nodded. "He will yet think it needful."

"Mari," Karel had a thought that gave her hope, "when he did it to you, did it make you angry?" If anger was customary…

Mari shook her head. "These brutes do only the Wishings of The Mother, Karel. There can be no anger at the Wishings of The Mother."

Oh, yes, The Mother is punishing me. Fortunately, only for small sins.

"You mean the they are the instruments She uses to carry out Her punishment?".

"That," Mari protested, "and a great moreness."

"Please tell me more."

"You must know of our history," Mari said, "that this understanding come to you."

I would love to know your history. There was no better way to arrive at a broad-based understanding of people than to listen to their history of themselves. Even when it was inaccurate, it provided insights.

"It came to be," Mari said in the tone of a lecturer, "during the time inside our ship of space, that there were dames of such great sinfulness that The Mother sent a 'hulbreech' for their punishing. This word is in your understanding?"

"I know what a hull breach is," Karel said.

"Many dames came to their dying," Mari said, "their sinfulness being that they were dames full grown and yet unmarried."

That's a sin in Term? They can choose, but they can't decide not to choose?

"In afterness to the hulbreech, there were two brutes for each dame yet living. Brutes must have a place to take their ruttings, or they will become Plotters. Many solutions were discussed, but none found agreement. The Captain of the time made no decision, thinking it could wait until we found a world we could colonize."

"You found this world."

"Shortly after the hulbreech, there was landing on this world, but there was one among the brutes whose name was Tervil."

"Wum Tervil?"

"William," Mari corrected. "He was leader at the first taking of dames. There was, already, a fewness of dames, and Tervil's crew took more, but only those who were yet of great sinfulness. These brutes return, betime, to Term and also to Poly, for a new taking of dames of sinfulness."

If they are taken, they automatically become sinners!

"The Mother makes of this a testing of our worthiness. A testing I failed."

"How did you fail the test?"

"The Mother," Mari said sadly, "can look into a heart and see the thing that is there. There is a softness in me, Karel, that would have fondness for a brute, even in my knowing of his uselessness and stupidity.

"For myself," Mari dropped her eyes in embarrassment, "I can think of no time that I have done this thing, but The Mother has seen in me a potential for such a doing.

"Not for my once-fathers," Mari insisted, "not even for my *uncle* did I know fondness."

I wish a certain 'brute', of whom I am very fond, would hurry up and come get me out of here.

"In Term," Mari said, "there are brutes of trueness who make remembering of the Law. A few Plotters, but they come swift to their dying. The most would never allow harm to come to a dame."

"The brutes in this place make forgetting of The Mother's Law," Mari declared.

"Which Law?"

"That She is of Motherhood to All Things and we, in our sameness to Her, have also sacredness."

"And they violate that Law by taking us?"

"But they make no killing of dames," Mari assured her hastily, "Tervil brought them to the way of wrongness, but they must not give such a greatness of hurt that a dame makes dying. Even now their Death-trackers seek a wife-killer. He will come to his own dying when they make his finding."

At least, I don't have to worry about being killed. Sang hadn't saved her life just to turn around and throw it away.

Men taking the women The Mother wanted punished. Doing The Mother's Will by breaking Her law. It didn't make sense, but it was a local belief, and Scouts never challenged local beliefs. First contacts had to remain *friendly*. She wondered if 'brutes' shared those same beliefs.

"In Term, there is ever two brutes to each dame."

Stealing wives from neighboring tribes had been a common enough practice on Earth. The difference here was that the theft had preceded the establishment of a second tribe. Since that second tribe definitely existed, that much of the story was probably accurate.

"Betime," Mari added, "the small ones of the Raiders came to the fullness of their brutehood and made, again, a Raiding of Term for the taking of such of the dames as had angered The Mother. There is ever a newness of their comings, but it is a thing of goodness. It means, of the dames who are *not* taken, that they have nothing in them of this thing that brings The Mother to anger. There was also the taking of the refmats."

"Refmats?" Karel was very much interested.

"Of this, also," Mari said, "it is known that The Mother had come to anger. In the things of Tervil, She made special punishings for a few. In the taking of the refmats, She punished the allness of the crew.

Reference materials? "How did She take your refmats from you?"

"After the reaching of New Earth," Mari failed to notice the laugh Karel was fighting to suppress—there were over a hundred planets on record called New Earth, "there was landing of the crew. It was a folly of her who was Captain, that she allowed landing of the allness of her crew and made waiting for the landing of supplies, equipments...and computers containing the refmats.

"When the crew had come to safeness on the planet, those among them who were pilots of the ships of smallness went again to the ship of bigness. But these were pilots of inexperience, Karel. The allness of their living had been in space. One of the pilots made crashing, causing such damage that they came no more to us. Of this, The Mother gives hardness to our punishing."

Well, Karel though, *that's how people who know how to build spaceships wind up living at this technological level.*

Beyond a certain point, a technology becomes dependent on its reference materials. No individual is capable of retaining all of the data relating to even a highly specialized area. Charts, tables, volumes of information are compiled, and the data is retrieved and utilized one item at a time—it is not memorized. Mari was describing a society suddenly cut off from those materials.

"There was trying," she said, "to make writing of refmats of newness, but it was a thing of hardness, and much was lost."

Karel had a vivid mental picture of what must have happened. Every member of the crew straining her memory—or his if 'brutes' were educated—and trying to recreate the refmats. *Impossible task.*

"This rewriting of the refmats," Mari said, "is yet the greatest work in our doing, both in Term and in Poly."

Poly? Now that she thought about it, Karel realized that it had been mentioned before, but it had not really registered. Poly must be a third place.

4 CHAPTER 4

Karel was about to ask another question when she heard Tami pounding across the porch. Mari collapsed in on herself as she had the time Sang had entered with the Elder, and Karel turned her head just in time to see the boy catapult through the doorway.

He had crossed the porch at a dead run, and too late he saw that his uncle had stretched himself across the doorway to sleep. There was no time for Tami to stop himself, but he tried, at the last instant to leap over the body of his uncle. He lost his footing, however, pitched forward, dived across Sang, caught himself with his hands and somersaulted into the room. He sat up slowly, rubbing one of his wrists.

The boy presented such a ludicrous figure sitting there that Karel laughed, but she sobered instantly when he shot her a look of almost pure hatred. She noticed that Mari had shown no signs of amusement. The girl was almost as withdrawn as she had been in Sang's presence.

Tami's attempt to avoid awakening his uncle had failed, anyway, Sang was sitting up and looking at him.

"Speak your news," the man said.

"They have made catching of Torn," the boy announced excitedly.

"Heyn," Sang grunted, "hell of a time for it."

"He will live long, and come hard to his dying, uncle." For Tami seemed delighted at the prospect.

"And end my sleeping with the noise of his mouth," Sang said. "Hell of a time for catching a wife-killer."

"May it be that I have the watching of it, uncle?"

Sang was awake now. Yes, the boy would joy at this seeing, but perhaps there was also a goodness to it. He nodded.

Tami left happily and Sang composed himself across the doorway again. In a moment he was fast asleep.

"Who is Torn," Karel whispered as soon as she was sure their talking would not disturb Sang.

"You will remember my saying," Mari answered, "that the Death-trackers made seeking of a wife-killer?"

"Yes," Karel had been more interested in other parts of the story.

"Torn," Mari said, "gave great wrongness to the way of the chair. He joyed in the hurting and forgot the time it must be ended. She came to her dying, Karel, and now he comes to his."

"I see." And Tami wants to watch!

"There will be sending for the belted-ones, and they…"

"The belted-ones?"

Mari sneered contemptuously. "It would be, would it not, that they would make differentness between the wives who are taken and the daughters who are born to them?"

"Yes," Karel had wondered about this, "I'm sure they would."

"These bitches of Raider birthing, when they come to such age as to be mistaken for a dame taken from Term or Poly, are given belts to show their differentness, and knives to hang from those belts. They name their belts a thing to mark their betterness to us," Mari's clearly did not accept them as her superiors, "but it is a goodness that they will come in soonness and bring Torn, with much pain, to his dying.

"It is a goodness," Mari continued, "that they give this doing to their daughters. A betterness if we, who have sat the chairs of these bastards and felt the pain of their giving, had the killing of them when such killings are allowed."

This was Karel's first exposure to the reality of intelligent beings actually killing each other. It was one thing to read about violence as an integral part of the history of most species, it was another thing to know that it was going to be done here and now and be done by her own kind. Mari's desire to participate was something Karel found difficult to understand.

Karel thought of any IL as a fellow creature, and she had worked hard to eliminate all forms of prejudice from her thinking. Not knowing what an IL they discovered might look like, Scouts could not afford to be fearful, repulsed or disgusted by anyone if they were to establish a friendly first contact. She had worked hard at overcoming those reactions. She had trained herself to understand, to feel, that any and all IL were 'people'. To Karel, Torn was a person, to Mari he was—not even a 'brute of trueness'.

"Mari" Karel asked cautiously, "would you really do it, if they'd let you?"

It was a relief to watch the girl's eyes drop in embarrassment. She shook her head. "It is not even that I can help Sang with his healings," she admitted. "It is not in me to look on bleeding."

Karel smiled her understanding. "Mari," she said softly, "would it...bother you...if I helped Sang with his healings?" Her training in first aid had been extensive. In case of an injury to her partner, she would be the only help available. But she wanted to avoid antagonizing Sang's first-wife.

"You have this doing?" Mari was awed. Anyone who could stand the sight of blood! "It would be a goodness. He has need of an otherness of hands, betime, and mine..."

"You won't be jealous, then?"

Mari took a deep breath and let it out slowly. "I will speak on this thing of jealousness, Karel. Before your coming, I was the only dame here who made no sharing of a brute. Sang had no wish to make a second going to Term or Poly. Perhaps he has it in him to remember more of the Law than these others. It was a goodness that I did no sharing of him."

"Why is that? I mean, why is it better not to share?"

"The ways of marrying," Mari was lecturing again, "are three. In Term a dame makes choosing of a brute for one hundred and eighty days. Then ends her living with that one and makes choosing of another. This is the way of rightness. The bitches of Poly," a great deal of contempt showed on her face, "choose two brutes and keep to them for always. This is not the Law of The Mother, Karel, it is a thing of their softness. The Polyan bitches smile in fondness on their brutes."

"I see," Karel decided to shift the conversation back onto a more useful track, "and the third way of marrying is the way it is done here?"

"Truth," Mari said, "each brute makes taking of two dames, keeps them for life. The great wrongness of it is in the sharing, that we have lost so much of our goodness that we may not even have a brute to ourselves."

Karel mentally ticked off another discrepancy. If it was against the rules to become fond of them, what was wrong with sharing the task of despising them?

"It was mine," Mari said almost boastfully, "to make only a small sinning, and this is known because my taking was made by Sang. He made only a small hurting of me, and it came soon to its ending. He took no second of wives."

"At least," Karel put in, "not until he had no other choice."

"Even of that," Mari finished smugly, "you have said that you are soon to a running, and there is a place of closeness for your going. My sinning was tiny." She held up a thumb and forefinger to show how tiny.

I hate to tell you this, but mine was huge—what's taking Mik so long?

Mik must know something she did not, otherwise he would have been here by now. Or, perhaps, he had been here and discovered the same thing she was learning, divorce required escape.

Well, she could stay married to Sang for a while. She was in no shape to run, anyway. Not yet.

"Mari," she said, "I appreciate everything you've told me, but I think I'd better rest now."

Mari looked at her fearfully. "I have made your tiring?"

Karel shook her head and Mari relaxed. Apparently she had been sternly warned against wearing the patient down. She went to look after the baby, and Karel slid easily into sleep.

The first scream brought Karel awake.

She lay there quivering, trying to orient herself. What was going on? *Torn!*

Oh, no, no, NO! They were really doing it. She had listened to Mari and pretended that she understood what she was being told. She had not believed it.

The reality of it drove into her like a knife. She opened her eyes and saw Mari hovering anxiously over her. The girl's face wore the same tortured expression that must have been on Karel's, and she flinched—they flinched together—as each new scream split the air. Mari's hand crept slowly into Karel's and they clutched at each other, cringing at each new blast.

Why do they do it at night?

Would it be worse in the daylight? Would it be any better? Karel kept her eyes open. If she closed them her imagination would take over. She watched Mari.

Mari's face danced and flickered in the light of the…

Oh, God, they're using fire?

Karel's mind and soul were reaching out to the man—wishing she could find a way to make it stop.

That's a human being out there!

She tried to sit up. She had some wild notion of rushing outside to…do what? To do something—anything! She could not just lie there! But she could not get up. She was too weak. She fell back panting heavily, with sweat pouring out of her.

Die, you idiot!

It would stop if he died. She could not tell whether she wanted it to stop because she could not stand it, or if she wanted it to stop because he could not stand it. She wanted it to stop. She wanted him to die. Mari had said they would keep it up until he did die. So, the sooner the better.

She would take any way there was to make it stop. She would accept anything. She could take very little more of it before she collapsed.

She hung on to Mari with the desperateness of one human being reaching out to another. They were a pair of children, clutching at each other in the midst of a world too big and horrible for either of them alone. They were drawing strength from each other in a time when neither of them had any strength of her own, and Karel almost screamed when Mari suddenly jerked her hand away and went into her submissive posture. Sang was there.

He reached down and touched Karel, unwilling to trust his eyes in the flickering darkness. His hand came away covered with perspiration, but he had felt the racing of the pulse, the tension. He could see her flinch every time…

"You have spoken of this," he demanded of Mari.

"Yes, Sang-ser," she replied meekly.

"You know, then," this to Karel, "the reason of this doing, that it is a wife-killer who comes to his dying."

She could not speak, she only nodded.

"She fears the time when the pain will be hers, uncle," Tami said maliciously. He had slipped into the room without being noticed.

"I had thought," Sang answered, "that you wished the seeing of this thing. You would do well to remember it."

"There is time," the boy answered, "the thing is not done in swiftness."

Sang caught Karel's reaction to the remark, but he kept his attention on the boy. "Get out," he said, "and make watching of this thing. *Remember the reason of it.*"

He turned back to Karel as soon as the boy was gone. "He speaks rightly? That you are come to fear of…"

"No," she gritted her teeth and waited for the next scream.

"I thought not," he said, but he came to much worry. There was yet poison in her body. "The thing is needful, Karel. Were there no doing of it, there would be many to become wife-killers." His eyes drifted to the door, and somehow she knew he was thinking of Tami.

"Sa…Sang-ser," she had to say it, and she had to try to believe it herself, "your ways, and the ways of your people…are yours. What you…whatever you think you need to do…is…right for you." *It doesn't matter if its right for me.*

Mari let out a startled gasp and Sang's face took on a puzzled expression. A Terman would have named others of his ways wrongness and this a goodness, and it was thus, also, with Polyans. A belted she would have made no speaking of *his* ways, they were also hers.

"Your saying," he said, "is that my ways have rightness?"

"Yes."

"What," he asked, "is the reason of this rightness?"

"Be…because the ways are *yours*."

Another scream tore through the air and Karel shuddered. The look of puzzlement on Sang's face grew more intense.

"You *feel* for this wife-killer?" It was incredible. Others of the shes…

"He's a human being, Sang-ser," Karel answered painfully.

Truth, but a strangeness to her way of saying it.

"His dying is a thing of my ways, Karel. *My* ways which have rightness."

"I…I'm trying to know that, Sang-ser, but…" she shuddered again. "I wish I didn't have to listen to it."

"I have said that if it were not done there would be others to become wife-killers," he argued. "A wife-killer has no manhood, Karel." He made wishing that Tami heard this saying. "Of manhood is the using of a knife. With a wife-killer it becomes the knife that uses the man." Hell with it—why make explainings to shes. "I have no liking for the quickness of your heart. There is yet much poison in you. I will make a drink and you will have sleeping until the noise has left the air."

He went to his storage cabinet and took some leaves from it. These he boiled slowly until he had created a sort of tea. He returned to Karel with the drink in his hand.

"You must make drinking," he said, "of only half. I have done a wrongness in the making of it." He carefully avoided looking at Mari. "There is more than is needful. To drink the allness of it would be death. Drink only half." He handed it to her and immediately turned his back.

Karel glanced at Mari and then at the cup in her hand. *So, he made a mistake, did he*, she thought. *He accidentally made exactly enough for two people.* She smiled at Mari. They knew that he would never ask what had happened to the other half.

Another scream tore through the air and Karel drank hastily. She could already feel the drug beginning to work as she handed the cup to Mari. A blissful calm was coming over her, and she gave herself over to it and slid into a deep sleep.

5 CHAPTER 5

The drama that had been generations unfolding on the floor of the forest was about to add another piece to the puzzle. A thrill ran through the Advocate, and the People—an unusual number of them—joined her Thinking to watch.

A southern two-leg, her two-leg, crouched beneath a tree and waited. Three of the northern two-legs were moving toward it. Between them ranged one of the fanged killers that the southern two-legs befriended. There would be a fight.

There would be a fight and her two-leg, her pet, or her friend, might die. With it would die any chance of proving, or disproving, the one thing of which she, alone, was convinced—that a two-leg could think, even if it could not Think.

She was forbidden to touch the mind of her two-leg. In the early days, when the two-legs had first come into the world, crashing down from the sky in their shiny changed-thing, attempts had been made to Think with them. But the mind of a two-leg was a tangled mass of nonsense, wave upon wave of sound-linked garbage thrashing about chaotically in minds that were incapable of either organization or control. A careful search might reveal an occasional pure thought, an emotion that was *felt* rather than warped into a sound pattern, but such searches were arduous, invariably futile and, if the two-leg woke, it was terrified. So Thought with the two-legs was forbidden, except to the two-leg healers, and then only a small alerting message that barely touched the surface but let them know that an injured two-leg was coming.

The Advocate was in the position of having to prove that there was a mind in the body of a two-leg without touching that mind. She had become convinced of it herself when a two-leg, this one, had saved her life. It had killed a snake that was slithering toward her, impaled it with one of those flying sticks that they used, and it had done so for no other reason than that the *snake was coming toward her.*

Time and again she created the scene for the People, let them feel the cold, angry hunger radiating from the snake, the quivering terror in a body, her own, too full of children to run, and the flaming hatred that came screaming out of the two-leg and struck the snake long before the arrival of the spike that killed it.

The People hesitated. The People debated. The People decided to reconsider the matter of the two-legs. The argument that had been killed by lack of interest was revived.

Explain the Contradiction!

This fight, the one in which her two-leg might be killed, would explain nothing. It would only demonstrate, once again, the first half of the Contradiction. The two-legs fought. Two-legs killed each other. Two-legs hurt each other. Two-legs were *able* to hurt each other.

A Person could never hurt another Person. A Person could not conceive of hurting another Person. Therefore, a two-leg that could not Think, but could do these horrible things, could not be, as the Advocate claimed, a different kind of person.

DeMyrn Tan crouched beneath to a tree, shaking with a muchness of fear.

Because he was near to his Time, he had allowed it that his hair made growing, and it had come to lie in long blackness against his skin. The hair of his face had come also to fullness, and a goodness that it was so. A goodness, but a thing of danger in the forest.

It was yet another vileness of the Raiders that they would tear a man's hair when they fought and kept their own to a shortness. Zek had once lost hair to the hand of an Ugly, and Zek had spent that of his Times among the Unchosen. With sorrow, Tan remembered the scarring that meant Zek must now spend all his Times among the Unchosen.

The thought of Zek brought remembering of their speaking together on the thing that must be done when the hunting had such a far northness that it was a near certainty that some of the ugly, hairless Raiders ranged to the south of him.

Was there yet no changing of the wind?

Of no goodness the changing of the wind until the coming of the vark. The vark was his eyes, his ears, and, of moreness, his nose. Half the tallness of a man and twice the strength, fanged and clawed and of such swiftness that no two feet could flee from the vark's four. The vark made tracking of the things Tan hunted and helped in the killing of them. The vark warned of the coming of Uglies and helped in the killing of them. Such warnings could only be made when the wind had rightness, and there was yet no changing of the wind.

There was no changing of the wind, but much danger in waiting for it. The Raiders would be coming, ever they made patrolling. They would strike Tan's trail, and he had sent his vark far south, that it might learn of their coming.

Did the wind make no changing, however, Tan had only one choice. At the coming of the vark, they would make running southward, hoping that there would be no meeting of Uglies as they ran. He feared the Uglies. He feared his own dying, feared leaving hair in their hands, feared their scarring of him, and he hated killing them.

A curl popped out from behind a tree and made staring at him from a small distance. This was the curl who was friend to him, the little dame whose living would have ended were it not for his arrow taking her dying and given it, instead, to the snake. He smiled on her to see that she was again in the heaviness that speaks the coming of small ones. It had been thus with her in the time of the snake, and this had been the thing that had given anger to the arrow.

Tan had much love for the curls, the tiny leapers who gave joy to the trees. The delicate bits of movement, of such smallness as to make hiding in a single leaf, which yet made dancings in the allness of the leaves. Dancings that were things of happiness to the watcher.

In Tan there was much love for the allness of curls, but it was only the little dame who came to nearness of him. Betime, even he had touching of her. She would make sitting in his hand to do her eating, and the others of the curls *permitted* it. In a time of pastness there had been some who thought to make hunting of curls, but the killing of one brought a hundred others down on the hunter. The harming of curls was death, but this one made sitting in his hand without fear.

He reached into his pouch for one of the berries he kept for the little dame and placed it on the ground exactly halfway between them. The little dame smiled on it. He knew it was smiling she made, though others would name him fool for the thought.

She stopped her smiling and quivered, and he knew that the other curls made speaking to her in ways that were not of his hearing. There had been those, in the early days, who claimed that the curls could make touching of a man's mind, but this had come to be of things not spoken of only on dark nights, along with stories of ghosts and witches.

The little dame pounced on the berry and was gone up the side of a tree. The vark was back.

The vark. More friend to Tan than the allness of men. Only in his Time, when he married, when he made no hunting's, when he had no need of it, did the vark leave his side, except to obey an order. When Tan was in his Time, the vark was friend to Zek who was in his Lonely Time.

The catching of varks, and their training, was a hardness. The Hunters shared their varks, so that none must make his hunting in loneliness, and in Tan was much joy that it was with Zek he made this sharing.

Zek, only, had understanding of their vark as great as Tan's. Other Hunters thought of their varks as fangs to make tearing of Raider throats, as noses to speak the coming of an enemy. To Zek and to Tan the vark was a friend.

It was time for going.

Tan came to his feet and took to himself a deepness of breath, as of a swimmer about to make diving. The vark sensed his doing and made readiness.

They ran.

In togetherness, they ran, with the vark holding its speed to one the man could match. There was hope that there would be no meeting of Raiders, but there was also holding of knife to the hand. The vark ran in front, the man behind. Together they flashed through the trees, made skirting of clearings, made silentness with their feet. Did they meet with Uglies, there would be no warning of it, but neither would the short-hairs be warned of their coming.

The Uglies would come in preparedness, but they would expect no running. Other Hunters hid. They leaped on the Uglies from concealment. Of the allness of the Hunters of Term, only Tan and Zek made this running when trapped upwind of Uglies. In the allness of the Hunters, only Tan and Zek had been caught thus many times and lived.

Their success was in the running, not the waiting, and often such running brought them to a place of safeness without a meeting. Not this time.

Man and vark were among the Raiders before either side knew the presence of the other. The vark struck for the throat of the lead Raider with a swiftness that defied the eyes, and the Ugly had no time to ready himself. He had time, only, for throwing forward of his shoulder, that the fangs make tearings in a place of less vitalness. He went down beneath the fangs of the vark, but there was no stopping.

There was never stopping at such a running. Tan's knife entered the belly of a Raider and tore itself out again, and he missed no step at the doing. His feet fought with the cry that was ripped from the Raider along with the knife, fought to bring the cry to such distance as to be lost to the hearing before it was lost to the making.

There had been a third Raider, and it was he that Tan feared. He who had taken no wounding made raising of his bow, and there was a place in Tan's back that could feel the arrow that would be coming soon. He made leapings to one side and then to the other as he ran, that perhaps the arrow would come to the place he had been, and not to the place he was.

The first of the arrows came and passed, and now feet fought with arrows, fought to make it that the Raider ended seeing before an arrow ended living. The second arrow came to Tan in the betweeness of the place he had been and the place he was. His leaping to the side had slowness, and the arrow took the inside of his arm. He grasped it, held it to his side, and continued the fighting of feet with arrows.

The third of the arrows fell short. There was no fourth, and yet Tan kept running. There must be sureness that the Raider had lost sight of him, and it must be before…

The thing came to his stomach.

He stopped. He had no choice, he must stop. He must stop and make doing of the thing that always came to him after a fight.

He puked.

He tasted the vileness that came from his mouth, and he felt the shame that went with it.

It was *unfairness*. He had taken a wounding. He would need the strength from the food that was leaving him.

He puked.

For this he had no stopping. To know the vileness of the Uglies, to think on the wrongness of them, the wickedness that allowed them to lay hands on a dame and take her to a place of wrongness, these thoughts gave no stop to the thing of his stomach.

He puked.

By The Mother! A Raider is also a man!

6 CHAPTER 6

The chair rose up out of the floor. It was central, it as universal, it was larger than necessary, it was to be feared. After the coming torture, the chair would remain. No matter where she tried to look, the chair would remain.

Thank God it's going to be today!

The waiting had become part of the torture, although Karel could not bring herself to call it a deliberate part. As far as Sang was concerned, she needed to regain her strength, and he was allowing her to do so, sound medical practice. Now that she had regained her strength, he would do what, to him, constituted completion of the marriage ceremony. There was no sense of enjoyment.

Not from Sang, that is.

Tami was another matter. He sensed her fear, preyed on it, reveled in it. Yesterday he had sat gloating as the afternoon wore to a close, as the chair had seemingly become larger and more ominous, as Karel's apprehension had mounted, and then…

"How is it, uncle, that you make this waiting? Of betterness that the thing be done now—while she is yet in her weak…"

He had chopped off the sentence in the middle of a word when he saw the look on his uncle's face. Calm, emotionless, infinitely patient, Sang's eyes had frozen the boy, and they continued to hold him for a long, uncomfortable time. Tami was fidgeting nervously by the time his uncle broke the silence.

"The she is mine."

That was all. No anger, no hint of resentment, no trace of any emotion at all, but the boy had dropped his eyes and sheepishly withdrawn.

This morning had been different. The instant she left her bed, Karel sensed that this would be the day. She did not need the look of anticipation on Tami's face to tell her that, and she certainly did not need to see his erection.

Of all the ridiculous, adolescent...

Sang had also noticed. It was almost a relief to see that he was nearly as disgusted as Karel was. Karel had never particularly liked the boy, but now she found herself developing a very strong dislike of him.

Sang finished his breakfast without haste, and his first comment was to Mari. "You will make your chattering with other shes," he said. "Make no returning until I have asked it."

Mari's eyes lifted the tiniest fraction of a centimeter from the point just in front of his feet where she normally kept them. She was losing her fight to keep the gratitude from spreading across her face, and to cover it she rose hastily and left the house. Karel guessed that this must be another of the ways in which Sang was 'less cruel'. Other wives were probably required to stay and watch.

"May I have the seeing of it, uncle?" Tami's voice vibrated with anticipation.

It was not the indifferent stare of the day before that raked the boy this time, and Sang's voice was cold and hard when he spoke. "Your grandfather had an otherness of sons."

The statement carried a significance that was lost on Karel, but not on Tami. "I have made choosing, uncle," he said almost defiantly, "I make no change to it."

"Perhaps," Sang replied nastily, "my brother would allow that you have sight of his doings with his shes."

"But I am soon to my manhood, uncle," the boy protested, "I have need of this learning."

Invoke the law, will you! You little shit!

"Truth!" For a moment Sang thought he had found a way out of the dilemma. "You are soon to your manhood. Name the man who stays in another's house when..." *Oh, hell! Why did I make that saying?*

The boy was getting up, and his disappointment was turning to pride. He literally swaggered out into the street.

Fah! Betime there will be meeting of his friends, and the saying will be that I have named him already of manhood. Damn it! Why could the little fart not have chosen the other of his uncles?

He turned from the door and looked at the she.

Karel rose calmly, walked to the chair, seated herself in it and placed her arms against the crossbar and her head against the back. She sat there waiting to be tied in place.

Sang stood staring at her. There was a strangeness in this she, a strangeness of her thinking.

"Explain," his chin jerked in her direction as if there might be some doubt as to who he was addressing, "this of your doing."

"Sang-ser," Karel tried to keep her choice calm, but her heart was pounding, and the fear was rising in her, "I could try to resist, but I'd wind up here, anyway. This saves time."

Truth, he thought, *her resisting would be useless*. Spoken thus, her doing made sense, but another of the shes would have tried. Mari had struggled.

"Come from that place," he growled.

He led her to a corner of the room and seated himself with his back to one of the walls. A wave of his hand indicated that she was to join him. She sat down and waited.

Sang looked on the face of the she, and saw, again, a thing that was not of shes. At her taking there had been anger and nothing of fear. Now there was fear, but her going to the chair was not the thing of a fool who thinks to end the coming of hurt by such a doing. Her going to the chair was a thing of controlling the fear, of keeping the mind to thinking of clearness in a time of fear. This was not a thing of shes.

"This," he said, "is *truth*."

"I…don't understand."

"Your doing," he pointed to the chair, "a thing of truth."

"You expected me to lie, Sang-ser?"

"You are of shes."

Well, so much for the stupidness of 'brutes'. The frankness and simplicity of his answer totally discredited Mari's belief. Karel was a she. Shes lied. The fact was noted, classified as part of the way things were. Nobody was fooling anybody.

"All right," she allowed her shoulders to sag and dropped her eyes to the exact point in front of his feet where Mari always kept hers.

Another truth, damn it! Sang saw how exactly, how perfectly, she copied the lyings of a Terman, but in Karel it was not a lie. It was…

"A thing of my ways that have rightness because they are mine?"

"Yes," she admitted without raising her eyes. Her voice had the same meek quality that Mari always used.

"You have liking for my ways," he demanded.

"I didn't say that," she said, "but I...I have no right to ask you to change, Sang-ser. I'm the stranger here."

A stranger, he thought, *also a strangeness.* He came to disappointment that her eyes had left his face. On the floor, they named him 'brute'.

"That," he said, "is the way of Terman shes. It was your saying that *my* ways have rightness."

Karel accepted the statement and straightened herself into the posture that came more naturally to her. Sang relaxed.

"I had no wish for a secondness of wives," he said.

"I know," she said, "but it's one of your ways. I remember the Elder saying he didn't understand..."

"My foolishness," Sang chuckled.

The Elder, he thought, *is a man of small understanding in many things.*

The Elder had named him, Sang, the best among the healers, and the saying was that of a man who thinks another's usefulness ends with the steadiness of his hands. *Korl* was best among healers, best among thinkers, best among men, and it had been Korl who had given Sang his reason for wanting only a oneness of wives.

It had been in the time he had gone to Term and returned with Mari.

He had kept his hurting of the she to smallness, he had made no marks that she would carry for the allness of her life, he had ended the thing as soon as it could be done. He had come to understanding of a hair-face, the one they named 'the Puker', having come near to puking, himself, because of his doing.

When it was ended, he made going to Korl to speak of the thing he had done.

"Of me," he said, "you have made a healer."

"Such," the old man replied, "is my hope."

"You have taught me," Sang went on, "of pain. That it is a goodness. That it names the place of damage in the body and gives a healer knowledge of the thing to be done."

Korl's only answer was a grunt of agreement.

"We spoke, also, of surgery," Sang said, "that when the healer, himself, makes the damage, there is no need of pain. The patient can be made to sleep, and not feel the damaging."

"Ah," Korl smiled. "You have taken yourself a wife, and you have added the noise of her mouth to that of the others this day."

Sang made no answer. He waited the saying of his teacher.

"You would know," Korl said after a pause, "of the damage that was ended by the damage that was made, after the way of surgery."

"You have taught me," Sang answered, "to think on pain as a tool, a thing that can be used for the making of goodnesses."

The thinking was in you, the old man thought, *I gave it words.* He closed his eyes and remembered the meeting of a boy. A boy who could throw a stone with such straightness and such hardness as to kill a pisone at fifty paces. A boy who could throw other stones with such crookedness as to miss another boy who had been sent, knifeless, into the street by a father who wished him punished with stones. Other boys had joyed in the stoning, this one had missed and missed again. Korl had been old at the meeting of that boy, but it had yet been that his hands did the things he asked of them, he was yet a healer. He had taken a second apprentice and taught him healing.

He sat now, beside the man that boy had become, and heard his saying that he had been taught to think on pain as a tool to be used for goodness. This, perhaps, was a truth, but the teaching had been done by another. In Korl, there had been seeing of a thing that was there.

"It is the way of a knife," the old man began, "that a man gives it to his son, and a son becomes a man, and a man gives it to his son."

Sang waited to learn the way in which his question would be answered.

Will he see, the old man wondered, *that to speak of a knife is to speak of the thing that hangs from a man? That the entering of a knife into the skin has much sameness to the entering of a man's thing into the place that was made for it, and that the slit made by touching a knife to a she has sameness of appearing to the slit she was born with? Yes, he will see.*

"With the blade," Korl continued, "he gives also knowings. A knowing of the way a knife is used, and a knowing of the ways a knife must be cared for. This was so with you, eh?"

"My son is yet of much youngness," Sang answered.

"Your father," Korl said, "has made these givings?"

Sang nodded. Korl held out his hand and Sang drew his knife and passed it over to him. The old man made a show of looking on the blade, tested the edge with his thumb, and gave a nod of satisfaction.

"This," he declared, "is well cared for, it has much sharpness?"

"Hehn." Sang grunted agreement.

"Your father," Korl repeated. "has given you knowings of goodness, not?"

"Truth."

"It is the way of a knife," Korl said again, "that a man gives it to his son, and a son becomes a man, and a man gives it to his son. With the blade he gives knowledge of its use and knowledge of its care—honing, protecting from rust, other things. He gives, also, knowings of the ways a knife must not be used, lest it come to dullness or be broken, eh?"

"This also," Sang agreed.

"What," Korl looked hard at the younger man, "what if the last of these knowings was not given, or given wrongly? How of a son who, lacking knowings of rightness, tried using his knife in ways of wrongness?" He took his whetstone from his pouch and, without actually touching the stone, pretended to try and saw it in half.

"The blade," Sang replied, "would come to dullness."

"It would make no change to the stone."

Sang made no saying, but he had begun to take meaning from Korl's words.

"It is the way of a knife," Korl repeated for the third time, "that a man gives it to his son, and the son becomes a man, and a man gives it to his son, this also of knowings."

Sang considered for a moment. "You speak, then, of one who was given a knife, and wrongness into his knowings of its use?"

"I speak not of one, but of many who were taught to use a knife in a way that has wrongness."

It was then that Korl gave him a thing for his reading. A fiveness of times Sang made reading of it, and there was yet much that came not to his understanding. He knew of the writing that its having was death, that its reading was treason. He knew, also, that it named the man who had taught the first of these ways of wrongness.

"When a father," he said finally, "has given knowings of wrongness, where can a son find learnings of rightness?"

Korl signed that he had no answer.

"Should the many be told," Sang wondered, "that a knife was never made for the cutting of stones, that there should be an end to the foolishness of wrong usings?"

The old man shook his head sadly. "There is no wisdom," he said, "in naming a fool for what he is. He will hear only the insult, never the truth behind it. When there are many to share in a foolishness, a wise man hides his differentness."

"A lie must be told, then, a pretending to be also of foolishness."

"It must be told," Korl agreed, "but it need not be told often, long at each telling, and, perhaps, it is better told by one who knows he is lying."

Now Sang was come to another time of this lying. He had another of shes to be put to the chair, and the saying of Korl was truth. There was need that the lie be told to the many who would wonder of it otherwise.

He stared at the second of his shes. The she looked back at him.

"The Elder spoke of she-whisperings," he said, "this is remembered?"

"I remember he talked about them," Karel said, "I'm not sure what they are."

He gave a derisive snort. "It is a name we give to a thing feared, when we shame of the fear and pretend we have it not."

"What she-whisperings was he was talking about, Sang-ser?"

"It is spoken among the shes that betime The Mother will make her coming and," he chuckled, "end the ways that have rightness because they are mine. There are some to think that you are She."

"I am not The Mother, Sang-ser."

"This is known to me," he said, "nor are you of witches."

"No," she tried not to smile at the idea, "I'm not."

"There is strangeness in you, Karel, but it is not such a strangeness that a man could walk from you in fear. Were it so, I would have done it at the time of your taking."

And if I had only known enough to claim a little sorcery in my stockpile... Too late for that.

"Is there anything you *are* afraid of, Sang-ser?"

"You ask if I would have feared you had you been of witches?"

"I don't believe you would have."

"You would need more proof than your saying of it."

There was a long, pensive silence. Karel refused to squirm under his scrutiny as Tami had done, as Mari would certainly have done. She was aware of the fact that he was considering what he would say next, but by the time he spoke she had forgotten the question.

"My fear," he said, "is of death, that it come to one I have said I would heal."

"Is…is that why you saved my life?"

Once again she was subjected to his heavy scrutiny. "You ask if it had been a betterness to let you die?"

"Better for you," she said, "and for Mari."

"I had no wanting of you, Karel," he said after a pause while he considered what she had said, "but your taking was needful. I made finding of a she who saved me the trouble of a going to Term. Had I not taken her, the Council would have brought me to trial, and, perhaps, ended my living. Had you died of stepping in stakur," he shrugged, "freedom from an unwanted second wife, but failure as a healer."

"Patients die sometimes," she said, "but you couldn't let me be one of them."

"It is foolish," he interrupted, " to speak of what might have been. As well to make wishing that you had been of men, that I might have made your killing as well as that of the other."

Sang had seen pain before, on a manyness of faces. It had never been, however, that he had seen pain begin to grow and then be ended almost before it had filled the face of the one who felt it.

The she cut it off. He had no knowing of the way it was done, he knew only that the pain was there in her face, and then it was not there and the she was looking on him as calmly as before.

"I didn't know," she said, "that you had killed him."

"He was husband to you?"

"He was my friend."

"Friend!" He literally exploded. "I know of you," it was partly a statement, partly a demand for verification, "that you are a teller of truths. I have seen of you that, even when you try to make lyings, you are a teller of truths."

"I'm not lying," she said bitterly. "Mik was my friend, and you've killed him, and...I will try...very hard...not to hate you for that."

At last, he thought, *she does a thing that is truly of shes.* Hating he knew. Shes made hating from the day they were taken to the day they died. But this one had said she would try to make end to her hating, and its reason had differentness. It was hating for one who had killed a friend.

"Is there no end to your strangeness, Karel?"

"Sang-ser," she said coldly, "can we get this...business of the chair over with? I...I'll try to be...whatever you expect of a wife...afterwards. But let's get on with it. I don't feel much like talking to you right now."

She started to rise and go back to the chair, but he put out a hand and stopped her.

"Is it, even yet, that my ways have rightness because they are mine?"

She took a deep breath and let it out slowly. Was she still a Scout? Could she still live up to everything a Scout was supposed to believe?

"Yes," she said finally. "It...it'll be much harder now, but I'll...I'll try."

"Is it ever thus with you," he asked, "that you make doing of another's ways?"

"Sang-ser," she said angrily, "I want to get *this* thing of *your* ways over with." What is he waiting for?

"I have asked a thing," he said. "I will have answer. Is it ever thus with you?"

"I try," she said. "Sometimes I can't do it, but I try—except when I'm at home, among my own people."

"Among your own people," he repeated. "I am among my own people."

She waited for him to go on. There was no sense in commenting on the obvious.

"I have said that I had no wish for you, when I made your taking."

"You said the Council would have...punished you if you hadn't taken me."

He nodded. "But the thing was done because of the wishings of others, Karel, from fear of their sayings and, perhaps, of their doings." He glanced at the chair and then back to her. "The chair is a thing others think needful. In your everness of following the ways, and doing the wishings of others, do you sometimes tire?"

"I don't have that right," she began, "I..."

"Right be damned," he cut her off. "I ask if you tire of it."

"Yes," she admitted, and she could not help glancing at the chair when she said it, "sometimes I do."

"I tire of it," he announced emphatically. "It is now that I am tired of it. There will be no chair."

Because you're tired of...

No, there was something else involved. Something he was not telling her, something he would probably never tell her. This was only his excuse.

"All right," she said. "I...I'll try to..."

"You will follow my ways because they are mine," he finished for her. "That is your way. There will be no giving of pain in my chair, but none must know that there was not. Especially Tami must have no knowledge of it."

"Why him, particularly?"

"He joys at pain," Sang said cautiously. "He would sorrow to know that it was not given. He would speak of the notness of my doing in places where I would not have it known."

"All right," she said, "I won't say anything."

She was about to say something else, but she saw him flinch as if he had taken a physical blow. He sat there staring right through her as if he had forgotten her, as if his attention had been called away.

7 CHAPTER 7

A two-leg was hurt. Badly. Other two-legs were carrying it toward a two-leg healer.

Pain was shared among the People. When a body was damaged, others, as many as necessary, absorbed a small portion of its pain, none taking too great a share, and relieving the damaged body of all but its own share.

The idea of a damaged body being alone with its pain was as intolerable to the People as that pain would have been. Pain was a thing to be relieved. Damage was a thing to be repaired. The idea of individual pain was inconceivable. Another's pain? Impossible!

Impossible among the People, but not among animals. That it was possible in two-legs should have been proof that they lacked intelligence, but it was not. Isolated as they were, trapped in solitude by their inability to Think, and despite their capacity for hurting each other, two-legs occasionally broadcast an emotion that was impossible, but not uninterpretable, to the People.

Sympathy!

In the People, such an emotion would be a waste of mental energy, a distraction from the effort of repairing the damage. In a two-leg it was valid. Sympathy could be felt by any two-leg, but there were special two-legs whose duty it was to remove the cause and eliminate the need for the emotion. The two-legs had healers.

The methods used by the two-leg healers were different. They could not Think. They could not enter a mind, strengthen it, and direct the flow of mental energies that sought out damaged tissues and caused them to regenerate. They could not bring two, three, four, a hundred mentalities to bear on the task so that the healing took place with a speed and correctness impossible to a single mentality. What they couldn't do mentally, the two-legs did physically.

The two-legs liked making physical changes. There were many things that the two-legs did that made the world different. They cut down trees and built things with the wood. They dug up the ground and forced plants to grow in unnatural ways. All but one of the changes two-legs made were unnecessary, destructive, or both. For the sake of healing, however, the two-legs changed each other.

This, then, was the second half of the Contradiction.

The two-legs could damage each other, but two-legs healed each other. When a two-leg was hurt, as now, the nearest healer of its own pack was warned.

A dainty tendril of mind went out from the People, cautiously, carefully touching just below the level of consciousness, strengthening until it created a faint stirring of uneasiness in the two-leg healer, and then withdrew.

He would know. He had felt such things before and learned to trust them. He would know that a two-leg had been hurt and was coming to him.

"We must end our speaking together, Karel," Sang said. "It is soon that a patient comes."

This was no scheduled treatment he was talking about. It was something he had just discovered. "How do you know, Sang-ser?"

"The curls speak it," he said.

"The curls?"

"The small ones of the trees," he explained. "In the whispering of shes it is said that they have speaking to the mind."

The little squirrel-like creatures! Telepaths? Unrecognized IL? Telepaths were notoriously non-technological, and this would not be the first time they had been mistaken for animals because they did not build things, because their civilization consisted of games played in the mind, and because they could communicate only poorly with members of other races.

"You said she-whisperings, Sang-ser," she suggested cautiously, "what do you think happens? Do they speak to your mind?"

"There is a feeling that comes to me," he said, "and it is ever that a patient follows it."

"Is this feeling ever wrong?"

He shook his head.

She of Strangeness

Well, well. Complications are upon us. The tiny creatures were telepaths, definitely. Which meant that this was their world. The human colony was trespassing, and the Federation would remove it.

And, she added mentally, *a patient is coming.*

"Sang-ser, Mari tells me you could use help with your healings."

"You have this doing?" It should not have been a surprise, this she was ever a strangeness.

"I know a little," she admitted.

"I had no wanting of you, Karel," he said, "but, perhaps in this you can be a goodness."

Now that I'm useful. She hid her amusement. "I know you don't want me, Sang-ser," she said, "perhaps I can help you there, too. I'll be leaving the first chance I get."

He looked at her aggressively. "You would make a running?"

"At the first opportunity," she confirmed.

A foolishness to speak this thing before its doing.

"For a running," he said, "there is punishment."

"I'm not afraid of you, Sang-ser."

Truth. Her fear of him had ended. Perhaps, if it came to a punishing, the fear would return, but it would never come to such greatness as to end her running. A thought of strangeness came to him.

"We will make contest, then, you and I," he said. "at my winning, there will be punishment. The punishing will be of hardness, and it will be done in a place where it can be seen by others of the shes. This is law, Karel, it is not a wishing of others for which I can know tiredness."

"I'm not afraid of you," she repeated.

"Make no thought," he warned her, "that I will come to carelessness because I have yet no wanting of you. You are mine."

It was not a matter of peer pressure, nor the more direct coercion of the law. This came from within. It was part of him.

Two men burst into the room carrying a third between them, the patient Sang was expecting.

Sang leaped to his feet and began directing the placement of the patient.

"Vark?" He directed the question to one of the men.

"And a Terman with him, healer," came the reply, "they came on us running, and hit us before…"

"The Puker," Sang spat.

"Belike, healer," the man replied. "We wasted no time seeking the pace where he left his pukings, but there are only two Termans that make such runnings."

"It is not the time of the other," Sang grunted. He clapped the man on his shoulder. "You have kept your living after a meeting with the Puker. Did you get him?"

"I put an arrow in him, I think, but he lived. We'll get him, healer."

"Shit," Sang snorted disgustedly, "your grandson will get him, and then only because he's too old for fighting." There was grudging admiration in his voice.

"Karel," he ordered brusquely, "look on the patient and speak me of your seeing." It was a test.

He watched approvingly as she bent to examine the wound. Pleased that, unlike Mari, she could stand the sight of blood.

Speaking of Mari...

She kept her eyes on the floor, mimicking Mari's meekness. In public, she should be careful not to do anything that would cast suspicion on Sang. She studied the unconscious man as he had ordered.

"Whatever a vark is," she said, "they have long teeth."

"Unh!" He held up a thumb and forefinger to show how long.

"Can...can you save the use of his arm, Sang-ser?" The muscles were laid bare, but not severed. There was reason to hope.

"He will keep the using of his arm," Sang said to the men who had brought the patient, "there will be stiffness, and he will make no huntings for a time. He will be second to keep his living after a meeting with the Puker." The statement seemed to satisfy both men, and they filed out.

Sang went to his storage cabinet and brought out a large, cloth-covered tray. He handed Karel a small flask full of some kind of liquid.

"If he starts to wake," he said, "give me the sleep potion and hold him down until it begins to work."

He's not going to wake up, he's hurt too badly.

He handed her a mask made of leather and donned one himself before opening the pack. Then he began arranging his instruments on the tray—using one of them to move the others and placing them so that the handles stuck out over the edge of the tray. Karel was struck with a sudden horrifying thought.

"Aren't there any gloves, Sang-ser?"

He smiled bitterly. "Korl remembers a time when there was one."

Oh, my God! "What do you do...without..."

"I wash," he said. "I touch only the handles. I take care that nothing of my hands enter the wound."

And you watch a lot of wounds get infected. On closer inspection, she could see that his instruments must have come from the ship. They were well cared for, but ancient, and without gloves...

He began washing the wound carefully, using a clamp to hold a piece of cloth that had been dipped in a solution that Karel hoped was antibacterial. When the area was clean enough to suit him, he set to work.

In the early stages of the operation, there was very little that Karel could do to help. Working under ideal conditions, her duty would have been to hand him the next thing he needed, but these were far from ideal conditions. The handles of the instruments were contaminated and had to be kept out of the wound. There was no way she could pass him anything without increasing its contamination, he had to select them himself.

In spite of the handicap under which he was working, Sang was performing an excellent repair job. Her respect for his ability grew at each stage of the operation.

A clamp snapped off in his hand, and he tossed it aside and selected one of the remaining three. This one refused to stay shut, and Karel had to reach over and hold it in place until he had finished what he was doing and took it back from her.

Karel wondered how he had managed without her, how he had kept the handles out of the wound, how he had been able to do, with only one pair of hands, things they were finding difficult with two.

He carefully debrided the wound, cutting away the dead bits of flesh, straightening the edges so that, when he sutured, he had a straight line to work with. When he began suturing, his technique was the strangest of any he had used thus far. He held the ends of the thread in a pair of clamps, keeping the free end up high while he hooked the needle through the area he wanted to secure. He used his clamps to tie the knot as well, but when it was tied, he passed one of the clamps to Karel and used his free hand to take a knife and cut the thread. This done, he set the knife down, retrieved the clamp that Karel was holding, and began the next stitch.

"Sang-ser," she said quietly, "it would go a lot faster if you just pulled back the ends of the thread and let me cut..."

The violence of his reaction startled her. He was on the verge of striking her, then he calmed.

"I had forgotten your strangeness," he said. "You had not the knowing."

"What is it?" *Not another not-thing!*

"Betime you will walk in the street," he said. "You will see a she with one breast."

"I've seen her," she told him.

"That she," he went on, "made touching of a knife, this was the punishing." He was reluctant to continue but decided to go ahead and tell her. "I made fighting in the Council that the taking be only of one, the other being needful for the feeding of small ones." He had not spoken in Council, nor would he speak now, that it had been in his knowing that this she would have no more small ones.

"It was proven," he continued, "that her husband knew nothing of her doing, else he would have ended his living."

I see, Karel thought. *Captives must not have access to weapons. We might use them on our captors.*

The operation continued without further incident, and when it was ended they both knew that, barring infection, the man would recover. He would be scarred, but able to use his arm.

Sang strapped the man's arm tightly across his chest and stepped outside. He returned leading the two men who had brought the patient.

"He will wake soon," Sang said. "Tell him to make no moving of the arm until I have said it may be so."

"The price, healer?"

"The debt is his," Sang grunted. "We will speak of it when I come to look on his arm tomorrow."

The man nodded and Sang supervised the removal of the patient. Then he set himself to the business of cleaning up.

The first thing he did was pick up the clamp that been broken during the operation. He carried it over to the storage cabinet, pulled open a drawer and began inspecting a small pile of broken clamps that lay within. He appeared to be searching for one that had broken on the opposite side, so that the two good halves could be combined into one instrument. Eventually he gave up and tossed the whole pile back in the drawer.

"Ever the same place of weakness," he muttered to himself.

He washed each of his good instruments thoroughly and laid them out on the tray in exactly the manner Karel would have expected.

"Sang-ser," she asked tentatively, "how do you sterilize them?"

"In the Other Place," he said, "there is an oven. In beneathness to it is a place that holds water. When a fire is put to it, the steam fills the oven and sterilizes the instruments."

She nodded her understanding. The method would be more or less effective, depending on how tightly he was able to seal the oven. Sang picked up the package and left.

The idea that came to Karel surprised her. She could do it. As a Scout she could bend the regulations at any time, but such bending had to be the result of rational thinking. This was not rational, it was something she wanted to do.

She was alone in the house. It was safe to think about the reason she wanted to do this thing and decide whether to act on it.

She had not thought about Eric for a long time. She had not wanted to think about him.

It had happened during survival training. A large carnivore had lunged up out of a hole directly in front of Eric, and the initial swipe of its clawed foot across his abdomen had brought his intestines into view.

Karel had heard his cry and managed to put an bullet through the thing's throat before it had time to lumber up out of its hiding place and finish him. It was, for her, the most amazing shot she had ever made. The combination of the adrenalin and the size of the target had somehow conspired to allow her to hit the thing. It was dead by the time she crossed the ten meters that separated her from her partner.

Karel had sat there helplessly watching Eric die. She knew what to do, she could have repaired the damage, he could have survived, but she had nothing to work with.

All right. She knew the reason for what she wanted to do, but it was against her principles. A Scout was not supposed to introduce any technological advances. The Federation, when it arrived, would provide these people with technical assistance, but it would be done cautiously, after a long period of study by experts who were supposed to be able to predict the changes such assistance might bring about in the overall society, and it would be done after negotiations with the leaders of these people. It was not the Scout's province.

She could argue with herself. She could tell herself that she would not be introducing an advance. She would only be replacing something he already knew how to use, but she would be exceeding his ability to provide his own replacements. She would be giving him something he could not have made for himself, and she would be doing it because she wanted to.

It was several hours before Sang came back with his pack, presumably sterilized, and put it back in the drawer where he kept it. By that time Karel had reached her decision.

"Sang-ser," she said, "I...I have instruments in my ship, new ones, and...gloves."

Gloves!

Could she know of his pain, of the anger that was in him when he watched the redness and swelling in a wound and knew that its cause was the dirtiness of his hands? And caesarians! Rarely had he done a caesarian without infecting the mother. The lifting of the child needed putting of hands inside...

Could she know of this? She had worked beside him and felt with him. Even when she had spoken of touching the knife, it had been a thing of bringing the work to betterness. Ever she was ready with the towel, and betime she had demanded of him that he stop for its using. He had sensed her fear that sweat would fall into the wound.

He had sensed, also, her fear when the clamp broke. He knew that the she looked to the day when the last of his clamps would break, and even to the day when one would come to his dying because of clamps that broke and gloves he had not.

She knows the hating of death!

"You would do this thing?"

"Sometimes," she closed her eyes for a moment, "I get tired of doing things the way other people want me to."

"Speak your meaning."

"When I get back where I came from..." she saw the look on his face and modified what she was about to say. "I will get back, Sang-ser. You can't stop me forever, and I'll keep trying forever."

"Speak me this tiring." His tone said he disagreed with her but did not consider it worth arguing about.

"When they find out about I gave you those things, they'll say I shouldn't have done it. That you shouldn't have anything you can't make for yourself."

"The reason of this?"

"Sometimes, Sang-ser, when you give somebody something, or show them how to do something, it changes them in a way that they're not ready to change. It can be very bad for them."

"You think, then, that I have readiness for this change that comes with the having of gloves?"

Was he actually showing a trace of amusement to go with the irony of the question?

"I had to watch a man die, once," she told him, "and there was nothing I could do about it because…I didn't have any gloves."

"There is," he said, "a thing of the contest." Strange. In a time of short pastness he had heard himself speak of competing with this she, and now he heard himself speaking of truce. He wondered how he had come to such a thing. The she was making a look of disgustedness. A thing to speak the wasting of his breath in such a saying. He nodded into the look of her face.

"When do you want to go, Sang-ser?"

"Tomorrow," he said, "but in beforeness to it, I would make speaking with Korl."

8 CHAPTER 8

It was the first time since her arrival that Karel had been given an opportunity to observe the village while it was populated. When Sang had dragged her through the gate on the end of his rope, the people had been there, but her awareness had been limited to the pain in her foot and distorted by the effects of the poison.

Now, with a clear head, she was able to look around the village.

A population going about the routine of its daily existence is, to the observer, a purposeless mass. The man engaged in repairing his house could be understood, the cluster of boys gathered around the well taking turns operating the treadmill contraption that raised and lowered the bucket announced that such work was given to boys, and the line of women who waited by the well to have their jars filled provided a further insight into the division of labor. None of these things spoke of purpose, of attitude, of value.

It would take a great deal of observation and questioning before Karel would begin to understand these people. There would always be things she would miss, overlook, block out because of her own prejudices. She would never completely understand them.

Her observation period was too brief, anyway, as Sang led her across the street to the house he had chosen to visit, but two things managed to impress themselves on her mind. The gate was guarded, but the guards faced inward. It seemed strange to her until one of the guards stepped forward and turned back a woman who had crossed an imaginary line which was as close as she was allowed to come to the exit.

The children are all boys!

Of the two impressions, the first made sense, the second did not. Then she remembered Torn. They had needed to send for the 'belted ones', and it had been some time before they arrived from the Other Place.

That did say something about values. Unfortunately, it was tied in with something she already knew about. It also meant that the Other Place was considered safer than here, safe enough for girl-children and belted women to live there.

"Korl-ser," they had arrived and Sang's voice interrupted her reverie, "is there room in your house for another?"

One other, Karel noticed, *he didn't mention me.*

"Sang-ser," a delighted voice came from the house, "for you there is ever room in my house."

A verbal entering ritual, then, with a ritual answer. They went inside.

Korl had once been a large, powerful man, but the bulk of the flesh had faded from his bones. Wrinkled lips curled back over toothless gums and, partly, explained his thinness. A long, sharp nose, emphasized by the sunken cheeks, jutted out from behind a pair of hard, clear eyes that avoided Karel and drove straight into Sang.

Sang squatted on the floor directly across from the old man, but it was a long time before he spoke.

Karel was unsure of herself in this setting. She did not think it would be proper for her to sit with the men, she was not even sure it was proper for her to have entered the house. She had not been mentioned in the admittance ritual. She huddled into a corner, hoping that she had guessed what Mari would have done.

Sang stared at Korl. Korl stared at Sang. They sat with their eyes locked together and their bodies still. The morning sunlight coming through the door struck Sang full in the back and cast a shadow on the old man, and the shadow had shortened considerably before some signal passed between them and it became appropriate to speak.

"There is a new she to my house," Sang announced quietly.

"I have heard," the old man's voice was harsh, "that a healer who has yet to make choosing of his apprentice made risking of his ass."

It is ever thus, Sang thought, *that first we must speak of the apprentice.*

"Were it only," he said, "that I seek for a boy, the thing would be easy. I must make finding of a thing that is in a boy, a thing he would hide from me."

A thing of rareness, the old man thought, *a thing that was not in the first of my apprentices. A thing from which to make a healer and not a damned seller of healings.*

"You must choose," he snapped. "Be it wrongly—you must choose." He glared at the younger man. "There must be no moreness of ass-risking until the choosing is made."

"The ass is mine," Sang answered, but the anger in his voice was tempered by respect.

"It is not yours," Korl retorted. "If your thinking is thus, I have failed in my teaching."

"I remember," Sang said almost sarcastically, "the name of a healer who risked his ass in a time of plague."

"It was not mine," Korl shouted. "A healer's ass belongs to those who sicken. He risks it only for the sake of those who sicken."

"When fighting men fear to hunt," Sang said, "their shes starve and their small ones with them. Nutrition is also a thing of healing."

Korl threw back his head and laughed until it brought an ache to his side. He reaches far to find his excuses.

"When fools will quiver in their holes and babble charms to ward off magics," Sang continued the argument, "there is need of one who will face the thing they fear."

"It is not needful that that one be a healer who has yet to make choosing of his apprentice," Korl shouted.

"I will choose, damn it, but I will not choose wrongly."

No, the old man's anger began to leave him, *you will not choose wrongly. There are ten, now, among the healers, and I have made you the best. You will take of that bestness and give it into one who has its keeping.*

"I am come," he said, "to my twenty-seventh year."

That would be eighty-one ship's years, Karel made a quick calculation.

"My teeth are gone from my head, the weight of my body is of more greatness than the strength of my legs, my arms have no strength for the pulling of a bow. I make no huntings. Betime I had two wives, and they have ended their living. Betime I had a son, and his ear hangs in the cave of a hair-face. The only goodness that was left to me was my knowing of healings, and this I have given into you. I would live to see its giving into one who will have its using when your hands have ended their usefulness. When you risk your ass, damn you, you risk also my knowings."

These things were known, the allness of them, and the fear that was in the old man was not of things Sang could take lightly.

She of Strangeness

"I will choose," he repeated, "in soonness."

"How is it with the nephew?"

Sang shook his head. "In a time of short pastness, there was noise in the air from the mouth of one who had sameness."

So? He sees in the boy the making of a wife-killer?

"Speak him," Korl said slowly, "the betterness that a man be of Death-trackers than have his name given to them."

"Such a choosing," Sang answered when he had recovered from his surprise, "is the right of the one who makes it, it is not the thing of an uncle."

"Speak," Korl answered, "not to him, but in his hearing, of the courage of the Death-trackers, that they take to a trail and keep to it even if it lead into the caves of the hair-faces. Speak that, when they have taken a man's name they will find his place."

Sang nodded and kept nodding for a long time. There was wisdom in the saying of his teacher.

"I will give the thought," he said, "what he does with it is his business. My choosing will be of another."

Korl stuck a bony finger in Sang's face and shook it fiercely. "There must be no more ass-risking until you have chosen."

"Betime," Sang replied, "the thing to be gained gives worth to the risking. I have come to speak on such a thing."

He came, Korl remembered, *with a thing in his mind.*

"There is gain worth ass risking, in this new she of your house?"

Sang shook his head. "There is a strangeness in her."

"Strangeness, Sang-ser? There are things in the knowing, things yet to be learned, and shes. Is it that this one has more strangeness to any other, or is it," he smiled a little, "only that this one is yours?"

"She has made twice—no three times—a doing of truth." *I had forgotten her hating of me, and the reason of it.*

"It is not," Korl was suspicious, "that there is newness to the way of her lyings?"

"It is not," Sang insisted.

My Polyan she came to doings of truth, Korl remembered, *but only after the passing of many years.*

"Doings of truth," he repeated, "this also of sayings?"

"Heyn," Sang agreed.

Korl rubbed his chin slowly. "She has named the place of her coming?"

"Only that it is another of suns," Sang replied.

"Unh," Korl nodded. "A belted she makes fewer lyings. Perhaps in this place of her coming she is belted. Perhaps, in this place, she needs to learn the ways of shes who are beltless."

"She spoke me of ways," Sang said, "that hers have differentness to mine. But she has said she will do of my ways because she is a stranger among us and has no right to bring change."

"She speaks of rights!"

"Heyn."

"A she speaks of rights!"

"She does."

"But," Korl went on, "the bringing of change is not among the rights she would claim?"

"She speaks of our ways," Sang said, "that they have rightness because they are ours."

"She gives no other reason?"

"This only."

If, Korl thought, *there can be a threeness of ways, there can be a manyness.* Of his wives, he had taken one from Term and one from Poly, and he had learned of them that their ways had differentness, not only to his, to each other. There had been surprise at the learning. This thing that she had spoken to Sang came not from surprise that his ways had differentness, it came from her knowing that there are a manyness of ways.

"The she-whipped," he said, "would give change to our ways. Their coming will be of an army, Sang-ser, not a oneness of shes."

"There was another," Sang said, "a man. He, too, was a strangeness. He made twisting of his hair, after the way of the Polyans, and yet there was no hair to his face. He made also a great noise, as of a gezel when it charges. I walked," he held up his hands a short distance apart, "that close behind him, and he had no ears for my coming." He made a quick stabbing motion and then a flicking gesture with his thumb, as if he were flipping something aside.

"Again of the ass-risking," Korl snapped.

Sang shook his head. "There was no risk. He heard not my coming." He paused for a moment and then went on. "It is another of her strangenesses, Korl-ser, that she spoke of this one and named him *friend*!"

Korl closed the eyes of his body. In the eyes of his mind, he saw again his Polyan she as she had been at her taking, barely a woman, in the fifth year of her life. The thought moved, and he saw again the gleaming of her body, felt the wetness of it as her shoulder touched his own when they worked together in the time of the plague.

From that time, from their going together to the helping of the sick in a time when others, even other healers, feared the touching of the sick, his Polyan she had been first-wife to him. First in all things but name, second, thank The Mother, in her leaving of him.

He had counted the teeth that fell from her head. He had watched each new wrinkle that made change to her face. He could yet hear her voice at the saying of a thing that was his. At her saying that she would wait, beside the Door of the Place of the Dead, so that she would have togetherness with him when he made entering of that place.

It was a saying of one for whom, until now, he had had no name. He had been given a name.

"Friend," he repeated softly.

"The thing is impossible," Sang snorted. "No man has the doing of it, even less a she."

Korl reached into the pouch that hung from his belt and took out a small stone. He handed it to Sang and waited. Sang examined the thing carefully, holding it where Karel could not see it clearly. There appeared, however, to be something extremely interesting about it.

When Sang finally looked up from it, Korl drew his knife. This, too, he passed over to the younger man, and Sang began a second careful scrutiny of the thing in his hand. He stared at it for a long time before testing it gently with his thumb. Then he drew his own knife and tested its edge, comparing the two. Finally, he started to hand the old man's knife back to him, but it was refused.

"The stone," Korl said, "fell from the sky, perhaps from another of suns, it has more hardness to any that can be found in our world."

Sang did not answer, but he tested both blades again and then reached over to return Korl's possessions. Korl accepted the knife, but he waved the stone aside.

"I am come to an age," he said, "when there is no more to my needing of such things. What is this gain that gives worth to an ass-risking."

"She offers instruments of surgery, Korl-ser, new ones," Sang told him, "also of gloves."

"Eh?" The old man leaned forward excitedly.

"In the thing of her coming," Sang jerked his head in the direction of the ship.

Of this, Korl thought, *his care to name her a teller of truths. Belike her coming was from a place where such things could yet be made.*

"She has named," Korl asked, "her reason for this giving?"

"It is known to me," Sang replied, "but it is not of things to be made easily into words."

"Heyn," Korl grunted, "but it is not of tricks? It is not that she will make your killing and her own going?"

"She has said she will make running," Sang said, "but not in beforeness to this giving of instruments."

"She has said it," Korl snorted derisively, "a foolishness to make such a saying before the doing."

"Another truth," Sang disagreed, "as it is with her."

"She could have held the thing in her mouth," Korl mused, "also this of the instruments. I would have sight of your she, Sang-ser, and also her speaking."

"Both are yours," Sang said, "her name is Karel."

For the first time Korl turned and looked directly at Karel. She had been wondering when, if ever, they would stop talking about her as if she were absent.

Now, suddenly, Korl's attention was on her. His eyes had been riveted on Sang from the moment of their arrival. It was as if he...

He couldn't, she realized with a shock. *I belong to Sang. He needed permission to speak to me, and he had to have a reason to ask for it.*

He was aware of her now, and his eyes drove into her as if he could reach into her soul and drag out everything that was there, everything she was. She was undergoing the most intense scrutiny of her life. She met his gaze, stared back at him, and tried to do the same thing to him. His face was completely impassive. If he gave any clue to his thoughts, it was hidden in a nearly invisible twitch of a cheek, a minute shift of one eyebrow, a vague movement of the lips that could have been meaningless. She studied his face, memorized every wrinkle of it and finally turned her attention to his eyes.

She of Strangeness

If they were really the windows of his soul, then she lacked the skill for reading them. They were more like a power, a magnetic force that took from her and gave back nothing. She collapsed and showed him everything that can be shown in a face. She ceased to care, to concern herself with holding back, with concealing anything, and, gradually, a silent communication began to build.

She could not tell whether it was because he was relaxing his guard, allowing her to see more than he had permitted earlier, or whether it was simply that she as beginning to learn how to read that craggy face, but there was definitely communication. She had respected the old man, admired him, and now she grew to like him as well. She had listened to him before because she was interested and because, she told herself, it was her duty as a Scout to learn everything she could about him. Now she waited for him to speak because she wanted to hear what he had to say.

He leaned back at last and returned his eyes to Sang. "I have found the strangeness of your she," he said, "it is that she looks on a man to learn who he is."

"There are others to make this looking," Sang said.

Korl shook his head. "A Terman does it not. Polyans will look, but the thing of their seeing is as they were told it would be, not as it is."

"How of the belts?"

"Shit," Korl dragged the word out. "They look on a man to see of his strengths and his weaknesses, and then to find the thing they can gain from him."

Sang felt of the scar on his arm and remembered the teeth of his sister. The sister who had waited the death of a Terman and made her marrying into the house of an Elder. The things she had gained from her marriage were partly his, he was yet brother to her, but it was truth that the belts looked only for gain.

"Karel," Korl's attention shifted back to her, "name the reason of your speaking of gloves and instruments."

My reason? She shrugged. "He saved my life," she said, "I think I owe him something."

"A she who speaks of rights," Korl was highly amused, "and also of debts. The payment is greater than the owing."

"You give her the debt!" Sang was indignant.

"I do not," Korl answered. "There is nothing in the having of a she that does not belong to her husband. Yet another had hidden the having, this one spoke when she could have held the thing in her mouth."

Sang shook his head. "She could not have held the thing in her mouth, Korl-ser," he said, "she has in her the thing I would find in an apprentice. She spoke me of one who died because she had no gloves."

Korl nodded. He had seen this thing in her face. "Karel," he said, "this thing of your coming, it is a ship of space?" Her surprise must have been written all over her face and he smiled at it. "You thought I knew nothing of such things?"

"I had been told," she said carefully, "that it…uh…that it was a secret that had been kept from you."

"You were told," he chuckled, "that a 'brute' has no brain for such learnings."

She dropped her eyes, but not the way Mari would have done it, this was real embarrassment. She should have known better. "I was told that," she admitted, "but I had my doubts about it, Korl-ser."

"You had wish to wait, to make your own learning of its truth or falseness."

"If a man," she said carefully, "is told often enough, and by enough people, that he is stupid, he begins to believe it."

"He believes himself stupid and becomes it." He chuckled again. The more he thought on it, the more he saw that it was the truth of a thing that happened betime. "Sang-ser, was it ever mine to speak on my meeting with a hair-face?"

Sang shook his head.

"This also," Korl said, "a thing of gain that gives worth to the risk. Needful," this by way of explanation to Karel, "that a healer make gathering of a thing we call stakur."

"Diluted," Sang cut in, "the poison has usefulness."

"It was in the part of the year," Korl continued, "that the growing of stakur had far southness. My years were ten, my wives were living, I was of healers. A foolishness, then, to make such ass-risking—not?"

Sang was still holding the stone Korl had given him. Now he leaned forward and placed it on the floor between them closer to Korl. "A betterness," he said, "to make ass-risking than to go to another of healers and ask for a giving. 'Better dead than in debt.'"

"Your learning," Korl said, "has slowness." He flipped the stone so

She of Strangeness

that it rolled over to Sang's side of the imaginary line between them. "A son takes the knife of his father, and there is no debt. An apprentice takes the tools of his teacher, and there is no debt."

Sang, the former apprentice, picked up the stone and dropped it into his own pouch.

"I spoke of my meeting with a Terman," Korl went on, "and his vark with him. Mine was a great southness, and it was not his to expect such a meeting. We surprised each other."

"You went in loneliness?" Sang was horrified by the idea. A man with shes kept himself to a northness, and even the Death-trackers went in pairs.

"But," Korl made a sweeping motion with his hand, "he waved back his vark."

"Unh," Sang turned to Karel, "that the fighting have fairness."

She nodded her understanding.

"We made speaking together, he and I," Korl said. "I named him shithead as well as she-whipped. I spoke that, when the thing was ended, I would hang his balls from a tree.

"He said," Korl stopped and chuckled gently to himself, "that it was needful he take my ears. Of balls, did I have any, there would also have been hair on my face." The old man closed his eyes and sat there rocking with silent laughter. "A truth, is it not, that his insult was better than mine?

"He said also," Korl sobered suddenly, "that he would joy to rid the world of my ugliness. You know this word?"

"A thing of the she-whipped," Sang said, "I have heard that they say this of us."

"You have meaning for this thing? This ugliness?"

Sang shook his head.

"Karel?"

She hesitated to answer. During her training there had been a demonstration of the variability of this particular concept, and planet of origin had proven to be the key to the differences.

Physical attractiveness, or lack of it, was a prejudice—prejudices have to be taught. In societies such as this one, where mating was non-selective—Sang hadn't cared what she looked like, only that she was female—there was no need for this prejudice. So, it had died out.

"I...I know the word, Korl-ser," she said.

"Is it truth that I have it, this ugliness?"

That, she thought, *depends on where you are.* "In his mind, the Terman's, yes, you did."

"My point, Sang-ser," he cried triumphantly, "that a man speak an insult, he must know its meaning. My need was only to know that I had been insulted, but his…" A sudden thought struck him, and he swung back to Karel. "Of the she-whipped, Karel, you would name their ways also of rightness?"

"Uh…right now I'm here," she said, "and I intend to do things your way. If I went there, I would do things their way."

"If I went there," he chuckled, "they would kill me, rid the world of my ugliness. This is also a rightness?"

"It would be as right for them," she said, "as your killing of them if they came here would be for you."

"You hear it, Sang-ser? The same rightness. No more, no less."

"I hear it," he did not sound as if he agreed with it.

"It is mine, Karel, to be a seeker of truths."

Tell me something I don't know. "I understand that, Korl-ser," she said. "The reason I came here, to your world, was to learn what was here. To learn new truths."

"I spoke of this thing, this ugliness, only because, at the time, there was in me a wish for knowing of a new truth. When the Terman named me thus, I downed my knife." He made a motion with his hand as of a man sticking a knife into the ground. "He honored the truce," the same gesture with the other hand. "We sat together between the blades and made speaking. How much, Karel, is your knowledge of the she-whipped?"

"Very little." She had only just begun to understand that the name referred to Termans—brutes of trueness.

"This also of mine," he admitted, "but this I know, that a she speaks and the hair-faces make doing of her wish. It would be, would it not, that a man who thought himself stupid and became it, after the way of your saying, is more like to be of them than of us?"

"I…would think so." Or they could be faking stupidity.

Korl laughed to himself. "Yet, in the allness of our talking together, it was never mine to see him as a man who thinks himself stupid. He spoke many things that I would name foolishnesses, Karel, but they were things of his ways, not of his mind. Of his ways…I have come to think differently."

Possibly, she thought, *but certainly not because of me, or because of anything you've been told that I said.* "Because you're older now?"

"Because of a thing that has come to…" No, this learning he had made was a thing to be spoken of later, if at all. "How is your knowing of our past, Karel?"

"I was told one version," she said, "I think you might tell it differently."

"I to tell it differently," he muttered. "How have you come to this thinking?"

"Well," she began, "people always tend to tell their own history in a way that presents them in the best possible light, in a way that makes them seem…"

"I take meaning," he interrupted, "from this bestness of lights, but my tale has much differentness, Karel. How will you know which is of lies?"

"Not lies, Korl-ser," she said, "sometimes a history…changes a little, because the people who tell it don't know exactly what happened, because one person can't quite believe what he's told, and alters it so he can accept it. After several people have made small changes, the story is very different from the way it began, but it's an error, not a lie."

"Unh," he nodded, "and how of an Elder who makes such a change because he would have it so?"

Sang started. "Your saying, Korl-ser, it is…"

"I know what it is," the old man snapped.

"But to speak on such a thing in beforeness to a she!"

Korl regarded him for a long time before he spoke. "Betime," he said, "you will go to this ship of hers. You will touch nothing she has not said you may touch, you will walk only where she has said you may walk. It is truth, Karel, that there are things of danger in your ship?"

"Yes…uh…well, I suppose something could happen, but…"

"You will make this going, Sang-ser?"

"It is of gain that gives worth to the risk."

Korl looked deeply into Karel's eyes, then he leaned back and smiled to himself. "This," he pointed with his chin. "is a she. Her thinking is not that of a Terman, of a Poyan, of a belt. Her thinking is that of a she from the place of her coming. In that place, Sang-ser, shes make bargains and keep them. There is no risk."

"This is known," Sang said.

"Karel," Korl swung on her, "I will speak a thing that is not known. This Elder, if there was one, who gave change to our history—there are yet many among us who have sameness to him. They would have my life for the thing I have said."

"Especially," she agreed, "since you said it to me."

"You see, Sang-ser! She will hold my life in her mouth. It would need a knife to draw it from her, perhaps not even then. This tale of your hearing," he was back to Karel, "a hull breach?"

Note the correct pronunciation. "Supposedly sent by The Mother as punishment for sinfulness."

"We are told," Korl indicated himself and his people, "of an accident, a meteorite that breached the hull. Shes died of it, but not because of their sinning. There was losing of air for breathing.

"We spoke of an Elder who may have given change to the history," Korl said. "such an Elder could be ours, could be Terman, or one of each. Karel, how can we know truth if both tales have been changed?"

"The best way," he said, "is to read something that was written by someone who was alive at the time, but, even then, they might…"

"Wish for the bestness of lights," he finished for her. "Were you not told, also, that a brute has no brain to learn of reading?"

I wish I was more comfortable with that word of yours—shit?—it seems to express what I'm thinking. "I was told that the Termans are trying to rewrite their books," she said. "Judging from what Sang knows about surgery, I'd say your people here have also done that."

The look that passed between the two men was hard to read, a mixture of shock, anger, and…apprehension?

"I told her nothing," Sang's voice came out in a squawk.

"It is, with a seeker of truth," Korl answered calmly, "that, betime, they need no telling. Karel, it is law that shes know nothing of this thing you have said. If there were such a book," he smiled to himself, "and I make no admissions, the shes would seek its place to make its burning."

It was Karel's turn to be shocked. She said nothing, but he read the question in her eyes and answered it.

"There was plague," he said, "and many to die from it. The shes, the Termans, at least, joyed at our dying, even when it came also to them.

What, then, would be their thinking did we lose our knowledge of healings?"

"They'd be happy to let you die." She shuddered violently.

It is twice in one day, Korl thought, *I have put my life in the mouth of a she, and there is no fear in me.*

"How of our Elder, Karel," he asked, "he who, perhaps, made change to the history?"

"It happens sometimes," she said.

"Yet we are seekers of truth, we three," he said. "We would know of the thing as it was, and not as another would have us believe, eh?"

Karel and Sang both nodded their agreement.

"The history," Korl said, "that was told to me in my youngness speaks an accident that came to be in the ship. Such an accident as to make a muchness of dying, but the dying was only of shes."

"Wh...how could it be selective?"

"In the ship, we are told, marrying was done in the lateness of life, and not as it is with us now. There was a place for the sleeping of families, a place for the sleeping of men who were unmarried, and a place for the sleeping of unmarried shes."

Kael nodded her understanding. If the hull had been breached in the single women's compartment...

"In afterness to the accident," Korl continued, "there were two men to each oneness of shes."

"That agrees," Karel put in, "with the Terman version. The number agrees, not the cause."

"So?"

"So, it's likely to be pretty close to the truth."

"In the ship," Korl went on, "there was taking, only, of a oneness of wives, and it was done by choosing, eh? But in afterness to the accident..."

"There was nobody to choose from?"

"A few," Korl said. "There was never a time when the allness of the crew made sleeping."

Of course not! Some of them must have been on duty at the time— probably a third, or at least a fourth of them.

"But," Korl continued, "the men who had already made their marrying had no wish to share. There came to be killings and...a thing called raping?"

Which you couldn't define any better than you could understand ugliness. Here it's a way of life.

"To give stop to such killings and rapings, the Captain asked a voting on changes to the ways of marrying."

"There was suggesting," Sang put in, "of the way it is done now in Term and of the way it is done now in Poly. The vote was to keep to the way it had been."

"We are told," Korl said, "thus we are told."

"You don't believe it?"

"There was, perhaps, an Elder who wished for a bestness of light," he replied, "but we are told that it was the foolishness of this voting that brought Tervil to such anger that he…"

"Just took what he wanted and got out," Karel finished.

"He was yet unmarried," Sang said defensively, "and would have remained so for the allness of his living."

"The taking and the leaving are of sameness between the two stories," Korl cut in, "and thus a probable truth, eh?"

Karel agreed that it was.

"So," he went on, "there was, probably, a dying of shes and a taking of shes. But how of Tervil? Was he doing the Wishings of The Mother, or had he been angered by the voting?"

"Either way, the result was the same."

Once again, Korl threw back his head and laughed uproariously, but this time Sang joined him.

"For us, " Korl said, "in our seeking of truth, how can we know which history is correct?"

"Without written documentation," Karel said, "I'd question both versions. They agree that there was a hull breach, that women died, that men outnumbered women, that Tervil and some others took additional women and moved to a place where, to this day, their descendants build houses with chairs in them and torture captive brides."

The two men exchanged a quick glance, and then Sang spun on her. She had thought she was growing accustomed to the sense of suppressed violence she got from the man, but once again it caught her off guard.

"In the place of your coming," he demanded, "the houses have no chairs?"

"Not…not like yours, Sang-ser."

She of Strangeness

He turned back to Korl, and they stared at each other in silence. Having been exposed to it, having participated in it, Karel could be aware that communication was taking place, but she was watching two very close friends, men who knew each other intimately, men who could draw on years of past association. She was cut off from whatever passed between them.

When they spoke, when they finally broke the silence, she was still cut off in a different way.

"It is the way of a knife…"

"That a man gives it to his son…"

"And a son becomes a man…"

"And a man gives it to his son."

A ritual? A code? It was something! She was not, she realized, supposed to understand, but she knew they were no more talking about knives than they had been talking about…

"The stone," Korl said quietly, "has more hardness than any we find in our world."

The stone, Karel thought, *fell from the sky. I fell from the sky.* She didn't understand why she was being equated with the stone.

"Karel," Korl had swung on her suddenly. "In my having is a document."

"Fool!" Sang was shouting and rising to his feet.

"Fool, yourself," the old man said. "Make softness to your voice and draw no attention to my house. I have come to a deciding."

Sang looked as if he were about to argue the point, but he thought better of it. He had, Karel guessed, learned better than to try to sway Korl when he had 'come to a deciding.'

"This thing," Sang glared at her, "is of death that it be in his having."

"It is twice, now, that she holds my life in her mouth," Korl said, "there is no harm in a third."

He went to his storage cabinet and took out several items, carefully laying them aside, until he found the thing he was looking for. In talking to him, Karel had forgotten how old he was until she saw him move with the deliberateness of age. He brought her a piece of paper, incredibly ancient, and very fragile. He handed it to Sang who reluctantly passed it to Karel. She began to read.

Bill Tervil died last night.

Just before he died, he confessed that he was the one who planted the bomb in the single women's berthing spaces and started this whole mess.

I don't like being used. Bill knew I wouldn't like it, that's why he got a kick out of telling me.

I don't really believe he planned things from the beginning, even though he said he did. I think he planted the bomb, for whatever reason, and when he saw what he had done to the sex ratio and the trouble that was causing, he came up with this other idea.

I can see him carefully going through the files, deliberately selecting people with known sadistic tendencies. I can believe that because I know who's here—including me.

I believe what he said about manipulating us into thinking it was our idea, not hard after that stupid vote, but his real objective was to get the girls out here in the middle of nowhere so he could do anything he damn pleased with and to them.

He let it build up slowly. He started by slapping Becky around the first day, and then he just sat back and waited for the rest of us to realize we could do that, too. When she tried to run away that time, and he tied her to a tree and beat hell out of her in front of everybody, it really started to catch on.

I'm as guilty as anybody, and as stupid, but it's too late to change things now. The pattern's been set. The others probably wouldn't believe me if I repeated what Bill told me.

I'm writing a book, trying to put down everything I can remember about medicine and surgery. All right, so it's only a matter of trying to assuage my own conscience, at least I'll know that there'll always be somebody around who knows how to patch the girls back up when...

That was all there was. If there had been another page, Korl did not have it, or did not want to show it to her. Karel sat in stunned silence for a long time after she had finished reading. When she finally looked up, Korl and Sang were both watching her. She wondered if they knew how clearly she understood what she had just read, and how much possibility of understanding it their own culture had bred out of them. She wondered...

"Why did you show me this, Korl-ser?"

He did not answer her, he turned to Sang.

She of Strangeness

"Betime," he said, "even the knives among those instruments of newness will end their sharpness. The stone has much hardness, Sang-ser, it will give betterness to the way of your honings."

9 CHAPTER 9

Time crept slowly through the mouth of the cave and seeped into the darkness to pile itself, layer on layer, in the empty stillness. Ages had passed since the cave had been formed. Ages of silence broken only by an occasional animal that slipped into the cave for a flickering moment, made its home there, died, and left the cave to the stillness and the passage of time.

A man screamed in the blackness, and the echoes of his screams bought him awake.

He crawled painfully to the mouth of the cave, shivering with a fear that was real, and with a fear that was left from his dream.

It had been years since he had waked, bathed in sweat, from this dream. It was sickness that had brought him, once again, to dream of a thing that was ended, brought screaming to a mouth that had learned to hold the screams inside.

But screams could bring other dangers, and DeMyrn Tan looked from the entrance to his hiding place to learn if the noise had been heard. In silence he waited and he watched. When he was sure there had been none to hear the noise of his weakness and come to the place of its making, he would think.

This place had goodness for thinking. He drew himself back to a time of pastness.

"Cuts?" The Archer's knife came slowly from its sheath, and his face had on it a smile that was no goodness. "There was no need of looking on books to learn of cuts."

Who knows the reason of a name? A man goes to a place where a thing is done and learns the names of the things that are part of the doing. Thus had it been with Tan when he had come into the print shop and heard the knowers of printing speak on carved blocks of wood and name them "cuts" or sometimes "woodcuts". He had learned the making of such things. He had forgotten the time when the name had seemed strange. And now this Archer would make scarring of his face because of a word.

The Archer who stood behind grasped his head, that he have no moving of it, and the one before came slowly to more and more closeness. It was not the knife Tan watched, but the face of him who held it. The huge, bloated, grinning mask that floated above him, the eyes that glowed with a thing that was evil.

"Enough!"

The dame stood in the doorway and the archer, he of the knife, stepped back, but the other yet held Tan's head.

"I said *enough*," the dame spoke again, and Tan's head was released.

She stood looking at him for a long time before she came to nearness of him.

"This," she held up a book, "is of your making?"

"Partly, dame," his answer was truth, "the making needs many hands."

"Speak to me," she ordered, "of woodcuts."

"Their making must be done in carefulness, dame, that there be no building of ink on the lines. My once-wife is not of those who have the first books to come from the press, and…"

"You have looked on her book," the dame snapped, "this much is known. Speak me the reason of it."

"To see the work of my hands, dame," he said, "to know if it had rightness. If there was a wrongness, I would wish to make the next with more care."

She nodded and opened the book. She flipped through several pages and then stopped.

"This one," she showed him the picture, "yours?"

He needed only a glance. "I made this cut, dame."

"Speak me," she said, "the right and the wrong of it."

He looked again, and she held it to more closeness. He feared wait too long before answering, but the light of the place was no goodness, and the thing needed study.

"The most is of goodness, dame," he hoped she would not think him a braggart for the saying, "but there are some wrongnesses."

She took the page from him and looked on it. "To my eyes the allness is good," she said, "where is the wrongness?"

"If the dame will look," he suggested respectfully, "on him who has the honor of holding a dame-child, she will see of the place where his knee touches the floor, that the line has lost its sharpness."

"It seems well enough to me," she argued.

"There is more clearness, dame, to the line between him who stands and the boy-child he holds. There is also much building of ink between the points on the crown of the Priestess. If the dame will look she will see the differentness."

She studied the areas he had named. "Speak me," she said, "the names of the dames who have come to their Motherhood blessing."

"Dame," he protested. "I was given a drawing and told to make a cut. There was none to speak the names of the dames who kneel before the Priestess."

"You have no knowing of their names?"

"I...I could make guessing, dame." She had made a trap for him, and he feared that any saying would be turned against him. Safeness, however, lay only in honesty.

"Guess, then."

"The Mistress of Printings spoke me that the book tells of the years of the life of Captain Manijeh," this was truth, "I would guess that the picture is of the time when she came to the Temple with proof of her damehood, or, perhaps of the time when her mother was Blessed."

"You do not know which?"

"I do not, dame."

"In your Lonely Time," she went on, "I am told you are of Hunters."

"I am, dame."

She spoke, then to the Archers. "I have spoken to the Mistress of Printings. She has named me the same places of wrongness to this picture. Cut him loose."

"He is not of the Plotters, dame?" The Archer was disappointed.

"Betime," a hardness and much meaning to her words, "to this very room...came...another...of...Hunters."

To Tan the saying meant nothing, but the Archer jumped as if he had been struck across the face.

There was little caring in Tan's mind. His hands had come to freedom. He could walk from the place. Betime the marks of the beating would heal. Betime also…

He looked from the door of the cave, to have sureness that there was none in such nearness that he might be heard.

"Clar," he whispered viciously. "Clar! Clar! Clar!"

Five years since his marriage to her had ended, and yet he kept her name in his mind and, betime, spoke it.

There was no other among his once-wives whose name he remembered. He had ended the thought with the end of his connection to the name. Only Clar, she who had come to the house to find him with his eyes on a work of his own hands and given his name to the Archers. He remembered Clar.

A thing moved at the base of the hill below the cave, and Tan strained his eyes to see what it was.

The vark.

The vark had slowness to its coming because it had come to do, again, the thing that none but Zek would believe, to share its kill.

When Tan had first come to wakefulness in the stillness of the cave, the vark had been gone. The vark had returned to wildness, Tan thought, to range in loneliness and think no more on the man it left behind. The going of the vark could mean the dying of that man.

When the Vark had returned, Tan had joyed. When the vark had stepped back from its kill, when it had waited for the man to take and made no growling as he took, Tan had cried. Saving a man's life at a fighting was the way of a vark. Saving a man's life in a sharing of food was the way of a friend.

To Zek, only, would he speak of this thing. Zek would believe it. Others of the Hunters would make laughing, speaking that only a fool comes to nearness of a vark when it eats. That only a liar would claim to have taken food from the mouth of a vark. Zek would believe. Zek's knowing of the vark, and his loving of it, had sameness to Tan's. It was of this loving, and the vark's returning of it, that the vark had made a doing that none but Zek and Tan would believe. The vark would make the same doing for Zek had he taken a wounding.

They would wait, Tan and the vark, for the man to come to full strength. When it was so, they would wait, also, a change of the wind. When they went, their going would be as friends.

10 CHAPTER 10

"The guards," Sang said, "would stop your passing of the gate unless it be that you are bound." He slipped the rope from his shoulder and gestured with it.

Karel turned her back to him and put her hands behind her. She couldn't see his face, so she didn't know it bore a look of distaste for what he was doing, but she felt the gentleness of his hands as he tied her.

It was different this time. He kept to a pace she could easily match, but he sauntered—no, he swaggered—up to the gate. And yet, in spite of his attitude, his air of bravado, no one paid any attention to them. People painfully avoided noticing them. Eyes that happened to fall on them were whipped away, and the owner of those eyes was embarrassed.

As they approached the gate, one of the guards stepped forward and hailed Sang, he did not look at Karel.

"But one in beforeness to you, healer," the man said, "the place of two stones."

"The sky-thing," Sang answered.

The man's face took on a worried frown. "The thing is best done in a place of safeness, healer."

Karel was surprised to see Sang's hand flash toward the handle of his knife. "Your job," he said menacingly, "is to tell others the place of my going, not to make criticism of it."

The man took a step backward. His attitude was that of one who knows he has overstepped.

Sang led Karel out of the gate and into the forest. Once they were out of sight of the gate, his swaggering, boastful attitude dropped from him, as if he had been putting on a show that was no longer necessary. He continued, however, for a couple hundred meters before he stopped and came back to Karel.

Again, the look passed across his face, the nebulous flicker that was gone almost before it was there, the momentary lapse in an effort to maintain an impassive countenance. This time she saw it.

"Sang-ser, you were almost ready to kill that man, weren't you?"

"Not almost," he answered emphatically, " but he sorrowed of his insult."

"May I ask," she said hoping for an answer rather than a refusal, "what it was all about?"

"She-whispering!" Then in a mocking tone, "A daughter can be made anywhere. A son must be made in the forest where there is risk." He made a disgusted sound.

"Oh," she said. They weren't here to make a child of any sex, but everyone thought they were.

"'Oh', hell," he said. He glanced back over his shoulder. "*His* doings can also be done anywhere." He was still a little angry.

He spun on her irritably, flipped the loop from around her neck, and motioned her to turn around. A moment later her hands were free, and she was again facing him.

"This is another foolishness," he said. "To make a son, a man must free the arms. And yet it is law that the she be bound until the time of son-making." It was 'a wishing of others' he was willing to ignore. He held out his hand to her and she took it.

They walked together, now, when there was room. When the path was too narrow for both of them, he took the lead, but he kept his grip on her hand.

"Another law?" The question was slightly sarcastic.

"Eh?"

She raised their clasped hands to show him what she was talking about. He snorted.

"A thing of your *stupidness*," he said, "a thing of…" He jerked her suddenly to a halt and pointed.

It took a minute to see what he was pointing at. It was so still and so tiny, if it had not started to crawl away from them, she would have missed it altogether.

A curl! One of the tiny, treetop dancers, hurt, quivering, terrified.

"Oh," she exclaimed and started forward.

"I spoke," he yanked her back forcefully, "of your stupidness. First the stupidness of stepping in stakur, and now the stupidness of touching a curl. Their touching," he jerked his thumb upward, "is death."

The trees above them were alive with curls, hundreds of them. Every branch sagged with the weight of the tiny creatures. They were watching to see what Sang and Karel would do.

"But it's hurt, Sang-ser," she protested, "won't they let us help it?"

He shook his head. "Touch that one, the others will kill."

"Well," she said sympathetically, "I'm going to do something."

He kept hold of her hand a little longer, but he saw a thing of her eyes. They spoke a wish, and the wish was also his.

Strange, he thought, *I am healer to people, not animals.*

He released her hand and nodded. "Don't get yourself killed, I have ended my thought of its betterness."

Thanks a lot! She stood there trying to think of something she could do. There was nothing, no act or gesture, that would always be recognized as friendly. There was one thing, however, that usually worked.

For some time now she had been hearing the sound of a stream nearby. The sound had, until now, registered only on her subconscious. Now she needed it.

She turned aside from the path they had been following and made her way to the creek. When she got there she looked around. There. The remains of some shell creature, picked clean by scavengers. If the former occupant had been eaten, it was probably safe, no, she'd better ask.

"Sang-ser, would you drink out of this?"

He shrugged. "Why not?"

Nevertheless, she washed it carefully before filling it and carrying it back to where the little animal was. She stopped and set the gift down in front of the little creature, then she rose, backed slowly away, and returned to Sang.

She offered her hand, and he stared at it in amazement for a moment before he took it. He was shaking his head as he turned away.

"Another," he said heavily, "of your strangenesses."

They had only taken three steps when it hit them.

GRATITUDE!

No message, no symbol. Pure, undiluted emotion driving straight into the two humans. Thousands of minds delivering a feeling directly into the minds of those who had inspired it.

She of Strangeness

It lasted no more than a few seconds before being cut off, but the two humans were overwhelmed.

Hours later, Sang and Karel stumbled into the village, carrying the entire content of the ship's medical locker. Their memory of visiting her ship had a dreamlike quality. The message from the curls seemed more real.

She wasn't afraid, the Advocate Thought.

He was, came the answering argument.

She made a change for the sake of a Person, she sympathied him.

It had been one of their useless, primitive changes, the kind of thing they did for each other because they were incapable of Thinking, but it had been accompanied by the emotion the two-legs felt when they made healing changes to each other. She had sympathied.

The People had gratituded the two-leg so strongly they had been afraid she would collapse under it. Too many minds had felt into hers so strongly that some of it spilled over to the male. Two-legs were not built to take that much. The female was not frightened, the way the male was, she was just overwhelmed. For the first time in history, the People had entered a two-leg's mind strongly enough that the two-leg had been aware of their presence, and there had been no fear.

Next time, the Advocate Thought, *I'll touch her mind gently.*

Carefully?

Of course.

It will prove nothing.

Perhaps not, but it is worth a try.

11 CHAPTER 11

The opportunity Karel had been waiting for came several nights later.

Sang had allowed her a great deal more freedom since their return from the ship, not that there was any connection. She had been sick, she had recovered, and now she was allowed to do everything Mari was allowed to do.

Whenever possible, Karel took advantage of opportunities to leave the house, to study the village, to plan her escape. In the days that followed her return from the ship, she learned a number of things that influenced the plan that was beginning to form.

The gate was guarded. She learned, by experimentation, that she was allowed to approach no closer than three meters before one of the guards ordered her back. They did it with gestures, without speaking, but the message was clear.

At night the gate was closed, and the streets were patrolled.

At this time of year, the planet was subject to torrential rains, storms of fierce intensity and short duration. The storms were usually nocturnal, and Karel had seen for herself that they were blinding. She waited.

She had awakened to the pounding of the rain, and she had crept to the door and looked out into a solid sheet of water. She had almost gone then, but the rain quit before she managed to gather her courage. Visibility returned, and the first thing she saw was a guard not more than two meters from the doorway where she squatted. She went back to bed to wait for a better chance.

Every night since then she had lain awake long after the rest of the family was asleep. Next time it rained, she would be ready.

Time to go!

She slipped quietly out of the house and felt her way along the wall, working around to the back of the building. There was a distance of about three meters to be negotiated between the rear wall of the house and the stockade wall, but there was nothing to guide her across the gap. Once she let go of the side of the house, she would be on her own. She put both hands against the wall, oriented herself, established the line she would have to follow to reach her destination, took a deep breath, and plunged. Three meters. Six, seven, possibly eight steps. She counted. Nine...ten...she was off course.

There was no danger at this point. If the rain stopped, the guards would spot her, but she would have an excuse for being there. She was going to the latrine and got lost.

Eleven...twelve...she had to reach the wall soon. She had to have time to get over it.

Here it is. She struck the wall at an angle that explained the extra distance she had traveled. Now she had another problem.

She placed one hand against the wall as a guide and leaped upward.

The wall was only about two-and-a-half meters high. She could easily jump that high, but she also had to grab hold of the top without being able to see it. The stakes had been sharpened at the top and the wood would be wet and slippery.

She caught one of the stakes, but before her fingers could close on it, she felt herself slipping and dropping back. It was no good.

She had been hoping to get enough of a grip with one hand to hang on until she could get the other one up to help. If she got out of touch, if she lost contact with the wall, she would be lost again. She could wander all over without finding it. The rain might stop any second.

She tried again, desperately. Still using one hand as a guide but reaching as high as she could up the wall before making her jump. This time she did not even clear the top. Her fingers scraped bark as he slid back down to the ground.

She was terrified now. It was one thing to be caught outside the house, it was quite another to be found trying to climb over the wall.

She put both hands against the wall and lined up on it. Then she let go, bent her knees until they bumped against the wall and leaped up and forward with everything she had. She took a layer of skin off her arm on the way up, but she threw both her arms up and over, and one of them wedged itself into the notch between two of the poles.

There she dangled, gritting her teeth and fighting desperately to get a grip with her free hand before her arm came loose from its socket. She caught, she held, she heaved herself upward.

Her chin came up level with the poles, but her arm was still trapped. She wedged the other hand down into the adjacent notch and heaved herself up as high as she could. Her arm came free, and she grabbed the top of the pole just as she started to slip back.

Now she was hanging by her hands and trying to find a purchase for her feet on the slippery bark. All she was accomplishing, was an increase in the amount of skin she was going to leave behind. She quickly gave up on that method, chinned herself again, reversed the direction of her efforts and shoved downward until half her body was above the top of the wall.

She swung one leg over, followed it with the other, and dropped to the ground on the other side. She was out.

She crouched in the darkness beneath the wall, waiting for the rain to stop. It had been her friend until now, it had hidden her movements, but now she needed to see where she was going. The ship was not far away, and she knew the route, but not through a blinding wall of water.

She felt safe now. She would be missed in the morning, but by morning she would be inside the ship. She was past the major obstacle. There was only a short trip left to be made. Once she was inside the ship, Sang, the whole village, could come and stand around outside, but they could not get in.

The rain stopped, but Karel continued to wait. She strained her ears as hard as she could, trying to catch any sounds from inside the stockade. She had no idea how they would react if they became aware of her escape. If they raised a hue and cry, she could make a run for it, but she had also heard Sang telling Korl how easily he had slipped up behind Mik. If they came silently, she'd be finished.

When she thought she had waited long enough, Karel began to move carefully away from the wall. The whole world had been drenched, and the moisture would reduce the amount of noise she would make, but she remembered Sang's condescending remark about the amount of noise Mik had been making when...

She crawled with agonizing slowness, planting one hand and easing her weight onto it gradually before bringing a knee up beside it. For at least an hour, she kept it up examining the ground in front of her carefully before planting a limb on it, and in that hour she covered less than three hundred meters.

She was trembling.

She kept trying to tell herself that it was excitement rather than fear, but her whole body was tingling in anticipation of the hand that could fall on her at any moment. When she was no longer able to stand the snail's pace, and thought she was far enough from the village to avoid being heard, she rose to her feet.

She wanted to run, but it would have been foolish, a waste of the energy she might need later, and dangerous. The stakur had nearly killed her. Sang had held her hand to protect her from her 'stupidness'. The ship might be less than a kilometer away, but the distance between held any number of hazards she had not learned to deal with. She felt safe. Not so safe that she could afford to be foolish, but safe. The principal danger, Sang, was behind her. Ahead might be varks with three centimeters of teeth, gezels that made a lot of noise when they charged, injured curls that she could step on without knowing they were there, and a thousand other things that could kill her.

I am myself.

For days she had been a she, Sang's wife, the cause of Mari's jealousy, the only redhead on the planet, a host of things that other people ascribed to her. Now she was Karel.

She was alone. She would be alone until she got back to the Federation. Wherever she went, whatever she did, whatever decisions she made would be hers. Totally hers, without regard to anyone else.

Fear!

She was running in terror. Her thoughts of a moment before, her sense of security, her confidence, her self-control were gone. Wiped out by the sudden blind panic that drove her feet in a way her mind could not have driven them.

She knew Sang was behind her, awake and following. Coming to take everything she was away from her, coming to shove her back into the mold, coming to kill who she was and force her back into being someone else. Coming...

The fear solidified, became tangible, omnipresent. It obliterated rationality and filled her awareness. Feet became blurred motion in a world of whirling motion. Trees loomed and whipped past, branches reached out and tore at skin that had lost sensation, and the sum of the parts was fear.

Less than a kilometer, half a kilometer, and a trained distance runner for whom it should have been easy. Her training was gone, her ability to pace herself was gone, her ability to think was gone. She burned herself out.

Panic expressed itself in a burst of speed that covered half the distance. Panic in a body driven beyond its capacity. A good body, a healthy body, a strong body, but limited. She approached the limit, and its proximity slowed her to a walk, but she did not stop, and she did not allow herself to rest. At the slower pace her body could gain strength, could push back the limits of endurance until she was able to run again, but it was a much shorter time before she was reduced to a walk once more.

Walking or running, the fear was the same. Unable to walk, she would have crawled, unable to crawl, she would have died, but she would have died straining to get to the ship. The ship, the only thing in her mind besides fear was the ship. The goal. The direction the fear was pushing her.

A thousand times she saw herself reaching the clearing, dashing across it with the last ounce of her strength, laying her hand on the lock that would open the door. When the fear was not enough to drive her, the vision pulled, kept her feet moving, dragged her forward when she might have stopped—and then it was real.

She was standing in front of the ship and reaching toward the lock. The fear was still there, it had never left, but she was really here. She was really watching her hand as it rose toward the goal she had dreamed about. She was…

Biting, kicking, clawing, and screaming with rage. The fear cut off a fraction of a second before Sang reached her, and in that fraction of a second she heard him coming and turned on him.

He managed to dodge most of what she tried to do to him, but her fingernails ripped three long strips of flesh from his chest and her teeth sank deeply into the arm that held her. He grabbed a handful of her hair and pulled upward until she opened her mouth to cry out—and then it was over.

She was lying on her face, with her hands tied securely behind her, and she was hating him with a violence she had never known was in her.

He waited. Until the last possible second, he waited. Less cruel than the others, is he? Not much!

She felt her head being lifted, by the hair, so he could slip the loop around her neck, and she tried to catch the rope in her mouth, bite it in two. A great deal less satisfactory than his arm, perhaps, but at least...

No more, she thought. *He'll take me back, but he'll fight every step of the way.*

When he raised her to her feet, she waited until she found her balance, and then she aimed a kick...

He dodged, caught her ankle, and lifted. She landed on her back, but not flat. Both her arms were under her, threatening to break, and one of his was jammed across her throat. But she could still hate. She did hate. She would continue to hate, but she would never hate any worse than she did right now, because there was nothing he could possibly do to her that would be anything but an anticlimax to waiting until...

The fear wasn't mine!

She could control her own fears, she could think rationally when she was afraid, when she was angry, even when she hated. No emotion of hers had ever taken over so completely, so totally, so overwhelmingly.

If thousands of minds could be grateful, thousands of minds could project fear and force it into her so strongly as to disintegrate all other awareness. Thousands of minds could, thousands of minds had, and they had begun at the moment Sang left the village. When he started.

So, the only thing I can legitimately accuse him of...is being able to run twice as fast as I can.

The hating went from the eyes of the she. Sang made raising of his arm from her throat, lifted her that she could sit and make no more crushing of her arms. He watched the face to see of pain and there was none. He watched the face to see of hating, it had gone.

"I tried," she said bitterly.

IT WAS A MISTAKE!
She was afraid.
That was the mistake.

It had been intended as a simple warning of approaching danger, information regarding the location of the hazard and an expression of encouragement. Somehow, when it had entered the mind of the two-leg, it had become twisted, garbled, warped into something other than what had been intended. The two-leg had panicked.

Without breaking off the contact, the Advocate had tried desperately to find a way of altering the signal, of circumventing the distortion whose nature she could not understand. She had failed.

Failed, that is, with the two-leg, but not with the People. She conceived a plan, and her plan was accepted, tentatively. Application of the plan required special conditions, conditions that might not arise within the lifetime of either the Advocate or the two-leg. Conditions so specific and improbable that the bulk of the People considered their agreement a promise that need never be fulfilled.

Nevertheless, a watch was kept on the two-leg in the event that the coincidence did occur

12 CHAPTER 12

Sang did not start back immediately, as Karel had expected him to do. He led her over to the edge of the clearing and seated himself with his back to a tree. He motioned her to a spot beside him, but she continued to stand and glare down at him defiantly. He reached up angrily and grasped the rope, as if to drag her down. Then he muttered something and let her stand.

Karel did not want to sit because she did not want to turn around. Behind her was the ship, the objective. In front of her was the man who had kept her from reaching it. She preferred to face the man.

She had not lost, not yet. Losing would mean knowing, with absolute certainty, that she would never be able to win. What had happened was a setback, not a defeat. Defeat was a possibility, she had to admit that. If it happened, she hoped she would be able to accept it as gracefully as Sang would undoubtedly accept…

There was a barest hint of movement in the brush. Karel turned her head and found herself staring into a pair of blazing eyes. There was no sound, no growl of warning. She could see nothing of the thing in the brush except for those two circles of flame, but she knew, somehow, that behind those eyes a heavy body was crouched and ready to spring.

"Sang! Behind you!"

Sang's reaction was instantaneous. He became a continuous blur of movement. The knife flew from his hand before he had come completely to his feet. The blade struck the creature at the base of its throat with such force that it actually counteracted the momentum of its leap. The thing dropped at his feet dead.

Karel was shaking, terrified, but Sang seemed completely unmoved. He had eliminated the danger, now he waited patiently for the thing to stop thrashing so he could retrieve his weapon. If he felt any emotion at all, he kept it hidden.

When it was safe, he stepped forward and felt of the fur around the creature's neck, as if he were looking for something. He apparently found what he expected, and he used it to raise the animal's head so that he could extract the blade. He wiped the knife carefully on the thing's hair and stood up. He ignored Karel. He looked cautiously around, tested the wind, frowned to himself.

"The vark is collared," he told her. He kept his eyes downwind, and he kept the knife in his hand as if he were expecting a second danger to appear. "There can be no moreness to our waiting."

"You have made too much waiting, Ugly."

Sang and Karel both turned toward the voice. A man had stepped into the clearing with a drawn bow. He was short, stocky, bearded. His face, most of his chest, both arms and one of his legs were a mass of scars, the wounds were only recently healed.

The bow, however, was held in a powerful grip, and the arrow pointed steadily at Sang. It was not a clear shot, Karel as in the way, but Sang solved that problem by stepping in front of her.

"She-whipped," Sang said without menace, "you have come to a far northness."

"I had need," the man answered calmly, "of Ugly ears to show the mistress of huntings."

"I have ended your vark, hair-face," Sang said. "Is it not loss enough for one day? Would you lose, also, your life?"

He could take it, but he doesn't want to. Karel had just seen a demonstration of Sang's knife-throwing ability. He could, she was almost sure, throw and leap aside long before an arrow could arrive.

"The next life to be taken," Sang's adversary was saying, "will be yours." He lowered the bow, tossed it aside, and drew his knife.

That the fighting have fairness, Korl had said.

"Karel," Sang spoke without taking his eye off his enemy, "if I leave it that the she-whipped keep his living, will you hold the thing in your mouth as it has been with othernesses?"

Don't tell anybody you didn't kill him? My God!

She nodded and then realized sheepishly, that he could not see the gesture. "You know I will, Sang-ser."

"Dame! I can free you from this vileness! I..."

She of Strangeness

Sang was across the clearing and driving his knife into the man for the third time before Karel realized anything had changed. Again, and again and again he plunged the blade into what was already a corpse. He got up, kicked at the thing once, and came back to where Karel was staring at him in horror.

"WHY!"

His violent demand threw her into a state of consternation, but it also got through to her in a way that nothing else could have. She had never seen anyone killed before. There was Eric, of course, but he had been attacked by an animal, and…well?

No, it had not been an animal reaction. The dead man had spoken to her without Sang's permission, a violation of a taboo so deeply ingrained in Sang as to trigger instantaneous retaliation. A cross-cultural blunder that had proved fatal, and it had happened while Sang had been doing his best to talk his way out of the fight.

Now he stood before her angrily demanding to know the reason for something.

"Why…what, Sang-ser?"

"Your doing," his chin flipped the way it did when he was angry, "why?"

My doing? The only thing she had done recently was run away from him.

"You know why," she said disgustedly, "we have a contest, remember?"

"Contest be damned," he shouted at her. "You had won the fuckin' contest, and you spoke me the vark and took back your losing of it. WHY?"

Her mouth fell open and she stared at him, incredulity gradually being replaced by indignation.

"What did you expect me to do?" She spat the words in his face. "Stand there and let you get killed?"

"You are a she, damn you! Act like a she!"

"Not," she shook her head emphatically, "if it means letting you get killed. That wasn't part of the bet."

Was not? Of course, it was!

Did she think his only loss, at her winning of the contest, would be a wife that was not of his wanting? The truth was the thing that made it a contest. Did she make her running, were it known that she had gone from him, and he had made no stopping of her, the Elders would give his name to the Death-trackers.

She would stay!

Did she know if it, she would stay and be wife to him for the allness of her days. He could speak, now, and end the contest.

I will speak, he thought, *to Mari and also to Tami, that no foolishness of their tongues take from her this hope of running.*

He reached out and put his hand on her shoulder. She made no move to shake it off, but there was something in her eyes that said she would rather it had not been there. He dropped his arm to his side, but he continued to stare into her eyes. Finally, he bent down, picked up the end of his rope and turned away.

"There is no wisdom," he muttered to himself, "in naming a fool for what he is." He was not sure which of them was the greater fool.

13 CHAPTER 13

It was nearly dawn when they got back to the village. The guards passed them through the gate without comment. Sang led Karel directly to the house, but he did not go inside.

"Tami," he shouted.

The boy appeared in the doorway with a suddenness that suggested he had been waiting, just inside the door, expecting the call. His eyes lighted with pleasure when he caught sight of Karel, but it was the kind of pleasure that always made her a little afraid and more than a little disgusted.

"You have made catching of her, uncle," Tami crowed happily.

"There is a thing," Sang said, "needful of doing."

Tami grinned excitedly. "You would have the whip?"

"I would have," Sang told him, "only the gag."

"The gag, uncle! The thing is better done when there is scream…"

Sang had hit him three times and was standing over him threatening to do it again, when Karel's horrified gasp made him pause. Three times in one night, she had seen this man shift into sudden, violent action, and two of those three times had been totally unnec…

"Sang-ser!" She had never liked the boy, but this was unfair. "I'm the one who ran away! Hit me!"

He had turned at the sound of her voice. No, she had ever dared put such a thing in her voice when speaking to him.

Another of her fuckin' truths!

It was not the boy he had struck. He had struck once at the thing he had done, and again at the thing he must do. *I am a healer who has killed, and now I must cause hurting.*

"It is also," his voice was a cold, hard threat, "that you are mine. It is mine to choose the way of your punishing." He jerked his head savagely to indicate whose it was not.

Tami was back with the gag and Sang turned on him.

"For as long," he said menacingly, "as you live in my house, you will speak me nothing of my doings with my shes."

For answer, Tami held up the object he had been told to fetch. It was not an apology, it was acceptance of superior force.

Sang snatched the thing from the boys fingers and continued coldly. "A man," he said, "I would have killed for the thing you have said."

That, Karel shuddered, *is very true.*

"There is little," Sang's whole attitude shifted suddenly, as if the incident were forgotten and there were more important considerations, "of food in the house. When I have seen the sick, I must make hunting, not?"

Tami nodded.

"But," Sang went on, "the punishment of my choosing needs a longness of time, and one to watch."

"To watch, uncle?" Tami's eyes narrowed suspiciously. He had made his plans for this day. "How is your choosing?"

"She will work the well…ah…" Sang held up his hand to silence the protest that was building. "I know your thought, that the well is the work of boys. "

"Small boys," Tami obviously thought himself too old for the task.

"Or large ones needful of punishing," Sang countered. "Yours to remember the well, I think, how it is to work it for all of one day, and…" He hefted the gag significantly.

Understanding came over Tami, and a sadistic grin spread itself across his face. "And if her doing has slowness," he said delightedly, "there can be…"

"No stoning!"

Karel was not sure what was being planned for her. The punishment must be public, Sang had said, and harsh. She had, however, observed the operation of the well from a distance, and it did not appear to be all that difficult. On the other hand, Tami had agreed that the punishment was severe. Not, perhaps, severe enough to suit the boy's tastes unless he could also throw rocks at her, but he had conceded that the inclusion of the gag made it…well, Sang could be expected to obey the law to the fullest.

He led the way, with Karel following perforce and Tami following happily.

She of Strangeness

"Speak your fathers," Sang announced to the boys at the well, "that my she works he treadmill today, to learn of her running and the notness of distance gained."

He lashed Karel's wrists to the bar that the boys hung onto when they operated the well. Then he stepped up beside her and held the gag up for her to see. Apparently he expected to have to force the thing into her mouth, and he had an air of resignation.

We made a bet, she thought, *and I lost.* She opened her mouth.

When the gag was in place, Sang stepped back and looked at her. "You have breathing?"

She considered it. Yes, even if the thing swelled as it soaked up saliva, she would be able to breathe. She nodded.

He glanced at Tami. "No stoning," he reminded curtly and walked away.

Tami was delighted with his assignment. Not so long ago he had been given this same, exact punishment. Now he had charge of the she. Had she been his, there had also been stoning. No, the hell with that. Had she been his, there had been whipping—not that a she of his would dare a running. A thing of his uncle's softness that his she had the guts to run.

A woman came to the well, and nearly dropped her jar when she saw Karel. She recovered enough to keep from breaking the vessel, but she dropped her eyes and refused to look at Karel as she swung the bucket out over the edge of the well.

Karel discovered that the thing was not as easy as it looked, and she literally stumbled through her first attempt to lower the bucket. She had to watch her feet carefully to keep from getting them tangled up in the wheel, and she felt a tremendous sense of accomplishment when she finally felt the sudden jerk and gradual increase in weight that told her the bucket had reached the water and was beginning to fill.

Bringing it back up really was simple, a matter of climbing steps that kept dropping out from under her feet. She still had to watch what she was doing, but this part of the operation went smoothly. She had taken a long time, however, and when she looked up a line was beginning to form.

Sang's message had been delivered. The boys who had been released from their chores had run joyously off to tell their fathers that the healer's wife was on a treadmill learning to walk all day and get nowhere. Suddenly every house in the village had developed a need for water.

J. Sheldon Jones

The sun crept slowly over the tops of the trees surrounding the stockade, and the warmth of it began to seep into Karel's back. One woman after another came to the well with her jar, and the bucket rose and fell as quickly as Karel could manage. She was becoming adept. Each succeeding cycle was completed more quickly than the one before, and she began to look forward to the time when, having filled every jar in town, she would be able to rest and wait out the day with only an occasional customer. The line of women waiting their turn at the well never seemed to shrink, however, and she began to recognize repeaters.

As the sun rose higher in the sky and its gentle warmth changed gradually into searing heat, Karel finally recognized the true nature of the punishment. No childish prank, this, no comic symbolism. They would keep her busy, keep her working continuously until Sang came and released her.

By midday her body glistened with sweat, and the burst of courage, with which she had determined to meet this challenge, had slipped into dogged determination to last out the day. She trod grimly up and down on the wheel in a seemingly endless cycle of agonizing monotony. Tiny rivulets began to form under her hairline and run down the side of her face. Occasionally she would shake her head and send a spray of sweat about her, but the rivers would quickly return.

The thirst had been mild at first, and it was not yet unbearable, but it would be. Her throat was becoming parched, her breathing was a series of dry, rattling gasps, and the work was getting harder. Each time she brought up the bucket, it was a little more difficult to reach the top, and when she had succeeded, she had to listen to the water being poured into a jar. She had to listen, but she tried not to look.

It's foolish to look at it. Foolish!

She did look, however, with increasing frequency. She would catch herself with her eyes glued to a tiny drop as it slid down the trail left by its predecessors and finally seeped into the ground.

Then she would look up, and her eyes would fall on Tami. The arrogant smile, the calculating eyes, the air of waiting. She knew what he would do. When the time came, when she was at her weakest, she knew what he would do. It was so childish, and so like him, but it gave her a weapon with which to destroy him. She, too, was waiting.

Mari!

She of Strangeness

The other women had come sheepishly, Mari slunk. The others had been, unwilling participants in the torture of one of their own, Mari was ashamed. She had the air of someone who has been tried and convicted by her own conscience. The air of someone who...

She woke him up and told him I was gone!

Karel swore silently. Defiance raged inside her. She would win. Without them, in spite of them, she would win. With everyone on the planet trying to stop her, she would succeed.

The sun crawled across the sky and waves of heat drove down onto her and into her. Her anger subsided because she forced it to subside. Anger came easily now, naturally, but it was a waste of energy.

She set her mind back on her original objective, finishing the job. There would be plenty of time for planning her next escape, the successful one, when this was over. For now, the objective was to last out the day, and to reveal the absolute minimum number of signs of suffering.

It was not easy. There was that constant, tantalizing nearness of the water, and there came a time when she was no longer able to keep her eyes off the it. She had to watch. Her eyes were as tightly bound as her hands, captivated by the unfulfilled desire. Every drop that spilled was an ache inside her, and yet she could not stop herself from watching it, longing for it, reaching out to it with her eyes and trying to drag it to her by force of will. The want, the need, the proximity, the deprivation were tearing at her, ripping her apart inside. She could not take her eyes off that water.

This was the moment Tami had been waiting for. He stepped forward, took the bucket, tilted it to his lips, and took a long, satisfying drink. Rivers of the precious fluid splashed out over his chin, ran down the sides of his neck and across his chest, and finally dripped onto the ground. He was careful, so very careful, not to empty the bucket. There had to be some left for him to throw out in front of her, right at her feet, with a few drops splashing across her toes. And then, with a self-satisfied smile, he hung the bucket back over the well and nodded for her to lower it.

The instant she felt the weight of the bucket on the rope, Karel leaped off the treadmill. The bucket plunged downward, and the wheel spun unchecked. She arched her body away from the whirling blades and stood back, enjoying the breeze. The bucket struck the water with a sudden jerk and sank slowly to the full length of its rope.

Karel raised her head and glared defiantly at Tami. She was more than motionless, she was the embodiment of refusal to move. Even the gleaming rivers of sweat had ceased. Nothing moved. She was locked into position and daring him to do his worst.

Blazing eyes were the only outlet for the smoldering challenge she had become, but he seemed to feel the heat of it and fall back without moving. From somewhere in the core of his being a sudden chill rose up to meet that flame, and he felt a rush of cold that filled his body and left him shaken even when it had passed. He tried to kindle a blaze of his own, a flame to meet the inferno that was hers, but he was afraid. Afraid of a she.

His authority was being challenged. He was being challenged, and he had nothing of sureness that he could win. He drew in a breath of deepness to feed the fire that must grow in his heart and stepped forward to meet the thing that must be done.

"You will raise the bucket," he tried to put in his voice the thing of his uncle, the thing that expected obedience. Sang never demanded, he simply stated his wish. It was never coercion, never doubt—expectance.

Karel did more than ignore the command, she denied its existence. A refusal, a shake of the head, or any other negative gesture, would have implied recognition of his right to command. She was denying him that authority, robbing him of it. They were engaged in a clash of wills, and her attitude declared that she would not submit to his.

"You will raise the bucket," he repeated.

If there had been a trace of doubt in his voice before, now there was fear. Where he had lacked confidence, now he had lost it.

An air of quiet expectancy settled over the line of women behind him. He could not see the eyes on his back, but he felt them. He burned with humiliated rage at the knowledge that they were hoping to see him defeated.

He stooped and picked up a huge rock.

"You will raise the bucket," He tried to make it a threat, but his voice cracked.

Some of the fire went out of Karel's eyes. She glanced calmly at the rock with which he was threatening her, and then brought her gaze back up to his face. She was physically helpless, but she was master of the situation. She looked at the rock again and gave one short, derisive snort.

The gag would not permit her to laugh in his face, but she got the message across. He could hit her. His uncle would half kill him for it, but he could hit her. He could beat her senseless, he could kill her. He could not make her move.

A look of blind hate came into his eyes. For a moment she was convinced that he was going to hit her. Not afraid, convinced. He was shaking uncontrollably, and the hand that held the stone was drawing back. Then he whirled and flung it from him. He stood glaring at her for an instant, and then collapsed. She saw his shoulders sag, and a look of resignation came into his eyes.

"I will bring my uncle," he said tiredly.

It was total surrender. He turned away from her and started slowly across the compound. He had taken about five steps when Karel gave another snort and stepped up onto the wheel. The sound froze him in his tracks, and he looked back at her.

She was working again, but not because of him and not from fear of his uncle. Tami was no fool to think the she feared his uncle in moreness to himself. She worked now as she had worked the allness of this day, by choice.

He sat himself in a patch of shade and glared at the she who was not in his charge, who had never been in his charge. The she who had brought him to shame in beforeness to others of shes. He looked on the she—and he hated.

Betime he would come to have a she of his own, and this one had killed the goodness of that having. The she of his taking would not have redness to her hair, strangeness to her speech. The she of his wanting was this one.

He had wish to hear her screaming. He had wish to see her writhing in pain beneath the touching of his knife. There would be no joy in the parting of the skin, in the sight of the redness beneath, unless it be that the skin was hers.

Karel saw the boy's face, and read something of his thoughts, but it did not concern her. She had beaten him. Subtly, but very completely, she had whipped him. Let him have his childish dreams of revenge. When he had calmed down, he would realize that Sang would kill him if he ever laid a hand on her. Her problem at the moment had nothing to do with what Tami wanted to do to her.

She was no less tired and no less thirsty. Her sense of victory buoyed her up for a while, but only for a short while. Sunset, release, was still hours away. There was a limit to how long her mind could overcome the needs of her body. Fatigue was adding to the thirst, and thirst was contributing to fatigue.

Her legs, which had been aching for hours, were becoming difficult to control. Her muscles began to twitch involuntarily, to vibrate, to shake in oscillation between the tension of work and the need to relax. The shuddering continued even when she was waiting, supposedly at rest. Then it ceased, or she ceased to be aware of it.

She ceased, in fact, to be aware. Her eyes glazed and she grew numb. All thought and emotion faded into oblivion. She folded herself into a soft, warm shell, cut herself off from internal and external stimuli alike. Her eyes stared without seeing, her feet moved mechanically. Her body continued to follow the pattern set by her brain so long ago and repeated so often that the brain's participation was no longer necessary. Her mind quit.

This, too, was a moment for which someone had been waiting.

14 CHAPTER 14

The People stirred. The sentry, posted outside the stockade, signaled that the time had come, and thousands of tiny bodies froze as their minds focused on the experiment.

Everything was perfect. The Advocate was pregnant, and the two-leg was in a state of such complete exhaustion that her mind would be incapable of mustering any sort of defense.

There was no risk, no possibility of failure. The questions would be answered, the Contradiction would be explained, and no one would be harmed.

The People gathered in a Thinking. Thousands of bodies were locked into position, ignored by the minds that owned them. The totality of attention was fixed on the one body that still moved, the focal point of the experiment. The Advocate.

Moving slowly because she could not move quickly, the Advocate lumbered up the wall of the stockade. Inside her body nestled six tiny lives, one of which was about to receive a gift.

Sometimes, when a Person was severely injured, that Person was put into contact with an embryo. The warmth and security of the womb were transmitted to the sufferer, and the child remained unharmed. Unharmed, but not unaffected. If the sick one died, he died in comfort, and the baby was born into a world it had already helped to improve. If, on the other hand, the injured Person lived, there was always a special relationship between the two People who had existed simultaneously on the fringes of life's beginning and its end. It was the child who had changed most.

The mind of the unborn infant was not fully formed. Such a mind was capable of being altered. In this case it was hoped that the mind would alter enough, that the link between the baby and the two-leg, the special closeness, would be enough to allow real communication. The Advocate was only a buffer.

She would see, of course, that no harm came to her child. She would protect its mind with hers as she protected its body with hers. She would go first.

It was like walking into a deep, black cave. There was nothing. The Advocate had never before encountered such total blankness in a mind she touched. Tunnels, passageways, caverns that twisted, shifted, altered, and were everywhere empty. She went down when she could, up when she must, searching, reaching, groping through nothing in a quest for near-nothing. Probing through darkness in search of an imperceptible flickering of light, and, at last, something stirred.

Nothingness stirred. Non-existent moved. Unreality hovered just beyond the border of imagined perception. The probe halted, hesitated, moved closer to where the thing had momentarily seemed to be. The probe touched, withdrew, touched again, and tiny bits of unawareness began to gather about the probe, blending, fusing, combining to become.

Contact!

There was no shock. Nothingness became, and the becoming was smooth, gentle, barely perceptible, real. The probe held.

Another, stronger, less cautious probe slipped out. This time there was no hesitation, no blindness, no searching. This second tendril of mentality knew exactly where it was going and what to do when it arrived. This was only physical.

Straight to the base of the brain it flashed, to the point where each and every signal from the body must enter the mind, to the interception point. Pain is not a series of nerve impulses, pain is a brain's interpretation of a series of nerve impulses. Pain was taken.

This time there was a shock, among the People. A wave of thirst roared out of the two-leg and encompassed the People. Each took his share, each felt a part of it, but none was left to the two-leg. An instant before Karel's body had been screaming its messages into a brain that had ceased to listen, and now it was gone. Everything of thirst, everything of pain, every slightest discomfort was taken by the People.

As her body was freed of its pain, her mind was freed of its dependency on the body, to a degree. The People could relieve the bombardment of nerve impulses that contributed to driving Karel into her trance-like state, but they could not provide sustenance. Her body needed water. Her brain was part of her body. The People could intercept the signals that told her brain of her need for water, they could not relieve the need itself.

Her mind began to revive. Her awareness began to creep slowly up out of the hole into which exhaustion had driven it, but she could not come back all the way. She could not, fortunately, come back far enough to interfere with what the Advocate was doing. She could not have cooperated because she did not know how to cooperate, but she could have resisted. She would have resisted if she had been aware.

The People did not want Karel's awareness to sharpen too much. As soon as they had collected all the pain, the true experiment began. The probe, the contact, the link between Karel and the Advocate was extended backward. It moved down into the Advocate's body, into the mind of the unborn child, and then the Advocate withdrew herself from the link. She stood guard, but she did not participate further once that link was made.

A sense of well-being flowed into Karel, surrounded her, enveloped her. Warmth, safety, contentment, comfort. They had taken her pain and given...nothing. The nothingness of the womb. The bliss of mindlessness, the security of oblivion, the joy of pure existence. They had freed her from need, desire, thought, emotion, sensation. She had only to be.

15 CHAPTER 15

Karel was not allowed out of bed for two days. Sang's attitude toward her was gentle, concerned, professional. He never referred to what had happened. He never referred to anything but her present condition. His own part in causing that condition seemed to have been forgotten. She was a patient. Dehydration, sunburn, exhaustion, to be treated with fluids, rest, and an ointment he knew how to make. The manner in which her condition had come about had no bearing on the case, except as a diagnostic tool.

If he had done anything else. If he had gloated, as Tami would have done, taunted her with the past and threatened her with the future, she would have loathed him. If he had apologized, she would have despised him. He did neither.

He treated Karel exactly the same way he treated Mari, except for her illness and a few areas in which Mari seemed to enjoy privileges as first-wife.

Then one morning after breakfast, when Karel had fully recovered, he rose to his feet, collected the things he took with him when he made the rounds of his patients, and jerked his head in a gesture that ordered Karel to follow him.

"I have need of your hands," he explained casually, "and, betime, of your mouth."

So, a new pattern was set, new roles established. Mari the mother, Karel the nurse, Sang the paradox.

Karel was not surprised to learn that his attitude toward his other patients was identical to the one he had displayed when she had been ill, but she had trouble reconciling this with the times she had seen him turn into a deadly killing machine. She had seen him face death, missing it by a fraction of a second, without turning a hair. She had watched him fly into a murderous rage, actually commit murder, and then demand to know why she had not. Violently jealous of a wife he did not want, determined to perpetuate a marriage he had never consummated, he was scrupulously fair to both his wives, and…

All right. I'll take another look around.

To understand the man, she had to understand the society that had produced him. She did not delude herself, the objective was escape, but in the process of discovering an escape route she could fulfill her obligations as a Scout. Her new role as nurse provided her with numerous opportunities to enter other homes, to observe other men, other wives, and travelling from one patient to another gave her opportunities to observe the village life outside the homes.

She was developing something she would never be able to report adequately, awareness of the feel of the village.

Customs, values as far as she understood them, her evaluation of the social and political structure would begin to be recorded as soon as she got inside the ship and started home. This other would never be communicated, it had to be experienced.

She had known about it all her life. Survey knew about it. For want of a better name, it was simply called the feel of a place. It could be detected from the moment of arrival, but it could not be described. When it shifted, Karel felt the change.

Excitement, expectancy, anticipation. An event was coming.

The only unusual activity Karel could detect was a game. It was being played by a group of adolescents, boys Tami's age and a little older. They had a laid long plank across a couple of supports, and they were trying to cross it without falling. Alone, of course, it would have been a simple feat, but each contestant had a friend—opponent?—on his shoulder, squirming, heaving, writhing, and generally doing everything he could to throw the other off balance.

Games are important. Children's games develop skills that will be needed in adult life, adult games sharpen those skills still further. With approaching maturity, games begin to resemble their adult equivalents more closely, and these boys were on the edge of adulthood. What they were doing was, probably, only one step away from the reality it represented.

"Sang-ser, what are they doing?" She had hesitated to ask, not because he would refuse to answer, but because he seemed to resent her questions.

"Practice," he grunted indifferently, "they are soon to their raiding."

Karel wondered what connection this activity could possibly have to a raid, and she was about to ask when Sang stiffened. His attention was on something else, and he was staring with such intensity that she closed her mouth and followed his gaze.

A boy of between three and four local years was struggling alone at the far end of the compound. The task was to shape a board so that it fit the hole in the side of a house. The tool was a smooth plane of about twenty-five or thirty centimeters in length. The problem lay in the inadequacy of the makeshift vice the boy had set up, a pair of stones, neither of which was large enough.

While they watched, the boy tried several variations. He placed one stone at each end of the board, but it tipped sideways when he attacked it. He worked the board back and forth in the ground, digging a shallow trench, and finally butted one end of the board against the pile of earth he had raised, planted his stones on either side, managed one complete pass before the whole thing fell apart.

He was sweating, probably cursing, and failing, but he kept trying. His technique was faulty, and he lacked the strength for what he was trying to do, but he could not be faulted on determination. He would succeed or collapse. More likely he would succeed and then collapse.

Karel glanced at Sang's face. His attention was riveted on the boy. She could see nothing about the spectacle that should have aroused so much interest. If he had been amused, she could have understood, but he was not. Curious, mildly suspicious, but the twitch of his cheek each time the plane, board and boy came down in a heap was not laughter. Neither was it sympathy. She could not guess what it was.

At last, however, he seemed to have seen enough. He started across the compound with Karel following. He stopped just short of where the boy was engaged in his silent battle and waited for a few moments to see if his presence would be noticed. It was not.

"You!" The grunted demand for attention was stern enough to be frightening without the added element of surprise. The boy jumped back, almost a full meter. He recognized Sang, however, and relaxed somewhat.

"Healer." The greeting and accompanying nod were formal.

"You are son to Jamshi?"

The boy gave a grunt of acknowledgement. His attitude struck Karel as different from what she would have expected, but she had no time to examine the reason it was unusual.

"Your father," Sang demanded sternly, "he knows of this?" He waved a finger at everything the boy had been doing, but particularly at the tool he was using.

"My father," the boy answered with dignity, "has made his going to The Mother."

Now it was Sang's attitude that was strange, partly because it was the first time Karel had seen him allow a visible emotion other than anger. The grief in Sang's eyes was echoed in his voice when he spoke.

"This had not come to my hearing."

"A few days of pastness only, healer," the boy answered with equal sadness. "He met the knife of the Puker."

Sang nodded. At the time his concern had been with the casualty who had been brought to him. He had not thought to ask if there had also been one who had no need of him.

"The death of a friend is ever a hardness," Sang said, and then he flinched and turned on Karel so suddenly she was almost frightened. "If ever," his eyes blazed with fury, "I saw this Puker in nearness to death, I would shout no warning. That is the way of a friend."

You killed my friend, so I should have let you die?

"That's not something I could do, Sang-ser."

He continued to glare at her with his teeth grinding together, and then he shook his head. He turned back to the boy. "You have no uncle?"

"I have uncles, healer."

Uncles! Two, at least, and perhaps more than two. This thing needed learning. "There is a right in your having."

"The rights in my having, healer, are two. I have made choosing."

Truth, Sang thought, but there are few to choose thusly. Many times he had wished that Tami had chosen this of his rights, or the other of his uncles.

"I am called Sang."

Not that Karel had been disinterested before, but there was a new note in his voice that caused her to prick up her ears. Something had happened, something the boy had said had caused a drastic shift in the man's attitude toward him. In keeping with her resolve to learn as much as she possibly could, Karel was straining to absorb every clue to what had caused the change, to understand the nature of the change itself.

"I am Chars," the boy was saying.

Sang grunted and walked over to the house. He examined the hole in the wall, glanced at the rotten board that had been torn out and tossed aside, then returned to inspect the replacement Chars had been trying to fit.

"A two-man job, Chars-ser," he said quietly.

Neither of them noticed the start Karel gave. Chars was much younger than Tami, and Tami was 'not yet of an age' to deserve the respect syllable.

Chars' eyes narrowed. "I would not have debt, Sang-ser."

"I would have," Sang countered, "two bags of chukra berries."

Chars hesitated. He needed the help that was being offered, and Sang had given him a way to salvage his pride, but...

"One bag, Sang-ser."

Sang's apparent hesitation was a transparent lie. The payment he was demanding was only a token, anyway, but it was necessary to carry out the farce.

"Is it," he asked, "that I may see of your plane?"

A few moments earlier he had been demanding to know if the boy's father knew the tool was being used. Now he was asking politely for permission to look at it.

What do the boy's uncles have to do with it?

Chars handed over the plane with a quiet pride. Sang took it, admired it as he was expected to do, and examined it closely. He turned it over and over in his hand, sighted along the base, tested the edge of the cutter with his thumb, and ran his hand across the wood. Finally, he looked up.

"A goodness," he announced. "I have no such. One bag of berries and the using of this when it is needful."

"Done." Chars picked up the board and started to wedge it back into place, but a grunt from Sang stopped him and he looked up.

"There is no oil in your having?"

"Oil, Sang-ser?"

"To give ease to the work," Sang ran the plane through the air as if he were using it, "that it slide readily."

Chars frowned. "I have no oil," he had never heard of lubricating a plane, either.

"You know my house?"

"I know it."

"If my nephew is not there," Sang sad, "you may speak my other she. Her name is Mari. Say that I would have my toolbox. She knows its place."

Karel knew where it was, too, but neither she nor Mari had ever been allowed near it. She watched as the boy ran off and then Sang spoke to her very softly.

"If he looks this way," he said, "I would know of it."

He flipped the plane over and tapped out the wedge that held the cutter in place. Quickly, but carefully, he adjusted the tool, muttering something about it not being an axe.

"He's coming," Karel said when the boy appeared carrying the heavy box.

It did not matter now, however, Sang was already finished. "You will wait," he told her. "Our seeing of the sick will have lateness."

This was another indication that something very unusual was going on. Nothing had ever taken precedence over Sang's morning rounds, except the time when she had been close to death, and he had stayed with her.

Which is the same thing.

Well, for the time being all she could do was watch. She selected a spot from which she could lean against the side of the house and still have a clear view of what was going on.

The work, naturally, began to show a more progress now that Sang had taken over. The first thing he did was to devise a better method of holding the board in place. The plane, of course, was operating more efficiently now that it had been adjusted and oiled, but this was only one of several adjustments Sang made during the course of the work.

Whenever he drew a tool from his box, one of his own tools, he seemed to have some complaint about it. He would examine it, possibly make some minor adjustment, and always ask Chars' opinion. The boy would take it, hold it exactly the way Sang had held it, look at it with a critical eye, and hand it back with a nod of agreement to whatever Sang had said about it.

Karel could not hear what was being said, but it was easy to guess. Sang was making suggestions, and they were being followed. He was managing to take the heavier jobs on himself, without seeming to do more than his share.

A woman came out of the house and stood watching the pair as they worked. She was nearly a head shorter than Karel, and somewhat heavier. Her hair was showing the first traces of gray. The scars were old, and Karel had seen enough of the local women to know that they were typical. It was a long time before she noticed Karel sitting there.

"I am Dreena," she announced as she sat down beside Karel.

Karel introduced herself and they sat together watching Sang and Chars. It was a long time before they spoke again.

"How," Dreena asked, "is the payment to be made?"

"A bag of chukra berries, and the use of his plane whenever it's needed."

"Chukra," Dreena smiled to herself. "The berries that grow in such nearness to the river that they can be gathered with one hand while the other holds the line that waits for the pulling of the fish. He is a goodness, your husband."

A goodness? The highest compliments Mari had ever paid him were that he was less cruel and less stupid than most.

"In some ways," Karel agreed guardedly, "he is a goodness. In other ways…"

Dreena looked at Karel, glanced down at herself then back at Karel. "This thing of the well," she pointed with her chin, "it comes of running?"

"Yes," Karel admitted.

"Betime there was another who did this thing," Dreena smiled vaguely to herself about something. "My Jamshi thought it a day of goodness for the making of a son, but in that time the other of his wives was yet living. He could take only one of us, the other must stay and have seeing of the thing. She spoke me offlaying."

Flaying! My God! I am lucky!

"It is seldom," Dreena went on, "that there is running. Termans do not make running because they believe that The Mother is come to anger with them. Even did they come again to their homes, it would be known that She has hatred for them. As well to stay here."

"I…uh…I take it you're Polyan?" Karel was delighted. This was her first opportunity to learn something about the third society that existed on the planet.

"We," Dreena confirmed her nationality, "make no runnings because we know what we are."

"Which is...?"

"Tribute."

"I...don't understand."

"Tribute," Dreena repeated. "My mother's word. She knew much history, both ours and that of Earth. She spoke of many times that one people would make payment to another, stronger people for preventing of war. Betime these payments included people."

Karel nodded her understanding. "You're saying that if they have too much trouble kidnapping the number of wives they want, they'll just mount an army and..."

"Not these," Dreena cut in, "it is Term we fear to fight."

"Term!" Karel was shocked. "But..."

"Unh," Dreena nodded, "they believe they have come to be a matriarchy because of their fewness of women. So, to keep their fewness of women, there must ever be some who are taken. To give hardness to such takings would bring anger to the Raiders and then, as you say, they would come with an army. The Termans would win, I think, there are more of them, but in afterness to the war, there would be..."

Karel saw it immediately. Men would die in the fighting, and all of the women here, captive and belted alike, would suddenly arrive in Term.

"It would invert the sex ratio."

"So," Dreena agreed, "they lie to their people. They speak that there will be war as soon as there is finding of the Other Place, but..." she chuckled, "they make damn sure there is no finding of the Other Place."

And they've threatened you with a war if you don't contribute your share of kidnap victims? Well, the Termans were right about one thing. The matriarchy probably had come about and was being perpetuated by the scarcity of women.

"Even so," Karel felt vaguely guilty about projecting her own desires into the conversation, but... "It doesn't seem as though it would upset things too much if a few of us managed to get away."

"Truth," Dreena agreed, "and of this there are ever some who try. Betime I had thought to make such a doing myself." She looked down at herself, selected the longest scar, and traced it with a finger. Karel did not miss the significance of the gesture.

"Did you try?"

Dreena did not answer, and Karel followed her gaze. Sang had been watching Chars as he used a particular tool, and now he took it back on some pretext and "tested it out" himself. When he handed it back, Chars handled it differently.

"He teaches without seeming to teach," Dreena remarked.

Karel had noticed this earlier. She had also learned that these people were given to indirection. No matter how unrelated the beginning, they would eventually arrive at an answer to any question that was put to them, unless they refused to answer. She remained silent and waited for Dreena to go on.

"They were friends," Dreena said. "When my Jamshi needed help with a doing, he would ask it of the healer. Betimes, the healer would hear of it, and come before the asking."

My Jamshi. Karel caught the glistening of moisture in Dreena's eyes, and the catch in her voice.

"He has no right to teach, Karel. It is of things to be hidden behind a pretense."

"He does that a lot," Karel said, "hide things behind a pretense."

"It will never be yours, as it was mine, to hear the sayings of men when they speak of the healer in his absence."

What they say behind his back? No, I don't suppose I will hear any of it. "I think he knows some of what they say."

"He knows it all," Dreena corrected, "but did they say it in his hearing, he would kill, and he fights well."

"Yes, I know," Karel said. "I have seen him."

"The Terman?" Dreena shrugged. "That was no fight, he had come to die. He was scarred, not?"

"Yes."

"Badly?"

Karel nodded.

"A Terman must keep his beauty, or he comes to be Unchosen, eh? Unmarried in a time when he might have been otherwise? Some prefer death."

"The vark wasn't suicidal." *My God! I'm defending him!*

"I have said he fights well," Dreena agreed, "and for this they fear to speak, in his hearing, of you and of his other wife."

"And what," Karel wanted to know, "do they say about us?"

"They speak," Dreena said, "of his softness, that you have no scars, eh? How can it be, they ask each other, that a man takes a she to his house, names her his wife, and yet leaves her," Dreena traced another scar with her finger, "unbranded?"

Which explains why he hasn't... No, Mari did not have any scars, either, and Sang had taken her out son-making several times, leaving Karel to watch the baby.

"It was the healer," Dreena was saying, "who helped at the coming of my son. I remember his hands, and a thing of his voice.

"My Jamshi had courage, Karel, but it was the courage of facing a thing and ending it. The healer lives with..." She could not finish the idea, but Karel nodded her understanding.

"Thank you for telling me that, Dreena, it...helps."

"When a knife," Dreena said, "is honed to great sharpness, there can be much cutting, of scarring, and only a smallness of pain. I came late to this knowing, Karel. I learned it only when I heard them speaking of the healer. My Jamshi added nothing to the talk that was made, but...I saw of his face as he listened...I..." her voice finally broke, and she covered her face with her hands.

"You miss him, don't you," Karel said sympathetically.

"I loved him," Dreena answered fiercely, "and I am no Terman slut to shame at the saying of it. I would have said it to him, were it not that..." She glared at something imaginary for a moment. "He knew."

There was nothing to be said. There was never anything to be said in this sort of situation. All Karel could do was wait until Dreena had recovered and try to change the subject.

"Why do you call them sluts?" Karel was not even sure what the word meant.

"I said this?" Dreena seemed a little shocked at herself. "A wrongness. For truth, a foolishness. We name them sluts, they call us bitches because of a very small differentness."

Not so small, Karel thought. *I think Mari loves Sang, but she'd never admit it, even to herself.*

"Betime," Dreena said, "in my smallness, there was a child. His parents, all three of them, were dead. My mother spoke that she would take him for a time, until another could be found who had no small ones and wanted him." She stopped and sighed heavily.

"He was only with us a few days, but then he left, and it was never that I heard my parents speak of him. Never! I think now that it was never spoken of between them, either.

"There came to be another of orphans, this one a girl, and my mother was asked if she would take this one also. I was there at the asking. I saw her face." Dreena shook her head sadly.

"She asked of my fathers, I was not yet of an age to be included in these discussions, if they would have her. Not, she said, for a time. It must be that they would have the girl for always, or she would refuse her taking.

"My first-father," Dreena smiled and closed her eyes on a memory, "he was a goodness, that man. He spoke that there were other families with no daughters. An unfairness, he named it, to take this girl to ourselves when there were others who had more need of her. He cried, Karel, and I knew of him that his tears were for the boy who had been and not for the girl who was.

"He had been with us only a few days, and two years, nearly, had passed, and there were yet tears in my fathers. Tears for the day they had come to us and torn a piece of our family away. I went to my first-father, sat his lap, cuddled..."

"So," she finished brusquely, "how to live in a family from which a piece is torn four times in each year, eh? Learn no love for the pieces that come and go. Name them brutes, and fools, and..."

And why didn't I think of that? Defensive hostility.

"Uncles!" Dreena said it suddenly, as if she had just discovered something herself.

"I beg your pardon," Karel said.

"To grow in happiness, a child must be given samenesses," Dreena declared. "Same house, same things in the house, same people in the house. I had wondered how this could exist among the Termans, they make this changing of husbands, but," she was delighted with her own discovery, "they have ever the same brothers, and their children have ever the same uncles."

Of course! And again, *why didn't I think of that?* Mari had mentioned an uncle, denying any fondness for him.

"Uncles are important here, too, aren't they?" Maybe Dreena would offer some explanation of Chars' promotion.

"Ah," apparently she could, "when a man comes to his dying, it is the right of his son to go to an uncle and ask teaching of the things of manhood. The uncle has, then, a duty to his brother's son, as it has been with the healer. There is no refusing." She shrugged uncomfortably. "I have thought would have been a goodness if Chars had made this choosing."

"Why is that?"

Dreena held out her hands palm upward and waved them up and down, as if she were balancing something. "A selfishness," she said finally. "My Jamshi waits in the Place of the Dead. My starving had taken me to him in more soonness."

"Starving!"

"A man must keep food in the mouths of his wives," Dreena replied calmly. "If he dies..."

"They would just let you starve to death!" Karel was horrified.

"They are proud, Karel. Each must care for the things that are his. I am Jamshi's. None may speak me without asking it of him. None may touch me, none may feed me."

"No one," Karel was beginning to understand, "except your son."

"A son is of the father," Dreena confirmed. "He needs no asking. He has a right."

He has two rights, Karel remembered, *and Chars has chosen this one.* She wondered what had happened to Tami's mother. She was afraid she knew.

She was also beginning to understand, and agree with, the reason Sang was impressed with Chars.

The board fit now, it was being hammered into place. When it was set solidly into the wall, Sang packed his toolbox and sent Chars scurrying off with it. He seemed to suddenly remember Karel.

"He has wish to see my doings with the sick," he said to her, carefully failing to notice Dreena's presence for reasons which Karel had come to understand.

"Then, if you don't need me, Sang-ser, I could go..."

"I have yet," he said, "need of your mouth. You will speak the wife of Jamshi that I would have her son to my apprentice."

This was a familiar game. Karel had grown accustomed to it in dealing with Sang's patients. It was not necessary for her to actually relay the message, it was only necessary for Sang and Dreena to pretend their remarks were addressed to her, but it was, indeed, necessary. Karel had seen a man killed for speaking to her without permission.

"Speak the healer," Dreena said, "that in my son there is small having of payment."

The debt is his, Sang thought irritably, *I do not speak of it with shes.* He started to speak and then stopped himself. *If his knowing of huntings has sameness to his carpentry, small wonder she fears the time I would take from him. Already she hungers.*

"There is a gland in the throat of the pisone," he said, "from which I have making of a medicine. When we make hunting together, this gland will be cut from his half of the meat and given to me. If our killing is other than pisone…"

Karel caught the sigh of relief that escaped from Dreena, and she smiled inwardly. *I have every right, do I not, to be proud of my own husband?*

"Betime," Dreena was utilizing another version of the game, allowing Sang to eavesdrop on a remark he was supposedly not intended to hear, "my Jamshi spoke that the healer is closer to him than a brother."

"Fah!" Sang grunted disgustedly. "The gossiping of shes. I sorrow that I came to nearness and had the hearing of it." Chars was back.

16 CHAPTER 16

DeMyrn Tan stood at the door of the house of his sister and made careful hiding of the things in his hands. He was come for a reason, and the reason of his coming gave nervousness to his stomach. Before their speaking on the reason there would be giving, and much joy in the eyes of the small ones.

"Ho, Myrn," he called in the way of politeness, "is there room in your house for the brother?"

"Uncle Tan! Uncle Tan!"

The shriek of happiness came from the throat of Gido, the youngest, the boy, but two bodies struck him, and he made laughing as the small ones dragged him into the house. Since small Myrn had learned walking, his visits had been greeted with joy. The joy of his sister was not much less than that of her children.

She came now, to his kissing, and Dana, his other sister, came also. It was not since the last of her Motherhood Blessings that Tan had seen Dana. Their greeting had joyfulness, but there was also a pain in her eyes, and he knew she had seen his scar.

"Uncle Tan," this was Sare, the middle child, and the wrongness that a dame-child should speak with such shyness gave him concern, "I wish speaking with you in loneliness."

Tan's eyes made an asking of his sister, but she knew nothing of the thing in her daughter's mind. Dorn would know, perhaps, but a once-father finds a place to go when a thing of the family is to be discussed.

"Can there be waiting," Tan asked of his niece, "a time of much shortness only? I have first," his hands came from behind him to show of the things he had brought, "to make a giving."

"Oh!" There was dancing of small feet. "Which is mine?"

"Gido," it was an uncle who spoke now, sternly, "in the way of politeness, which giving should be first?"

"Small Myrn is not here," the boy spoke sullenly.

"So?" Again, the asking with eyes.

"She has need," the mother told him, "of a dress of newness, not? She is gone to a fitting of it."

"I will have seeing of her...?"

"Her return will be long before your going, Tan."

"Gido," the uncle spoke again, "you have another sister."

"She must have," the boy answered with sullenness, "the first of your givings."

"The reason of this?"

"She is older," the child hedged.

"And...?"

"She is of dames." His tone named the one reason of as much stupidness as the other. There must be speaking with Dorn on this thing. A once-father should permit no such attitude.

Tan made his givings then, and Sare thanked him with much politeness, but he knew that her thinking was on her wish for private speaking. As soon as it could be done, after giving to Gido, he made excuses and took her to a place where their speaking would be unheard.

The thing of her mind came with hardness to her mouth, but at last she spoke. "Uncle Tan, I have made fighting in school."

Fighting! The laugh of his mind touched nothing of his face. They made tapping of faces with fists and named it fighting. But Sare was not of those to come to this thing without...

"There was reason." His words were of sureness, not of asking.

"There was one who spoke me a thing."

"A great badness?" He did no doubting of her, but it was, perhaps, that she doubted herself.

"She spoke me," Sare continued uncomfortably, "that betime you had been taken to a questioning of Archers."

The words pained him. Did Myrn, also, and Dana make fighting for him with words, damehood ended the tapping of fists, when they heard these things? Did they hear them? Was it Clar who yet made telling of this half-truth, this thing to bring shame to his sisters?

"I named her liar," there was fire in the eyes of the child, "and I beat the shit out of her."

Shit? He blushed. Was she come so soon to the age that begins using of such words? The uncle looked at her, saw the beginnings, traces only, of breasts. Soon, then, he would fear for this one as she made picnicking, pride as she went to the first of her marryings. Small Myrn soon, this one later. He felt old.

"I was released," he said. "She who was, then, Mistress of Archers came to know of me that my doings had no wrongness."

The child that she yet was fought with the dame she soon would be, in the end she made accepting of the world as it was.

"I must make apologizing," she said.

"No." She had fought for his good name. Myrn, did she hear of it, would pride in her daughter unless there was apologizing. "You have a knowing now that was not yours then. It was given for speaking if ever you hear of this thing again. If they do not speak it, the thing is best forgotten, eh?"

"Will it be forgotten, Uncle Tan?"

"I am watched," he spoke truthfully, "and because of me, you are watched. Our family must have care in our doings."

"The fighting," she said, "will be remembered."

"It will."

"But it proves nothing," she went on. "She becomes no liar because I have pushed her face to the dirt and made her to say it."

"Truth, dame." Muchly surprised, she looked on him. None, himself least, had yet named her thus, but her saying had earned it. Her thinking was no longer childish. "You have much sameness to your grandmother."

She glowed. She would have run from him, shouting her joy of the thing he had named her, but he caught her arm, brought her back to him.

"This is yours and mine, dame," he spoke pretending to kiss her. "Not for the hearing of others, eh?"

"I am no braggart, Uncle Tan."

She ran from him, then, and he let her go. There was a sadness in him, though, as he walked to where his sisters waited him.

"So," Myrn was sarcastic, "the great healer of small troubles decides to join us. Did you sympathize well with the beating she got for the beating she gave?"

His head came around fast. "Do you know," he asked quietly, "the reason of her fighting?"

"Stubborn," Myrn answered. "Spoke me nothing. Not even Dorn

could get it from her."

He told her. He spoke, also, that the child must not know of his telling, or there would be no more confidences. There was a look that passed between his sisters when he had finished, and he knew of them, then, that they also heard these sayings.

"The bitch," Myrn's anger was ever of quietness, more terrible that she did no shouting of it, "to strike at me through my child!" They knew what bitch she meant.

"You have taken a scar," Dana wished to give change to their talk, not that this was better.

"It is small."

"It is ugly," Myrn snapped. "Do you know how hard we work to find wives for you? Soon you will bald, already you wrinkle, and there is ever that fuckin' knife on your belt, even in times when your trade could be hidden."

This was truth, all of it. At the Changing Time they became sisterly, introducing him to dame after dame after dame. It was sisterly, also, that they had no memory for the fact that his once-wives had never been one of their choices. He allowed them to think they took care of him.

"The knife must be worn," he told them. "This is law."

"Law?" To them it was also news.

"The city," he explained carefully, "will not be attacked. We are strong. The Uglies know this, they fear us. But, were it to happen, there is a place I must go for defending, and there must be no time lost in a searching for weapons."

"Why," Dana asked, "is this not made public?"

"It frightens," he answered. "It is known only by those who need to know." Of the wisdom in this, they had understanding.

"You change, brother, when you speak on these things. You show a hardness unbecoming in a brute."

This, too, was truth. It was a thing much discussed among Hunters. Be it born in them, or made by their work, they had hardness. And most dames feared to take such a man to their homes.

"Small Myrn," now it was he who had wish to give change to the talk, "is soon to her Coming to Damehood."

"Unh," Dana, at least, was willing to speak on the thing for which they had gathered, "she is yet to make her picnicking."

Picnicking! From his smallness, Tan had feared it. Feared when his sisters had gone to it, feared, now, that his niece would make such a going. Picnicking—why?

"She will be," Myrn announced, "among those who do the next picnicking."

"Is it," Tan feared the thing he would say, and yet he feared more the thing that could be, "known to you why it is never the Hunters that guard picnics?"

Both his sisters wore looks of confusion.

"My speaking," he said, "is not a thing of pride in the trade I have chosen. I speak from knowing that it is we, Hunters, who have knowledge of the things of the forest. It is we, Hunters, who have varks. Even without my vark I can see of the place where an Ugly hides long before I come to that place. I can see, and hear, the coming of an Ugly long before to his arrival. Would you rather your daughter be guarded by me, or by some deaf, blind townman who will fail at his guarding and die of his failing?"

"This," Myrn, the eldest, the name-bearer, gave answer, "is the way it is done."

"Myrn, I speak the safeness of my niece," small need to mention that it was also her daughter. "When I took my scarring there was one who died of its giving, and another who fell to my vark. *Who the hell have these bedamned townmen killed?*"

"I am your sister," Myrn was come again to her quiet angriness, "I bear the name of our mother. Choose your words with more carefulness, man-thing, I will have respect."

"I am hard," he answered softly, "and difficult to find wives for. Were I at this picnic, a man would die trying to take my niece. I could crawl under the nose of these townmen, Myrn, kill one twice before he knew of my presence. I could fight five who did know of my coming."

"You call them cowards?" In Dana, at least, there was the beginning of understanding.

"Untrained," he answered. "The thing needs learning they were never given."

"She bears the name, Myrn," Dana spoke.

The mother thought on the thing, and the anger softened.

"I have thought on these picnics," she said finally. "Not on the guarding of them, but on their making. They say it is thus that The Mother makes choosing of those to be taken and those to be saved. I have wondered…"

"With us at my picnicking," Dana said softly, "was a bitch that I hated. I feared greatly that The Mother would take me, take us all, because of her."

"Just so," Myrn was nodding, "all are taken, or all are saved. Nineteen to suffer for one who, perhaps, deserves to be taken."

The day and the time of the picnic were not known, the place was. They would come suddenly and without warning, taking small Myrn and the others immediately through the gate to the clearing where such picnics were held. This was, they said, a thing of safeness, that no spy could give warning to the Uglies. There were no spies.

It was not spoken, but it was known, that Tan would be in much nearness to this picnic.

17 CHAPTER 17

"His learning has quickness, not?"

Karel was surprised at the question. Her opinion had never been asked before, on any subject. Now Sang was asking her views on a subject of such importance that Korl had refused to discuss anything else until they had shouted at each other over Sang's failure to choose an apprentice.

"Yes, Sang-ser, he learns very quickly."

He was waiting, almost demanding that she go on.

"He...he asks the kind of questions that show he understands what you've told him. He can, almost, guess what comes next."

This was not what he wanted to hear, either, but there was something he wanted to hear, needed to hear, must hear. They had stopped in the middle of the street, and Karel sensed that he would refuse to move until she had said...

"I...I like him, Sang-ser, I..."

"You like him!"

The flash of anger was quickly replaced by amusement and then curiosity.

Had he a few moreness of years, I had made his killing for this saying of yours. And yet no other she of his knowing would have been able to make such a saying, even had it been a lie.

"You like him," he repeated. "For me you have no liking, eh?"

"No, Sang-ser," her hesitation had been brief, "I wouldn't do that to you."

He threw back his head and laughed, drawing, and ignoring, startled looks from a few passersby. Then a new thought struck him, and he grew serious again.

"For Korl," he demanded, "you have much liking, not?"

"Yes," she admitted. *But he doesn't resent it the way you would.*

The answer, essentially a rejection of him in favor of Korl did not seem to bother him. If it did, she had missed any sign he gave. He was behaving the way a man does on receiving a new piece of information, absorbing the fact without emotion.

"Chars," he said, "makes living with his mother. You know the meaning of this?"

"Yes," she said, "I assumed that was why you had chosen him."

Even if she had wanted to, she could not have concealed her approval of that choice, and her agreement with the reason it had been made. This, apparently, was what he had been asking all along. That it should matter, that he should want or need her approval, was as confusing as it was flattering. That it was so, however, was made apparent by the fact that he continued their journey without further discussion.

When they reached their house, Sang stopped stared at a dead animal that lay on the porch. Then he began to laugh uproariously, stooped, picked the thing up, and laughed again.

"Pisone," he muttered between chuckles, "and not even that he has made skinning of it."

"Wh…what is it, Sang-ser?" Karel's curiosity overcame her fear that he might resent the question.

"An insult," he answered.

"From Chars?" Impossible! The boy worshipped…but Sang was shaking his head.

"Tami hates you," he said.

"Yes, I know." She had not been overly concerned about it.

"From the time of the well, when you gave shame to him, I have made sleeping with one eye of openness, that he make no cutting of your throat in the night."

"What!" Sang knew the boy better than she did. If he had thought it was necessary to guard her, it probably was.

"A goodness, then," he hefted the pisone as if it should mean something, which, to Karel, it did not, "that he has ended his stay in my house, eh?"

"There is Dancing tonight."

This was hardly a piece of news. It would have been utterly impossible for Karel to remain ignorant of the fact that an event of such importance was about to take place. She had yet to ascertain what the Dancing was, but she knew when it was.

"Ever before," Sang went on, "Tami has made going to Korl, to be crutch to him, to help in his walking. Tonight, Karel will have this duty."

It was an order, but not one she would have difficulty obeying. She was delighted at the prospect of seeing Korl again. She could learn more from the old man in five minutes than Sang would tell her in…perhaps a lifetime. If only there were time, before the Dancing began, for him to talk.

The evening meal was earlier than usual that day. Apparently there were preparations to be made before the Dancing. They followed the family custom of eating in silence, but the conversation that usually followed the meal was omitted. As soon as she had finished eating, Sang dismissed Karel. He had already told her where she was supposed to go, and he did not repeat himself. He simply said it was time.

As she stepped out into the street, she noticed a number of changes that had taken place in the village. The gate, which usually remained open until dark, was closed. The number of guards manning the gate had been doubled, and the extra men had mounted platforms placed next to the wall and were watching outward.

The porches of the two houses nearest the bandstand showed empty spaces where a plank had been pulled up, and those planks had been stretched across the intervening space so that they connected the houses with the platform. Karel remembered the game she had watched a few days earlier, the boys who had been crossing a plank set above the ground in this fashion, and she mentally eliminated one of the questions she had intended to ask Korl.

That, my dear, is how tracks go in and do not come out.

The discovery embarrassed her. The simplicity of it was, no doubt, the reason she had overlooked it, but she should have been able to figure it out before this. The fact that the bridges were made from wood that was part of the houses themselves and which could be put back into position without showing signs of having been disturbed explained part of the ruse. The other part, the method of disappearing from the houses after the false trail had been laid, remained a mystery.

And no doubt, Karel thought disgustedly, *the answer to that one is as simple as this was.*

As a matter of fact, if she could find an excuse for doing so, she could probably snoop around and spot the answer right now. The gate was closed, guarded, and unused at the moment, but there were new faces in town. People she had never seen before—a class of people she had never seen before—thronged the street.

Belted ones! Arrogant? No, confident. Karel saw a captive woman step aside, stand with her head bowed, as a belted one passed. Contempt was there, a flash of hate in the eyes of the captive, the other was merely accepting her due, immune to the surreptitious glares in her wake.

The sound caught Karel off guard, made her hesitate, caused her to miss a step. It was a familiar sound, but it belonged to things that are not consciously missed until they come back.

I haven't heard a woman laugh like that since I've been here.

Not like that. Not freely, openly, unafraid of being heard. Mari would snigger occasionally, Dreena had a quiet, explosive chuckle. Karel had not heard a genuine female laugh since her arrival, and she had found very little to laugh about, herself.

And what that says about this place is not funny, either.

Right now, however, she had another problem. She had, per instruction, arrived at Korl's door. She had to get inside, and she was not sure she knew the right ritual for asking permission to enter. If she made a mistake, used an inappropriate phrase, did a not-thing, she could offend the old man.

Anybody else, I wouldn't care so much, but...I hope this is at least acceptable.

"Korl-ser, is there room in your house for another?" The instant she had uttered the phrase, she remembered that she had never been included when Sang requested entry to a patient's house.

"Karel," the delight in the old man's voice was genuine, "if a man has a house in the Place of the Dead, you will ever be welcome in mine."

Well, leave it to Korl to be original. She had never heard that particular response before, and she wondered if she flattered herself overmuch to think that it might be special.

In any case, she could go in now, and find herself face to face with the next problem.

Where do I sit, how do I act? If she imitated Mari, kept her eyes on the floor, the old man would slap her down as hard and as fast as Sang had done. *You don't lie with your mouth, don't do it with your eyes.*

She of Strangeness

The moment she entered, however, she saw that the question had been resolved for her in advance. Korl was sitting in a corner with his back to the wall, and this was the position these people took when they wanted to talk—a silent invitation. She accepted it gratefully and sat down to a discovery.

The last time she had been here, he had torn out her soul with his eyes, dissected her, examined every particle of what she was until he knew her. He had withheld everything of himself until he had decided to trust her.

This time he knew her. This time they knew each other, and they built on what they knew. Each had added a new set of experiences and a volume of thought to go with it. Things had happened, and the meaning of those things had been considered. It was Korl who had changed most.

The thing that poured out of him, rolled over her, engulfed her, nearly smothered her with its intensity, was purpose. Determined, driving, unwavering purpose. Final purpose.

Final!

One thing he wanted to see accomplished. One act yet to be performed. One thing left to be said. One process to be set in motion. One goal, and then he would die.

He would quit this world and joy to be shut of it. His Polyan she to end the waiting that was hers, he to end the waiting that was his. His Polyan she...

A fiveness, the years his Polyan she had looked on him and seen only a knife and its user. Fifteen were the years of goodness, when her seeing had come beyond the thing he had done to the thing that he was. Now he would come to her with a knowing, a truth given of the she from the sky, and he would take of that truth and make building of a house that had no...

"There is no other," his Polyan she had no need of this saying, it was her right, "that I have named to welcomeness in my house in the Place of the Dead. You will come?"

Karel was too shocked to answer for a long time. She had heard these people, particularly Dreena, speak of the afterlife in this off-hand manner. Jamshi was absent, not gone, and Dreena was waiting, somewhat impatiently, to join him. There was no trace of the misgiving, the doubt, that Karel had grown accustomed to observing in other peoples, had often felt in her own mind. The Place of the Dead was, to these people, a fact, but this...

My God, what an honor!

The casualness of his faith was an example of its strength, and he had just said he had never invited anybody else to visit him in the next world.

"Yes, Korl-ser," she could not keep the catch out of her voice when she said it. "I will come."

"I am come," he announced gruffly, "to my twenty-seventh year, and you to your eighth?"

Karel nodded. Back "home" she was most often fifty-seven, twenty-three and three-tenths of one, depending on the base she was operating out of, but yes, here she was eight.

"Nineteen years, then," he grunted, "to pass before your coming, eh?"

Don't show up, Karel thought with some amusement, *until I'm as old as you are now? Well, that's one way of wishing me a long life, would you care to throw in a happy one?*

"I'll try, Korl-ser."

"There is a truth in you, Karel," he said, "I am come only to a knowing that it is there, not yet to its understanding. I have need of nineteen years to make this learning. I need, also, a teacher."

He seemed to expect something of her then, but she had no idea what, and it was some time before he realized that she did not.

"The other," he said, "your friend."

"Mik?" Was he saying that when he got to the Place of the Dead he would look Mik up and...ask for lessons? In what?

"Mik," he repeated nodding to himself. He seemed to be absorbing the name, memorizing it, then he chuckled. "a fiveness of times Sang has come to me to ask of this thing that a she name a man 'friend'."

"Oh?" She had known it puzzled him, but she had not thought him greatly concerned about it, certainly not enough to ask about it repeatedly. "What did you tell him?"

"I have named," he replied angrily, "my own need of a teacher. Would you name me fool enough to speak my guessings as if they were truths?"

You mean, that's it? That's what you want Mik to teach you? He read her astonishment and flinched at it.

"Damn!" He struck the floor with his fist. "The knowing is yours with such fuckin' ease, and it is not I who have time to make its learning of you."

There was a long, pregnant silence, and when Karel broke it her voice was full of suppressed fury.

"Neither," she said deliberately, "has anyone else."

"There will be a second of runnings, then." It was a statement, carrying neither approval nor disapproval, intended only to convey the fact that he understood what she said, if not how she felt. It calmed her anger.

"There will be," she told him, "as many runnings as necessary."

Necessary! More than a needfulness! A word for naming a thing that must be!

"You think him such a fool, then, as to learn nothing from these runnings, eh?" Korl shook his head. "The truth is in you, Karel, and the learning will be made whether the teaching be a thing of your wishing or of accidents."

Just so it's understood, she thought, *that I'm not going to hang around and give lessons.*

"So." Korl seemed to be changing the subject. "Now there is an apprentice."

Karel looked at him suspiciously. So many of the things he said had more than one meaning—sometimes several. Was he speaking of Chars, of Sang, or of himself—all three had something to learn. She decided to take the remark at face value.

"Yes, now there is an apprentice."

"How is your thought on the boy?"

"He's not a boy, Korl-ser. You know that as well as…probably better than I do."

Not a boy? I must learn of this thing. "I was told," he said, "of the finding of one who has in him the thing that must be in a healer. I had thought him to be also of boys."

"You…you haven't met him?" She was flabbergasted.

"An apprentice," he explained, "must , in the early times of his learning, look on his teacher as a knower of allness. Only in laterness, when he has come to know that there is no allness of knowings, may he meet the one who taught the teacher."

"Then you…don't know anything about him?"

"Sang spoke that he had chosen. I asked nothing. Such an asking would be..."

She understood. "A friend of mine—Mik—used to say, 'Your opinion of me changes my opinion of your ability to form an opinion.'"

Korl began to laugh and could not stop himself. Every time he seemed almost finished, a new burst of mirth would hit him, and he would begin again. The thing was truth, but it was truth that came to meaningfulness only when the mind of the opinion former was known. And it spoke a twoness. First, that she understood the reason he had not asked of the apprentice—that it would insult the opinion forming of the chooser. It spoke also that, in his asking of it of her, he named hers an opinion-forming of goodness.

"His name is Chars," Karel told him, when he had calmed his laughter enough to hear. "He is about three, maybe four years old, but..." she saw him start and went on quickly, "he has two uncles, Korl-ser, and his father is dead. He lives with his mother."

A warm, calm pleasantness crept into Korl. He closed his eyes and began to rock slowly back and forth in the goodness of it. "An old man," he began slowly without opening his eyes, "ends his hiding of things the young would conceal. There is, perhaps, but one in a thousand who can be made into a healer, Karel, and that one will hide the thing in him that..."

Korl stopped speaking and looked on the she. Perhaps it was not thus in the place of her coming. This truth that was in her might well be, also, in others of that place. If it were so, the thing he would speak would come with hardness into her knowing as the truth of her came hard to his.

"I was healer," he drew himself back to the time it had been, "in the time of the plague. A hundred to die in a oneness of days, Karel, and it was mine to see nearly the allness of the dyings.

"There were nine, in those days, to name themselves healers. There was one to touch of the sick, to risk the death that was in them, and I was named fool for the doing of it. I make no boastings, eh?"

"You're telling me for a reason," she agreed.

Good! Her understanding has swiftness.

"There are healers, Karel, and there are sellers of healings. This is understood?"

It was.

"My living, in afterness to the plague, had goodness, but the goodness of it was only because that I made finding of one from whom I could make a healer."

"He's very good, Korl-ser," she said, "you've taught him well."

"I do not speak a skill of the hands, woman, a thing to be taught. I speak on a thing that must be in a healer. A thing he would hide, a thing the teacher must find in beforeness to the teaching."

"The…uh…thing Sang found in Chars?"

And I in Sang, damn it, are you blind?

"You know the meaning of this living with mothers?"

"I understand it," she said, "as well as an outsider can understand anything you people do."

"You have named his years three, perhaps four," Korl continued, "and yet, I would guess, when Sang speaks him, he is called Chars-ser, eh?"

"Yes," she agreed, "and he told me specifically not to address Tami that way."

"The thing must be earned, Karel, and the way that has usualness to such earnings is not of living with mothers. There is Dancing this night. You know the meaning of this?"

"No," she admitted, "I know it's a very important event, but…"

"When a boy would make Dancing," he interrupted, "he makes first his going to a place of loneliness. A place where the sky and the wind and the stillness will bring him to knowing of his own smallness. He will sit in such a place until it be that the smallness gives him to know if there be full readiness for Dancing.

"It can be that a boy lies into himself, that his wish for the Dancing is such that he names himself of readiness when there is no truth to the naming. There is much pain in the knowing of readiness yet to come. I," he tapped his chest, "made two smallnesses. When I had ended my second, I began the making of my house."

He stopped and chuckled. "There are some, of my years, to name it wrongness, now, that the young will choose of the houses that stand empty—of these , there are many, Karel, there was a plague, not? Those of my age would name such a doing a debt to the dead, and they ask how there can be paying of such a debt. I think…" he came to remembering that she would not know of such things.

"The houses of the Other Place are not made as these are, Karel. The tools for the working of wood are a fewness—and greatly cared for. In the

Other Place a house is made by choosing a tree of great thickness and hollowing it. The hollowing can be made with fire, with a stone for scraping what is burned, and..." he drew his knife and showed it to her, "this for the carving of the chair."

He saw her start at the naming of the chair, and he kept from her seeing the sadness it made in him. Even in her knowing of his ways, the ways of his people, she thought on a house as a place that had no chair. Such thinking was, for him, a near impossibleness, and he sorrowed that it was so.

Perhaps, he thought, *my asking should have been for a moreness than nineteen years.*

"Betime," he went on, "there will be an end to the trees of such size as to permit of such house-makings, and, of this, I name it a goodness that the young take from the dead, but I am one of a fewness to think thus.

"When my house-making was ended, I made a hunting in loneliness. Ever before my hunting had been done in the company of my father. I made, now, a hunting of loneliness, eh?"

"And they still do that," she asked, "even if they don't make their own houses?"

"You come swift to understanding," he agreed. "I will give a morness. The thing of my killing was gezel. You know of these?"

She did not.

"For a grown one," he told her, "it needs three men to make a killing. One to stand before that it will charge him, one striking from the side that the charge will end with a turning of the head, and a third to strike..." he pointed to a spot on the side of his neck, "in a place where the blade will enter. The allness of these doings...dangerous.

"My killing, of course, was a gezel of youngness. Their skin has more softness, and the thing can be done in loneliness." He paused, considered a stray thought, and then went on. "I do not speak you this, Karel, to make braggings."

"Oh, yes, you do."

He laughed. "I carried the meat to the house of my father," he went on, "and in afterness, I went to the house that was mine and not his."

"You...your debt was paid." It was not a question, and she could see that her understanding of it surprised him.

"Symbolic only," he grunted. "There can be no real paying of a lifetime's owing. But it was in afterness to this doing that my father named me Korl-ser, eh?"

"When you'd earned it."

"I Danced," he went on, "in the next of the Dancings, and in afterness to it I made going to Term and took the first of my shes. When I had taken my Terman she, my father came to my house and asked a speaking with her, but when he had spoken he went from me and said nothing. At the taking of my Polyan she, he came again, spoke her, and...made giving of the *stone that fell from the sky."*

And have you spoken to Mari, Korl-ser? Then again, what difference does it make? You gave it to Sang after talking to me.

"'Betime,' was my father's saying, 'it will come to be more friend to you than the knife it strengthens.'"

Are we back to that? I thought we understood each other.

"Betime," Karel said softly, "there will be a second of runnings."

"Necessary," he agreed. "Of this, when I came to a similar giving, it was of the stone, only. The words are...yours."

So, he had understood her, after all, at least better than she thought he had, but there was still that thing he wanted to do before he died, and all this was leading up to...

"I am old," he snapped, "and I have done you no hurt, eh?"

He might just as well have slapped her. In fact, she was not sure what he had done was not worse. He had accused her of the one thing that, as a Scout, she was not supposed to do—and he was right. Because of the well, because of the threat of the chair, because of the forced marriage—however unconsummated—she had allowed her resentment of Sang to override her objectivity. She had known it, been ashamed of it, but she had not, until now, truly admitted it to herself. She dropped her eyes.

So! The trap closes. "We spoke," he said, "on a thing that must be in a healer."

"That much I have seen, Korl-ser."

"Part," he countered. "You have seen only a part." *And in afterness to the raiding, your seeing will have moreness.*

"All right," she sighed, "I'll take a closer look. For your sake, Korl-ser, not for his. I don't think I want him for a friend."

"Nor he you," he countered.

Karel laughed. It was undoubtedly true, it was, probably, even a quote. She might even have felt insulted, if…

Oh, my God! Insulted!

"Korl-ser," he caught the fact that she was shifting the subject, "when you killed your gezel, did you skin it?"

The question puzzled him, but he nodded. "Skinned, butchered, much of it smoked. The allness of its eating belonged to my father, it must be brought to goodness that it would keep till his finishing of it."

"What would it mean," she asked knowing full well what the answer would be, "if you had given a pisone—and not even bothered to skin…"

"The nephew!" His reaction was so violently angry that it gave depth to her understanding to the viciousness of Tami's insult.

"Sang…laughed when he saw it."

"Perhaps, then, his is a moreness of the thing that just be in a healer. I would have killed the little bastard."

"Sang's comment was that he was glad to have him out of the house."

Korl smiled into the thinking that had come to him. The nephew would Dance this night, and of this was made a way of returning—in smallness, only—the insult.

"I have seen," the old man announced, "a manyness of Dancings. It is not in me to wish sight of this one. Speak Sang my thanks for the thought that was in him, but go, now, in loneliness. I would rest."

Karel thought she had been dismissed, but just as she reached the door his voice stopped her.

"When you look," he said insistently, "make seeing of the thing that is *there*."

18 CHAPTER 18

Not tonight!

Superimposed on Karel's vision was a series of images that were not her own. The stockade was surrounded. There was a ring of guards posted just outside the wall, and others farther out. It was as if Karel were making a near-instantaneous tour of inspection—from above.

The idea had crossed her mind casually and been answered emphatically.

Karel had, in the past, had some experience with telepathy. One friend, in particular, had sometimes gotten tired of trying to express himself in words, and had resorted to his natural mode of communication. Karel had been able to receive most of it, but this was different. This was very close to what it was like to actually be a telepath.

I am not going anywhere tonight, indeed not.

The Dancing, the distraction she had hoped might get her over the wall without being noticed, was about to begin. She might as well watch and learn. A crowd, like audiences everywhere, surrounded the participants, and Karel skirted the circle until she found a place where she could peer over the heads and between the shoulders of those in front of her.

When she could see, she noticed that the dancers fell into three distinct categories—two concentric rings of men surrounding a cluster of women. Most of the women were mature, all were belted. There was a wider age span among the men. The outer ring included Tami and members of his age group, all facing inward. The men in the inner circle were wore the only costumes, wigs and fake beards, and faced outward.

The drumming began.

It started slowly at first and then gathered momentum, and the rhythm of it began to stir an excitement in Karel that she could equate with no other sensation she had ever felt. The pounding of the drums seemed to actually drive her blood through her veins, and her heart began to race in time with the drums.

The Dancers began to move, slowly and carefully. The knot of women tightened, huddled together as if afraid of something. The beards became wary, staring out into the crowd, watching for something, but pretending to be unaware of the stealthily approaching youths.

The youngsters moved in, sometimes erect, sometimes crawling, sometimes dashing from one imaginary tree to another, but always in time with the beating of the drums. Close, closer, almost on top of the beards and then, as the drumming rose to a near-frenzy, they were on top of them. Each lad had drawn his knife at some point in the performance, and now he leaped forward, grabbed a man by the beard, pulled him in, and made a stabbing motion with the blade carefully pointed backward.

One by one the beards collapsed and writhed on the ground in time with the drum. Those who had struck them down leaped past them, each grabbing a woman from the knot in the center—a particular woman. Karel saw several of the lads dodge past the closest woman to take another.

The women began screaming the moment the attack was launched, and now they struggled in mock terror, pretending to claw and bite their captors. The struggles continued even after each lad had tied his victim in the manner with which Karel had become familiar.

It's a dress rehearsal! Karel had not expected it to be this literal. The purpose of the Dance itself was public declaration that the prerequisites, selection or construction of the house and symbolic payment of the debt to the father, had been met. The women, and the bearded men who lay in simulated death, had been recruited to help, but the thing was definitely a puberty rite. In 'afterness' these lads would go on their first raid. Here they announced their readiness for mating.

Very seldom, however, did a ceremony of this kind depict so accurately the reality to follow. Without ever having been there and never having asked, Karel could now describe exactly what took place during an actual raid, making only a few allowances for the fact that the Dance took place in a confined space.

And there's something missing, she thought. *No, wait a minute! Here it comes.*

One couple had separated itself from the throng and leaped up onto the platform, and now the thing being represented was lost in the intricate steps of the Dance. Each lad would have his moment center-stage, a chance to demonstrate his mastery of the complex set of foot and body movements he and his partner had obviously rehearsed.

The thong encircling the woman's neck was used to guide, to impel, to suddenly reverse her direction, with force but without violence. She stooped, she leaped, she swung, she slid across the floor of the platform to be brought up short with a suddenness that made Karel wonder how her neck could stand the jerk. They circled, danced around each other weaving patterns with the rope, and with their bodies, that threatened to drop them in a tangled heap at any moment. Then they would be apart again with the woman literally flying at the end of the rope. She came down, somehow, on her feet, and made a final, running leap at her partner. He caught her lightly on his shoulder and made a dash across one of the planks and into the house it led to.

The next couple took the stage.

Their dance was not a repetition of the first. It was no less intricate, and no less strenuous, but it was distinct in every other way. The rope was hardly used at all, it hung completely slack during the few brief steps the woman took, and then she was lifted from her feet to spend the remainder of the Dance on the lad's shoulder while he performed, essentially, alone. It was a boast, indicative, no doubt of the society's respect for displays of strength and the young man's pride in his own. It was also a mistake.

When it came time for the final dash across the plank and out of sight, he had exhausted himself. The feat was difficult enough without passing the limits of endurance before the attempt. He fell.

A hush fell over the crowd as the lad slowly and deliberately climbed to his feet. Everyone seemed to be waiting for something, and there was an almost audible sigh of relief when he drew his knife, poised it for an instant, and...

He's going to kill himself! By the time Karel finished the thought he had completed the deed.

A man stepped out of the crowd of spectators, kicked the corpse aside and helped the woman to her feet. They stood together for a moment looking down at the boy. The man's face was carefully impassive, the woman's filled with grief.

They're the boy's parents.

Most of the women who danced tonight would be aunts, cousins, sisters, family friends. This was a mother who had come to help her son become a man and seen him fail. The failure worked on the father, too, but differently. His face wore a disgusted expression as he yanked the knife out of his son, lifted the body to his shoulder, mounted the plank where the lad had left it, and continued the journey leaving his wife to follow or not as she chose.

There was a short silence and then the drum took up its beat again and the next pair of Dancers began. The Dancing continued without further mishap until the last couple had disappeared, then the crowd broke up.

So, now we do the disappearing act.

That the family was going somewhere was obvious. Everything that would move had been packed into three bundles and Karel had been assigned to carry the second largest of them. Sang would have the biggest load, and Mari, who also had to bring the baby, the lightest. The distribution was as fair as anything ever got around here.

As soon as they were ready, Sang led them out into the street and directly up onto the stage. The planks the Dancers had crossed the night before were still in place, and Mari, Karel and then Sang passed over them.

What would happen, Karel wondered, *if I lost my balance and left a track that's not supposed to be there?* She decided that it would be too dangerous to try.

Inside the house her final question was answered. Sang tilted the chair backward on a set of hinges that Karel had not noticed. There was a tunnel underneath. Simple and effective.

The chair, when it was back in place, would cover the hole with a fit so precise as to be undetectable, and there would be a way of locking it from below. The planks would be reset into the porches, and the tracks would center the immediate attention of pursuers on the stage.

But this has been going on for generations! Somebody should have figured it out. The pursuers had a vested interest in figuring it out.

The trip was a pain in the neck, back and shoulders, a matter of tramping along in the wake of the torch that Sang carried. When they finally emerged into the light, Karel was surprised to find herself looking at a small city, and her surprise was due to the fact that it was small.

Oh, yes, the plague. A hundred deaths, Korl had said, in a single day.

He had given no indication of how many days, but he had said there was too much work for one healer.

Sang tossed the torch aside and went directly to the hollow tree that was to be their new home. Unpacking was women's work, and he left almost immediately to find Chars and make his rounds. Karel found herself alone with Mari and the baby.

"You've lived here before, haven't you?"

"Most times," Mari answered. "After each of the raidings, a few are chosen for staying in the Other Place. Of these, there must be one who is of healers."

"I thought this was the Other Place," Sang had dropped the name once, the sterilizer was here.

"The other place," Mari answered condescendingly, "is the place where you are not."

Missing the obvious, Karel could feel herself blushing, *is what I'm best at.*

"Are you glad to be back?"

"It is of betterness here," Mari agreed. "There is a moreness of freedom, except during a raiding."

"Why is that?"

"This is an island," Mari replied. "Around us there is river, and there is no way of our leaving except through the tunnels. We are free to go anywhere, except that we may not stand in nearness to the shore."

Because you might be seen? Karel tried hard to conceal her elation. If she could see the other shore, she could swim to it. *Unless something in the water likes to eat people.*

That was something she would have to find out about, but not from Mari. Never again would she trust her co-wife. An idea came.

Karel waited patiently until everyone in the house was asleep, to begin her first conscious attempt to contact the curls. It was difficult because she had no idea how she had managed it before. She thought she might have projected an image of herself climbing over the stockade wall and had unconsciously delivered a message and triggered the answer she received. She had done it unconsciously and had no idea how she had done it.

She concentrated on water, imagined the feel of it sliding across her body. She tried to recapture every sensation she had ever felt while swimming, and then she imagined herself being attacked from below by something she could not see.

She let her mind go as blank as she could and waited for an answer. When none came she began again, trying for more and more realism, hoping that her ignorance was not a hindrance. She should know what color the water was, she should know what the riverbank looked like, she should be better able to locate herself, and she should, most importantly, know how to go about projecting the message she was trying to send.

She failed. She tried again and she failed again. Were they asleep? Were they too far away? Was she doing something wrong? If she did get through, would they understand what she was trying to ask them?

Then it came. A vague, blurred picture began to form in her mind, fading, receding and then materializing again. The image in her mind began to move, and it took a moment for her to realize that her communicant was leaping toward her through the trees.

It became a dizzying ride. A branch would come flying toward her, and, at the last instant, a pair of tiny paws that almost seemed to be her own would flash out and catch it. Then she would be flying through the air again or rushing down the trunk of a tree with the ground rushing up at her. She would bound across the intervening space and go sailing up the trunk of the next tree.

At last, she, or rather her friend, came to the bank of the river, dove in, swam across, immediately mounted the trees again, came to a particular one, scampered down the side, and Karel was looking at herself upside down. At the same time, she was seeing the curl peeping through the doorway. Then the nature of the communication changed.

Conversation is a mild word for what took place then. It was the first time in her life that Karel had not needed to make allowances for the possibility of being misunderstood. There was no possibility of being misunderstood. This was total communication. This was total friendship. Separate entities, individual minds, but sharing with each other. She absolutely reveled in it.

When it was finished, when it came time to break it off so that both of them could sleep, she felt a sense of loss, of isolation, of aloneness so acute as to be nearly unbearable, but her question had been answered.

If a curl can swim it, so can I.

19 CHAPTER 19

DeMyrn Tan stood in the Place of Picnics and made puking. It was ever the same. A twentiness of mere children, one dame muchly pregnant, and a fiveness of townmen to guard them.

Five!

The bodies lay, except that their knives had been taken from them, as they had fallen. As it had been known they would fall if the Uglies came. Four to one is no fight.

He had seen it before, found the bodies, and puked at the finding. Betime he had crossed the trail of a raiding party, seen here that a dame had stumbled and been dragged, that another had been knocked from her feet and then lifted again. The hate in him now was no newness.

His mind screamed what his mouth must hold. *My niece has been taken.*

And the slowness of the following. The time lost while the one who was left untouched by the Raiders waddled slowly back to the city, pushing her belly before her with difficulty, resting often, to speak on the thing that had been. Then another, swifter dame, also pregnant but not so greatly, to lead a following of townmen in the tracking of those who had fled.

Townmen! So greatly did they fear a scarring, an end to their beauty, a Time among the Unchosen, that they would flee from a fight as surely as they would come too late for fighting to be made.

There had been no sound, and the vark had given no warning, but a man stepped into the clearing. Tan's hand flew to his knife and his body bent to a readiness for fighting, then he laughed at himself and returned the blade to its sheath.

"I had meeting with Dorn," Zek said quietly, "he spoke me long and proudly that small Myrn had gone this day to a picnicking. I came to…I am come too late."

But you are come. And Tan came, nearly, to tears because of it. Of true friends he had only this twoness—Zek and the vark.

"Five hours," Zek was looking on the age of the tracks, "and they must rest the dames betime."

"And when we have made their catching...?"

"I am Unchosen," Zek pointed to the great scar that made his ugliness, "and not greatly fearful of dying."

Tan shook his head. There was no need in him to name his courage of sameness to that of his friend. Of cowardice Zek knew he had nothing. For prudence, Zek would have respect.

"There could be catching of a straggler, perhaps," he said. "to bring the dame home is my wish, Zek, not to die in a fighting of uselessness."

"And if she be other than small Myrn?"

"A Hunter takes what he finds," Tan replied. "He does not pass the pisone because it is no gezel."

But it was not to be. Had there been a straggler they might have taken, he had entered the hiding place of the Uglies a full hour before their coming. The Raiders had pushed, marching through the night and into the morning, more anxious, perhaps, for arrival than fearful of pursuit.

The gate had been, scornfully, left open. That the place was empty was known to Tan and Zek before they entered it. The vark spoke them that, leaping to the platform where the tracks obviously led, and then sniffing about the edges of it. The vark gave no warning of enemies here, only of a trail that was broken. Casting about for the place it began again, the vark found it.

Tan and Zek entered the house behind their vark to find his sniffing and whining at the chair in the center of the floor. They looked on each other with puzzlement, but neither made any doubting of the vark. The trail broke, came here, and broke again. The thing was no magic but only trickery.

They examined the chair and the floor about it and found at last the way of its moving. They learned, also, that it had been made immovable in afterness to the passing of the Raiders and their captives.

"Fire," Zek suggested when the thing was known. "Burn the place to the ground and enter the hole it hides."

"To meet a twentiness to our three?" Tan was dubious.

"Wait the coming of the townmen, then."

She of Strangeness

"Zek, have you thought on the sending of townmen?"

He had. Perhaps the allness of Hunters had thought on this thing, not speaking it, even to each other, for fear of being named as Plotters. They stood together, Tan and Zek, sharing an anger with dames for the doing of dames to others of dames. But the dames who made the doing commanded Archers.

"We must make a hunting," Zek said. "The covering of our tracks here is not needful, townmen are without eyes for following a trail, but you must have a killing to show for the time you have spent."

There was wisdom in this. Zek would not be missed. Unchosen, he came and went as he pleased, but the Mistress would ask of it should Tan return with hands of emptiness. And she would ask it of a man already watched and suspected. So, they would hunt. He would do what he must to keep himself living, but in beforeness to that doing he would speak, here, now, only once, the thing that was tearing at his heart.

"My niece was not taken, she was given!"

20 CHAPTER 20

The city had been deathly quiet ever since the raiding party had come boiling up out of the tunnel. Mari and Karel had been ordered to remain silent, and whenever the baby so much as stirred, Sang pounced on him, giving him either to Mari to be fed or to Karel to be cuddled.

The silence lasted for hours. It became oppressive, nerve wracking, intolerable. Finally, the word was passed that the Termans had, once again, given up and gone home.

The screaming began.

The one thing that Karel had never learned to deal with objectively was the screaming. The result, the scars old and new, she had come to tolerate, understand as this society's equivalent of a wedding ring, the sound that accompanied their making was painful to hear.

Always before she had retreated physically, gone far enough away to keep from hearing it. Always before it had been coming from only one house. Today it was everywhere. She began casting about for some thought or activity on which she could concentrate intensely.

Sang is waiting for something!

Karel clutched at her curiosity, the way a drowning victim would snatch at anything within reach. She had seen him this way before. When? Where? Why?

Then she got it. Today it was not necessary for the curls to speak him the coming of a patient—he knew. He did not know how many there would be, or how badly hurt. There were ten healers and as many as twenty girls who might need them. Sang was tensed like a drawn bowstring.

He's afraid!

He was that, and angry as well. Fearing for the one who might die before he could get to her, terrified that his opportunity to help might come too late, and angrily expecting the worst.

I begin to see the thing that must be in a healer. I'm looking, Korl-

ser, I'm looking.

When the man hit the door with a girl in his arms, Sang rose to his feet with a calm born of release from waiting.

"Healer, I have made too much of a cutting."

"You wish a healing?" Sang had not yet looked at the patient, he kept his eyes on her husband. His eyes were scornful, his tone mocking.

"I wish a healing," the man said. "Swiftly, healer!"

Swiftly? Did you think, as you stood with your dong stiffening in your joy at the noise of her mouth, to end the thing swiftly? In beforeness to this fear of her dying did you choose stopping? No, you son-of-a-bitch, I will not move swiftly. Sweat, you bastard!

"I must have," he kept his voice calm and irritatingly slow, "the touching of your she."

"Done, healer," the man's eyes were wide with fear.

"I must have," Sang drawled, "her speaking."

"Done again, healer."

"Her seeing."

"You have it, healer." The man was pleading.

Now, having gained permission, Sang deigned to look at the patient. He took in her condition with a practiced glance. A muchness of bleeding, a greatness of pain, no danger of dying. The man had no knowledge of such things, and of this he had come needlessly to his fear of becoming a wife-killer. *His problem, none of mine.*

"There is price." Karel, who knew him, could hear the things he was not quite able to keep out of his voice. Contempt, loathing, and an effort not to let it show.

"Name your price, healer."

"I will have a gezel."

"A gezel, then," the man's voice was relieved. It was as if Sang had already made the cure by contracting to do so.

"Not a young one," Sang went on quietly. "I will have all the meat of a gezel come to the fullness of its growth."

"Healer," the man protested, "it needs a threeness to make such a killing. I would have debt to the other two."

Debts, Karel remembered, *are greatly to be feared.*

"You can hunt again," Sang said, "and a third time to make your paying, but I will have the first of your killings. Or," he was letting some of his anger show now, "if the price is too great...there are other healers."

"You are nearest, and I am told you are the best."

"I have named my price. If you fear it, take your fuckin' she from my house."

"No, healer," the man almost screamed. "You will have your gezel."

Sang dismissed him with a jerk of the thumb and watched him go with the kind of resigned hatred that is no less potent for the fact that nothing can be done about it. When he turned back, Karel was staring in horror at the mess on the floor and he leaped to her side and gripped her arm so tightly that she winced.

"I know," he said close to her ear in a voice that was low and hard but not angry, "of your thinking. It is not the time of such thinking, Karel."

"Sang-ser," she said violently, "I absolutely hate that man."

"It is not," he repeated, "the time for thinking. Look down, Karel. You will see a thing that needs doing." He was right.

She was looking at the same mass of raw flesh, skin laid open in so many places that the body it no longer covered was, only just, recognizable as human. It was the same sight that had inspired the bloody hatred that was the first, and only, emotion she had ever shared with Sang. But he had felt it longer than she had. He had faced up to the futility of focusing on it. There were, as he said, things to be done.

"Do you want me to wash the cuts?"

He shook his head. "Washing brings, also, hurting. She is not mine to hurt."

But I am, and you didn't. She understood, now. She understood, among other things, why he had never approached her sexually. He was supposed to have done this, or something like it, to her. Instead, he had made Karel his wife in name only. With Mari he had, without leaving scars, at least gone through the motions. Karel could sense, now, what even that had cost him.

"Mari, take your pukings from the house," he snapped suddenly. "When they are ended, find Chars and speak my need of him."

Mari scooped up the baby and ran, escaping gratefully to the outside.

Sang went to the box where he kept his medicines and instruments and came back with a flask in his hand. He bent over the girl, and she cringed away from him.

"It is not a time for fearing," he said in a tone more gentle than Karel had ever heard him use. "It is soon that the pain comes to its ending. This," he held up the flask, "is a juice that brings sleep. Long before your waking the pain will be gone."

The girl watched him fearfully as he poured some of the liquid into a small cup. Her fear of poisoning was obvious, and it was no surprise that she clamped her lips tightly together.

"Shit," Sang said under his breath as he rose resignedly to his feet. "It is ever thus, Karel. They are told that we kill shes, even, that we eat them. Most times I must force the opening of their mouths and pour, and then they fight the drug, and it comes more slowly to its working."

"You want me to try." It was not a question, it was a shortcut.

"Quickly," he agreed. "The light goes soon from the sky."

Karel took the cup from his hand and knelt beside the trembling girl. "You have to trust us," she said. "I know it's hard after what's happened to you, but…"

"You are of *them*," the girl said suspiciously. "It is of this that you would have my drinking of this poison."

"It's not poison, Karel said. "I drank it myself, once. It only put me to sleep."

"How do I know that there is no lie to your saying?"

"You don't," Karel admitted, "but you did hear the man who brought you here say he wanted you healed. Before we can do that, we have to put you to sleep."

"There will be waking from this sleep?"

"Yes," Karel could understand, and even identify with the girl's suspicions, but she was also afraid of having to finish the job in the dark. "Look, if they were going to kill you, why would they bother with poison? He could have done it with a knife."

It worked. The decision may have been based, partly, on the idea that it was just as well to die and get it over with, or on having heard Sang say he could force her to drink it, anyway, but the argument worked. She tried to reach for the cup, but the movement was too painful, and Karel helped her sit up and held the cup for her.

Just as she was easing the girl back down, Chars slipped into the room. Sang had him examine the patient while they were waiting for the drug to take hold, but he refused to allow anyone to touch her until he was sure she was completely under. Then he set Karel to work cleansing the wounds while he laid out his instruments.

"You have not the touching of this she," he said quietly to Chars, "nor her speaking. He will, perhaps, forgive a looking if I name it needful," he saw the disappointment in the boys eyes and hurried on, "the fault is mine. I forgot these askings, but it is of betterness. I would not have your eyes, or your thoughts leave my doing. Karel will do the helping and yours will be watching. Would," he regarded the boy cautiously, "would you have it that I live to finish your teaching?"

The question was so startling that Chars blinked, and Karel looked up from what she was doing.

"Yes, healer."

"Mari, keep watch on the door," apparently she was done puking. "Speak me loudly the coming of another with a she who needs healing."

He watched her take her post in the doorway and went on. "Time passes quickly and soon the sun goes from the sky. Karel will do the cutting of the thread."

Chars flinched as he caught the implication of it. Scissors were used for cutting tissue, only. For thread they used a knife. He looked from Sang to Karel to Sang to Karel. He had been handed the power to kill one of them and maim the other. He would not use it.

The operation began with Sang, as usual, explaining quietly to Chars as he worked.

"This kind of shit," he said at one point, "is not necessary. The shes are so full of fear when they come to us that the thing can be done, almost, by shouting at them. This," he pointed, "wants debridement, eh?" He took the knife from Karel and did so with a few quick strokes before handing it back. "In the naming of price, you must give thought to the future. Ask a thing of such greatness as to make him think long and hard before coming to you with another such healing. For this one I have asked the allness of meat from a gezel, eh?"

"Will it stop his doing of it," Chars understood what was being said, "or only send him to another of healers?"

"Betime the one, betime the other," Sang admitted. "Worth a try. Karel, get this fuckin' blood out of my way."

Her hand shot in and out with the sponge.

"One more," he said at last. He inserted the last stitch and immediately took the knife away from Karel.

She of Strangeness

More often than not, he had Karel apply the dressings, but this time he did it himself after packing Chars off to clean and sterilize the instruments. Then he carried the girl over to the bed and laid her on it carefully. The anesthetic was still holding, and he was confident that when it wore off she would shift into natural sleep.

"Would you like me to stay up and watch her tonight?"

He shook his head. "She will do no waking, and if she does I will hear." He looked at Karel for a long time, saw what he had been afraid he would see. "It is your time of sleeping, woman, not yet the time of thinking."

"If you say so, Sang-ser."

She started away. She would lie down, she would make a pretense of obeying. His grip on her arm was gentle. She could have pulled away, he would have let her go. He wanted to say something, but only if she was willing to listen. She was.

"Do not lie in wakefulness, Karel." It was no order, advice born of experience. "For this thinking there is needing of strength."

Yes, she would need that. To bounce back from this one, she would probably need more strength than she had. The hatred she had felt a short time ago was ebbing. It was its cause, not the effect, she would deal with at the "time of thinking".

"You're right, Sang-ser. Good night."

It was the first time she had wished him that.

When Karel woke the next morning, her first thought was for the patient. She rose quickly and went to the bed, but Sang was already there, talking quietly to the girl.

"It is as I said," Karel heard him ask, "the pain has made its going?"

"There is no pain," came the answer, "a smallness of itching…"

"So soon!" He was delighted. "Yours is a great youngness. Your healing will be swift." He noticed Karel standing behind him and sent her off to fetch fresh dressings.

When she returned she saw that he had already begun to remove the dressings of the night before. He was working slowly, pausing often. At the first tug, the slightest sticking, he would stop and watch the girl's face while he continued to pull gently. If there was any sign of pain, he would moisten the dressing, soak it off. He would not hurt this child.

She was a child. Hardly more than that, anyway.

"I will have it," Sang told her when he had finished inspecting and redressing each wound, "that you remain here this day. If there is no wrongness, your going can be tomorrow."

The girl's eyes went wide with terror as she realized what leaving here would mean. "I must go back to him?"

"You are his."

"But..." She turned away from him, refusing to face him as completely as, a moment before, she had tried to reach out to him. There were tears in her eyes.

Shit! Sang thought. *He has hurt and I have helped, and of this she has wish to stay with me.*

"For a giving," he said painfully, "there must be a having. This thing you would ask is not in my having."

He turned abruptly and went over to the fire where Mari was preparing breakfast. Karel stayed.

"He would if he could," she insisted. "He would!" *And he aches because he can't.*

Even before they had finished eating, there was a call from outside and Sang rose to meet the visitor. It was the man who had brought the girl to them, her husband. From the corner of her eye, Karel saw the girl stiffen when he entered, as if she sensed who it was.

"I have come for my she," he announced stiffly.

"Tomorrow," Sang said.

"Tomorrow!" The man was instantly, violently angry, but Sang's face was also showing hostility. "I will have her today, healer."

"I have said it will be tomorrow," Sang answered coldly.

"The healing is done," the man growled. "How is this of keeping my she?"

Sang flinched as if he had been struck in the face. "It is mine to name the time when the healing is done." His voice shook. "Tomorrow!"

"The she is *mine*, healer!"

Sang's hand flashed involuntarily toward his knife, but he stopped himself and took a deep breath. When he spoke, his voice was calm.

"There is a wrongness that may yet come," he explained. "I must keep the she until I have sureness that this wrongness will not be. Did you place no trust in my skill, how is it that you made no going to another of healers?"

"You are yet the best of healers, Sang-ser."

You son-of-a-bitch! I gave you not the using of my name. Sang's eyes were blazing again. "Then it will be mine to say when the healing is ended," he said, "of betterness that you spend this day in the hunting of gezel. The gezel," he added forcefully, "is mine."

The two men stood glaring at each other for a full minute. Sang was confident, but reluctant. The other was angry and afraid. If knives were drawn, there was no doubting the outcome. It was not Sang who would die.

"You will have your gezel," the man said finally and stalked out the door.

Sang continued to stare at the door for a long time after the other had left. He was shaking with rage and breathing heavily. His right hand clenched and unclenched a few centimeters from the handle of his knife. He was exerting every ounce of his will to keep himself from plunging through the door in pursuit of the man who had said...

He spun around and caught the patient watching him. He went over to her and stood looking down at her with the anger still writhing inside him.

Several times he tried to speak and several times he started to turn away. The girl lay there watching the struggle that was going on inside him. She knew that his anger was not directed at her.

"One day," he spat. "For a giving there must be a having. One day is the allness of my having."

He was out the door and striding away. Karel and Mari looked at each other, and an understanding passed between them.

"The going is yours," Mari said. "I must stay with the small one." She buried her face in her arms and began to sob.

Karel flew out the door with her mind screaming. She stared wildly around for Sang and she was not even aware that it was the curl and not her own eyes that located him. She ran after him, nearly in tears herself and terrified that he would reach the tunnel before she caught up with him. She did catch him, but barely, and she fell in behind him gasping for breath. He seemed unaware of her presence as he strode purposefully toward the mouth of the tunnel.

He's going to walk right out and leave me standing there in front of the guards, she thought, *and then he'll be alone.*

As they reached the tunnel, he turned and looked at her. His eyes were glazed, and she was not sure he was seeing her, but he took her hands and tied them very, very gently. His hands, hands that never shook, were doing so now. He slipped the loop over her neck, rapped out a location to the guards, and led her through the tunnel.

Karel was nearly blinded by the tears of relief that began to pour out of her. He was going to take her with him. She did not know what was going on inside him, but she did not want him to have to face it by himself. She stumbled blindly after him, unaware of the fact that he was carefully choosing the easiest path for her to follow, oblivious to the fact that he was slowing his pace to match hers, completely isolated from everything but Sang and his need.

He did not stop until they were more than three kilometers from the city, and then he untied her and sat down with his back to a tree. She slid down beside him and waited for him to speak—if he was going to speak.

It was their time of thinking.

A hundred shes had come to him for this healing, and a hundred times he had come to this place when the doing was ended. His mind roared with seeing, again, a thousand cuttings, an eternity of screamings. There had been dyings for which he had no stopping.

A hundred gezels, a hundred arguings, a hundred shes to fear the poison of the cup, a hundred times of sending them back to, perhaps, a moreness of cuttings and burnings and...

"The others," he said, "come in laterness—infected."

Terrific! Something to look forward to.

"They name it a weakness in me," he went on, "that I ran from seeing of the thing of the well."

"Did you?"

A thing in her voice. A hoping that it was so, a readiness to joy of it, a fear of his denying.

"I ran," he admitted, "I have seen, and seen, and seen again. From the seeing of this, that I had done, I ran. Weakness."

"You said they call it weakness, Sang-ser. What do you call it?"

"Differentness?" He spoke it hesitantly.

"It takes...a lot...of courage...to be different."

Truth, but a man could keep as bravely to a foolishness, not?

"For you," he said, "there was no chair. Was it courage that I asked your holding of this in your mouth?"

Oh, come on! There's a difference between cowardice and stupidity.

"What was it," she asked, "that kept you from killing that man today?" It had not been fear, she knew that.

"Kill him," he snorted, "and in afterness to the one day that was my giving, kick his she from my house that she go to her starving? It was not his living that I let him keep, Karel."

Not many men in this culture would even think of that, or care?

"Korl," she said, "doesn't call it weakness, he calls it 'the thing that must be in a healer'."

He flinched. "The thing that must be in a healer is an emptiness. A place for the taking of sickness into himself, that it be ended in others."

He turned, then, looked on her, saw of her eyes a thing that had not been before. A moistness, a nearness to tears, but a joy of him for being himself. Not since the dying of his second-mother had a she looked on him thus.

"Sickness," he repeated. "When a man takes a knife to his hand that he will touch it to a she, there is a sickness in him."

She could tell by his face that he was seeing again the result of that sickness, the girl they had worked on yesterday, and others before her.

Talk it out, Sang-ser. I can't help you yet, but I will. I promise.

"They name it a needfulness, this doing, but I have seen of their eyes when they speak of it. They glow with the joy of it even in speaking and..."

He made search for the words to give rightness into his explaining. The thing was known, understood, but a hardness to speak it correctly.

"Tami," he began again, "was come to a hard-on when he thought on your sitting in my chair, not?"

Was come to a...oh that. "Yes, yes he was."

"And again, at the well, before your shaming of him, eh?"

She nodded.

"When I take a knife to my hand that I will touch it to anyone, the thing that hangs from me hangs. It is ever thus when there is doing of a thing that is needful. When this sickness comes into them, Karel, it is like a thing that lives, moves, longs for a place of otherness. It fills them till they would burst, and then it flows."

He drew his knife, looked at it, showed it to her, let the light play up and down the blade for a moment.

"You see the sameness," he asked quietly, "it can enter anywhere, it has no need of a place that was made for it. And this sickness flows into it, filling it until it, too, would burst, and it yet longs for a place of otherness."

The blade in his hand began to shake, and he sheathed it quickly. Then his hands came up in what began as a gesture of helplessness and ended with fists clenched in impotent rage.

"When the sickness," he said, "is come into the she, there is change. It comes to be of sickness that can be seen, diagnosed, treated. But, damn it, Karel, it begins in the man. It is there that it should be treated, and I have no cure for it there." The look on his face matched the anguish in his voice. "I name myself healer, and I have no cure for this fuckin' thing in the place where it should be cured."

"You do what you can," she said softly.

"I do what I must," he corrected bitterly, "when it is too late to do what is needed. The thing flows, Karel, from the man to the knife to the she, and even when it is in the she there is no end and to its wish for a place of otherness."

"That's when you take it?"

"Into my knife," he agreed, "into my needles, into the place of emptiness that must be in a healer. I am filled, Karel, I have no strength for a moreness of such seeings."

Now! His last cry of pain had been uttered. He was still hurt, wounded deeply, but he was so habitually self-reliant that it would never occur to him that help was sitting right next to him. It would not occur to him that he needed help.

"When you're filled," she said quietly, "the thing to do is share."

"Eh?"

"It'll still flow, Sang-ser," she turned, slid her arm around his neck and presented herself to be kissed, "give it to me."

He was surprised. More astounded than he had been by anything she had ever done, but he hesitated only for an instant and then responded with an eagerness that was violent in its intensity.

It was a release, an escape valve, a means of overwhelming an unbearable memory in order to drive it out. He was crushing her, driving into her, taking exactly what she had offered without preliminaries and without even a hint of consideration. It was rape.

It was what she had expected. It was what she had heard, and seen, him do to Mari. She could not have lived in his house for so long without knowing that this was his way, the only way he knew. She had expected nothing else. This was a gift, therapy, something she could do for him. She was surprised to find herself responding.

Her body began to twitch, and then to buck and to heave, out of time with his, but beyond her control. Small sounds escaped her, and she heard them, at first, as if they were coming from outside her. Then she exploded. She heard, and saw, nothing as she soared into an orgasm that met, matched and outlasted his, and then came drifting slowly back from a nebulous somewhere she was glad to have been.

Karel opened her eyes.

Sang was staring down at her with a bewildered expression on his face. He made no move to withdraw. He propped himself up on his elbows, eased some of his weight off her, and stared long and hard.

She had nothing to say to him, not even with a smile. Her face, she knew, wore a look of quiet contentment that she could not have erased if she wanted to, but that was what he needed to see. If, with her own reaction to him, she had surprised herself, she had demolished him. What Mari endured Karel had asked for and enjoyed.

When he shook his head it was a denial. He did not understand. He would spend long hours struggling to comprehend what had happened.

"I am not yet healed," he said at last.

"Nor I," she admitted, "but it helped."

She had been helped? On this, too, he would think muchly—that he had given strength by taking it. The thing was impossible. He had named himself filled to hide the truth of his emptiness, his weakness. She had given into him, but it was not enough.

"Karel!"

Her name was a cry of anguish, and he buried his face in her neck.

She held him, but that was all. She would do nothing, say nothing that he would remember afterward and resent. She wanted to pat his shoulder. Her mind was filled with little cooing, motherly sounds that she dared not make. He was not a child. He was a man who wanted to pretend, for a moment and not even completely, that he was a child. She was not his mother, but she was a good enough substitute to give him what he needed.

He needed to be held.

21 CHAPTER 21

The dame was once-wife the ninth to him, her name forgotten, as it should be. For the others, did he search through his memory, he could recall names. The name of Clar came to him easily. For the name of his ninth, he would do no memory searching, hers was his respect.

"There is proof, Tan?"

"I have seen it, dame."

You have seen it. You , and your vark, and this Unchosen.

"You are a brute," the word tasted badly to her, "and already suspected of Plottings. Much ease, then, to your disappearing, and none would dare ask of it."

This was truth. It had never been spoken in his hearing, but it was truth. Men disappeared, betime, and it was known that the Archers had them, although none had seen their taking. Were it a dame who had brought the thing he knew into the city, it would have been different. But he was, as his ninth said, a brute.

"But why is it, dame?" He had much wish for this knowing. "Why do they wish to keep from this finding, and yet speak often and loudly of the war that will be when the finding is made?"

"Perhaps," said his ninth, "there is fear in them of losing this war. You have spoken, with small respect, of those you call 'townmen'. Would they fight, Tan?"

Would they? Their following of the Uglies had slowness, and he knew of them that the thing that held their feet from swift travelling was fear. Fear of a scarring, such as that now worn by Zek, fear of coming to an ugliness that would place them among the Unchosen. And even if they did make fighting, they would not do it well.

"They would fight, dame," he answered with truth as he knew it. "For this, I think they would fight."

"How badly," she asked quietly, "would they need to outnumber the Uglies?"

"Muchly, dame."

"Three to one?"

"That would be enough, I think." He hoped.

"Then they have it, Tan. The Raiders have come again to a fewness. I do not know how this came to be. Perhaps a sickness among them, but their takings are fewer. For a taking, there must be a brute who takes. They are fewer."

"We could teach them, dame," he spoke it excitedly. "I, and the other Hunters, could teach fighting. We know it well."

"There must be proof, Tan," she spoke harshly. "A thing that can be seen, and not disputed. Your word is not enough. There must be proof."

"Then I will make finding of proof, dame."

"If," she shared not in his confidence, "there is such a finding, speak it quickly, loudly and to as many hearers as you can. If, as you say, there is wish among the officers to keep from this war, it must be that the allness of Termans hear you and wish for it as you wish for it. And they must hear of it before your mouth can be stopped."

"My hunting," much determination in his voice, "shall ever be to a far northness. I will find proof."

22 CHAPTER 22

It's time to go.

Now. Immediately. Two hours ago, would have been better, but the plan called for darkness, when red hair would look brown, when the only redhead on the planet would not be so recognizable. It was time to go.

Mari knows! Mari sensed what had happened the instant Karel and Sang had returned to the house, and Mari had spent the day sulking. Mari was jealous, and Mari's jealousy was not the reason it was time to go.

Mari loved Sang. Karel had always known it, Mari had just been forced to admit it to herself. She called it "softness", the thing that had angered The Mother enough to send her here in the first place. She was chastising herself as much as she was resenting Karel. She loved him and she was jealous of Karel.

Mari loves him, I don't. Karel had spent the entire afternoon coming to that conclusion, and it had been a difficult conclusion to reach. She did not love him.

*But, t*his was a difficult admission, *give me enough time and I will.*

How long? A day? A week? A month? She was that close. She could cut and run now, or she would stay. It was time to go.

She was still a Scout. She had a duty to perform, an obligation to the people who had sent her here. That was one of the factors that had tipped the scales. Mari was another.

The belt, and the knife that went with it, had been handed to her miraculously. She had wanted a knife. The idea of going without one had made her hesitate for a long time. With it she could make everything else she needed. But the risk of trying to steal one was too great.

Now Sang had brought one home at the exact time she needed it. He had been called away the instant they got back, and the search for him had been going on long before he was found. Chars met him at the mouth of the tunnel. A healer, he said, was come to his dying and at the dying of a healer the allness of healers are called. But an apprentice may not go to such a doing without his teacher, so Chars had waited.

Sang ran.

He had come home, briefly, to drop off the belt.

"He is gone," he announced, "and it was he who sat among the elders as one of them. I am called to a speaking with them, that they may think on my taking of his place."

"That's wonderful, Sang-ser."

"The hell it is," he sounded as if he meant that. "I will be late. Wait no supper for me." He was gone again.

Mari had gone out immediately after that, as if she could not stand to be in the house with Karel. Now, at last, it was dark enough. It was time to go.

She was not going to the ship. The last time she tried that, Sang had outrun her. This time, too, he would go straight to the ship, assuming that was where she had gone. When he did, finally, realize she was not there he would, hopefully, waste even more time searching the wrong side of the river for her tracks.

By the time he picked up her trail, Karel would be far to the south. Term as there, the curls had given her its location and its distance. Poly was further. Either place could offer sanctuary, and she should investigate both of them, and have a report ready when the rescue ship came to pull her out of here.

She would be three days in the woods, however. The curls would help. They would keep track of any pursuit, keep her informed, suggest ways of avoiding it. It did not eliminate the risk, but it gave her more confidence. Having a knife would improve even that.

She could get sidetracked. Sang, or someone else, could get in front of her, force her to turn aside. She might have to spend a long time living off the land. She might even wind up building the landing marker somewhere out in the middle of nowhere. She needed the knife.

The belt fit as if it had been made for her. The knife was razor edged and beautifully balanced. The patient was sleeping soundly, and even if she had not been, she was too new here to realize that there was anything wrong with what Karel was doing.

There was a horrified gasp from the doorway, and Karel whirled to find Mari staring at her with a look of utter contempt on her face.

"Go on," Karel challenged. "Go tell him. I won't try to stop you. I just won't be here when you get back."

She had handled a knife and been seen doing it. Now she *had* to go, in spite of the increased risk. She was not going to let herself be maimed without making them work awfully hard for the opportunity.

"To *do* such a thing," Mari said disgustedly. "To make pretending that you are one of *them*."

Us and them, us and them. I want to go home and be us and the rest of us.

"Get out of my way, Mari, I'm leaving now."

Now the girl was terrified. She slid along the wall, keeping her back to it, and made room for Karel to pass, but her eyes never left the knife.

She thinks I'd...

"I won't hurt you, Mari. I thought you knew me better than that."

Deliberately keeping her hands away from the weapon, Karel stepped past her husband's other wife and out into the night.

"Karel."

"Yes," she turned back.

"Not even a belt is allowed to pass the tunnel unless it be a brute is with her."

Do I really look stupid enough to try that?

"There's another way." It was dark, and she had already started to turn away again. She missed Mari's incredulous expression.

"Karel."

"Yes." *What now?*

"Thank you."

I'm not doing it for you, idiot. I'm doing it because if I don't, I won't. Maybe it was the same thing. From Mari's point of view, it would be.

"He was always yours, Mari, he never wanted me. I don't think he does yet."

"Perhaps not," Mari agreed, "but, did you try, you could give change to that."

Yes, I think I could.

"Goodbye, Mari."

It was time to go. Indeed, it was.

23 CHAPTER 23

The vark made the sound that spoke the coming of a dame. Tan stared at the animal with astonishment. There was never wrongness in a saying of the vark. Did he speak the coming of a dame, a dame was coming.

How could this be? Here, in the forest, in this part of the forest, a place of such nearness to the Uglies, how could this be? A dame walking in loneliness.

Tan came to a smallness of fearing. He knew of the forest, and it was a thing of wrongness that a dame be alone in his forest. It eased his fear, a little, that the vark gave no warning of Uglies, but it was a thing of strangeness.

None but a fool goes to a thing of strangeness without making first a checking of weapons. None but a fool allows himself to be seen until he has learned of the strangeness. He made sign to the vark that they would seek a place of hiding and wait the coming of this dame.

The noise of her feet came to his ears long before he had seeing of her. She made such noise that it was a thing of ease to know her place. It was, perhaps, a foolishness to make this crashing about, but it could also be from fearlessness. A witch, or The Mother herself, would be fearless, and not of things he wished to meet. Would it be well, he wondered, to observe this dame until he was sure there was no harm in her?

She came, then, to his seeing, stepping into the clearing and walking straight across it. She held a knife to her hand, and she looked in fear at the things about her. She was not of things to be feared because of their fearlessness. He came to his feet that she might know of his presence.

"Dame!"

When the man leaped out of the brush and spoke to her, Karel charged him blindly.

She had been seen entering the water. A shout had gone up behind her and a crowd had gathered on the shore to stare at the place where she had dived in. The knowledge that her escape had been detected, much earlier than she had hoped, had given her a sense of being pursued that was not eased by the fact that the curls insisted it was not so.

She had been running for two days, desperately afraid and certain that at any moment a hand would fall on her. There had been more than ample time for her to imagine what they would do to her if she was caught. The panic that this inspired in her hampered her contact with the curls. They would not touch her mind when she was afraid. Fear was contagious, it was like pain to them. Karel could not help being afraid and their minds would not come near hers when she was.

Now she was tired, exhausted, dragged down by emotional stress as well as physical exertion, but the fear had replaced itself with anger. She was being followed now, the curls said so, by three men who apparently picked up her trail by accident, Sang was not among them. And her visions of the torture she would undergo if recaptured had become a source of resentment rather than panic. The stolen knife was in her hand, and she was determined to make them pay as dearly as she could for the privilege of taking her back.

Here was one who had, somehow, gotten in front of her. She flew at him in a screaming rage.

Tan was so surprised by the attack that he almost forgot to defend himself. It was only at the last possible instant that his hand flew up reflexively and caught her wrist as she drove the knife down on him. The force of her charge drove him backward and they crashed to the ground together. He lay on his back with his arm locked against her weight and the knife only a few centimeters from his throat.

She was sobbing with rage as she struggled to shove the blade down just that much farther. The vark was whimpering off to one side, but he made no move to come to his master's aid. Nor could Tan do any more than fend her off. Had it been a man above him, he had long since killed the bastard, but he could do no harming of a dame.

"Please, dame," he begged it of her, "I am no Raider."

A number of things clicked in Karel's mind, and the pressure on the knife eased a little and then relaxed entirely. An enemy would not have escaped the notice of the curls, they would have warned her, and the man under her wore his hair longer than any Raider she had ever seen and had a beard to go with it. Dancers pretending to be Termans had worn beards, and among the names that Sang, Korl and the others had for Termans was 'hair-face'.

She stood up and stepped away from him. "I'm sorry," she said, "I…"

A dame speaks sorrow for a doing! He was more astonished by this than he had been by her attack on him.

"The sorrow is mine, dame, that I made your surprising, but there is gladness in me, that you made not my killing."

She watched him climb slowly to his feet, and she became ashamed of herself. She was supposed to be a Scout, a diplomat, an ambassador, a representative of a civilization. Wherever she went and whatever she did, she was under scrutiny. Her actions gave people their first impression of the civilization that had produced her. I just tried to kill a man.

Her chagrin was heightened by the realization that she had unconsciously placed herself under his protection when she realized he was friendly. It was logical. He knew his way around, she did not. A sense of security came over her. She felt a wave of relief at the prospect of being able to rely on someone else, of being able to lean on someone whose resources and ability were greater than her own. That was what had allowed her to get back into her proper frame of mind. Now that she was "safe", she could act and think like a Scout.

"Are you Terman or Polyan," she asked.

Again, there was astonishment. To be taken for a Raider in a time of surprising was one thing, but when she stood in calmness and had a fullness of looking on him…

"I am Terman, dame."

"I really didn't know," she said. "I didn't mean to offend you."

A second of apologies! And yet the fault was his that she had seen of his feelings. He must have more care to his way of holding his face.

"My name is Karel," she said.

Truth? He had no need of this knowing, but neither was there harm in it. Perhaps she had seen of his beauty and would wish it known that she would think on him in the Changing Time.

"I am DeMyrn Tan, dame."

This was her first encounter with a two-part name since she had landed. Sang, Mari, Dreena, Korl, none of them had ever mentioned more than one name. This man had been careful to give both parts of his name.

"What would you like me to call you?"

She of Strangeness

"You may have my calling as it pleases you, dame."

Very nice and very useless. "What do most people call you?"

"Tan, dame."

Good! The other was probably a family name, matrilineal, of course. "Tan, can you help me get to Term?"

"Such is my hope, dame," he said automatically, "but I can make no promise other than that I will die in the trying."

Well, Karel thought, *we have here a 'brute of trueness'.* It was going to be an interesting contrast.

"Is it, dame, that you have made escaping from the Uglies?"

The Uglies? Right. They're so ugly they don't even know what the word means. "Yes, I did, Tan. Two days ago."

"A twoness of days," he gasped in admiration. Then he was suddenly terrified. "They will have come to much closeness in their following of you, dame. We must give quickness into our going."

"The quicker the better as far as I'm concerned."

"It is mine to think that our going must be across the wind, dame. It is now that the wind comes from the north and makes its going to Term. We must wait its changing."

"Why is that?"

"The vark, dame," he answered. "The wind speaks him the coming of dangers and he..."

"He warns you?"

"Truth, dame, he makes noises in his throat."

"All right, then," she said, "if we go across the wind, where will that take us?"

"To a place of safeness, dame, for hiding until the changing of the wind."

"But," she protested, "won't they be able to track us?"

"There are no varks in their having, dame," he said, "and my hiding place is surrounded by rock. Without a vark there is no tracking to it."

"All right," she said, "I'll just put myself in your hands, Tan. You take me wherever you think best."

He made turning away, that she have no seeing of his embarrassment. It was a hardness to decide if the thing be of shame or of pride that a dame place herself under his care. Yet it must be so, and there was wisdom in her that she realized this.

He made sign to his vark that it circle about them. Of the trackers behind them there must be warning, and also of patrols beneath them in the wind. The vark knew of his fear for the safety of the dame and shared it. The animal gave wideness to his circles.

Far to the south was the going of the vark, but only a little to the north, and betime there came to him the thing he had feared. A threeness of Raiders moving northward and already ahead of them.

Like an arrow, the vark made running, coming to the place of his master with all the swiftness that was in him, and Tan read the saying of the vark when it leaped before him and made growling.

"There is coming of Raiders, dame," he said anxiously. "The vark speaks a twoness or a threeness." His knowing of this was because that the vark had set himself for fighting. From more than three, they ran.

Karel flashed a question to her friends in the trees and received an immediate answer.

"Three of them," she said, "about a kilometer south of us."

Tan had come to such fear that he gave no thought to it that she knew the number of the Raiders, also their place. In him was a sinking of the heart that she had named a threeness.

Betimes they had made killing of a threeness, he and his vark, but the risking had been only of self. Now the risking was also the life of the dame, and of shame to him did he fail to bring her to safeness. Yet the fighting must be, and the doing of it must be soon.

"I must make my going, dame," he said. "I would ask of you that you make hiding yonder." He was pointing to a small thicket. "If it is that I come to my dying, I will try to make loud screaming so that you will know. If you hear it, you must run with the allness of your speed, that the Uglies have no taking of you."

"Can't I help? She drew her knife determinedly. She had not changed her mind on the subject of being recaptured.

"Please, dame," there was pain and fear in his voice, "I would not have it that you come to hurt, and these vilenesses would do you hurt. I beg of you that you hide and wait."

Well, she had promised to do as she was told. She slipped into the hiding place. If he died, however, she was to run and, rather than count on hearing his scream, she linked herself with the telepaths to watch.

The Raiders were moving cautiously, but the Terman and the vark were clearly stalking. There was a special stealth in their movements that even Karel, with her limited knowledge, could understand. The vark had taken the lead.

When the animal stopped, Karel could see that the patrol was a scant hundred meters away. She guessed that neither the man nor the vark could see them yet, but they were apparently aware of the enemy's position and were coming to a spot that the vark had chosen for the ambush.

The first of the Raiders was allowed to pass unharmed, and it was not until the second was abreast of the vark and the third was directly in front of Tan that the attack was launched. Karel was unable to detect the signal that was given, but the man and vark moved in unison. Teeth and knife struck at exactly the same instant, and before Karel could even be sure of had she had seen, two of the Raiders were dead and the third had whirled to find himself facing a pair of enemies. The man had his knife out, but when he found himself outnumbered, he turned and ran.

The vark hit him full in the back before he had taken three steps. As they crashed to the ground, Karel's view was obscured by the vark's back for a moment. When the animal moved out of the way, she was looking at a corpse. An instant later Tan and the vark were racing back to her hiding place.

In his fear for the safeness of the dame, Tan had made a forgetting. The thing of his stomach, the everness that happened when he had made a killing, came to him just as he reached the place where he had left her. A muchness of shame came over him as she came from the place of her hiding and made holding of his head while he did the thing for which he had no stopping.

"I *make* killing of the Uglies, dame," he assured her fearfully. "It is only when the killing is ended this thing comes to my stomach."

"You don't enjoy killing, do you, Tan?"

She was not angry. Indeed, the sound of her voice was—of understanding? Yet there was no safeness in this, it might be only that she held her anger for another time. When they were come to a place of safeness, when she no longer had need of him, she might make a second thinking on this.

"I make their killings, dame," he insisted. "I know of their vileness. Many are the times I have done this killing—many. Yet it is in me to think, had they been of our small ones, they would have grown to be of trueness.

Their vileness is only that they came to their birthing among others of vileness. I think, dame, that my puking is only for the small one that might have been of differentness."

What is he afraid of? Mari had said something about "Plotters" who were executed without mercy. Was there such a paranoid attitude toward male Termans that they were forced to live under a cloud of suspicion?

"Our going must have swiftness, dame," he mumbled. "These of my killing were not those who follow your trail."

They traveled in silence after that. Karel was uncomfortably aware of the fact that he was afraid of her. She wanted his confidence. She wanted to talk to him about Term. She had Mari's point of view, she needed a man's. And if she were going to get it, she would probably have to do so before they reached the city. Out here, in his own element, he might open up. Once they got to Term…

They reached the cave shortly before sunset. As Tan had said, the place was surrounded by rock—a lava flow at the base of an extinct volcano—and their tracks disappeared when they stepped onto the rock. As an added precaution, however, he led her to the cave by a circuitous route, and it was only after carefully checking their back trail that he allowed her to slip inside.

"It is here that we must make waiting, dame," Tan said softly. "When the wind has made changing, we will go.

Karel was delighted. She hoped the wind would be kind enough to wait a few days before it changed. This would be her chance. She would move slowly, carefully, alert to the possibility of frightening him, but she would have time. If she managed it right she would have time to learn more about Term than she had learned about the Raiders in several weeks of living with them. She decided to begin.

"Tan," she said in the friendliest tone she could manage, "do you have to call me 'dame' all the time? I told you my name."

The cruelty of it! When he had brought her to a place of safeness, when he had killed to keep harm from coming to her, to make such a saying of viciousness. A saying like the those in the mouth of Clar—spoken to make hurting for the joy of it. Was it his puking that had brought the dame to such hatred of him, or another of his doings?

His chin began to tremble, but he held back the tears just long enough to lash out at the pain.

"I am in my Lonely Time, dame," the pain in his voice was palpable. *"I am not of the Unchosen."*

Karel sat horrified, listening to the agonized, racking sobs that were coming out of the man she had sought to befriend. The remark was intended as friendly but, to him, it was an insult, worse than an insult, an attack on the core of his being. By offering him the use of her name, she had…

Oh, my God! I've proposed to him.

24 CHAPTER 24

It took Karel a day and a half to begin to recover from the blunder. Tan would still guide her to Term. There was no question of his deserting her, but he remained sullen, refusing to speak to her. She had lost the thing she sought to gain—his confidence.

She began telling him her own story in the hope that, by repeatedly emphasizing the fact that she was a stranger, ignorant of local customs, she could make him understand that her intention was entirely friendly.

He listened, at first, with strained politeness, but as the story progressed, he began to take interest in it. When she came to the description of the Dancing, and the trip through the tunnel afterward, his mind seemed to leap ahead of her story, anticipating what came next, and he glowed with pleasure.

This is proof!

If the dame would speak, in Term, of these tunnels, there would be belief. None would dispute the word of a dame. There would be sharpening of knives, there would be much making of arrows. He, and the other Hunters, would teach the things of fighting to the townmen, and before the next taking of dames, there would be war.

Small Myrn, scarred, perhaps, and much saddened, would come again to the house of his sister, and the bastard who had given that scarring to her would be dead.

But would the dame speak? A bitch, so greatly of sameness to Clar as to have spoken such a thing to him—would she speak? No matter. The speaking would be his. Did she deny it, did she name him liar, he would die of his foolishness, but he would speak. Quickly, loudly, and to a manyness of hearers.

"You know of *swimming*, dame!"

Karel was delighted. She had startled him into breaking the silence with which he had been punishing her. He had given her an opening.

"Well, of course, I know how to swim, Tan."

"But, dame...I..." Then he remembered what she was—what he thought she was. "I sorrow that I have asked of your doings, dame, it is only that..."

"Only what, Tan?" She carefully kept her tone as neutral as possible. "Don't you know how to swim?"

"I, dame? But I am of Hunters, and of men. It is needful that I have this knowing, but you are a dame."

She did not want to prompt him again. Let him tell it in his own way.

"I am told, dame," he went on after a long pause during which she watched him slowly overcome his fear of her, "that in the first of raidings, the dames were taken as they were playing in a place of swimming. There have been none among the dames to make such playings since that time."

No, Karel thought, girls are not taught to swim—they just go on picnics. It did, however, explain Mari's assumption that Karel would try to pass through the tunnel, and the crowd that had gathered on the shore to stare hopelessly at the place where Karel had...drowned?

"Tan, you say Hunters need to know how to swim?"

"Betime, dame, it is needed," he shrugged.

"Would you like to tell me about hunting?"

"Dame?" She asks of my *likings*!

"I'd really like to know about you," she was careful not to make it sound like an order.

"Of me!" Yet, in the story of her telling it was ever that she asked this one of his doings, that one of his thinkings. "I would not have it that the dame come to boredom."

"You won't bore me, Tan, I assure you." He was not going to get out of it that easily.

"There is only a smallness to tell of the doings of Hunters, dame. We make going to the forest, then we make killing of things for eating. We carry the meat to Term, and it is given to the Mistress of Huntings that she may give it to the butchers."

Given, Karel noticed, *not sold*. Meaning what? A communal society, or only that males did not own property?

"The vark helps you, doesn't he?" It was a sudden inspiration. He was reluctant to talk about himself, but...

Tan made looking on his friend and again on the dame who had asked of their doings together. "He has the following of trails, dame," he said. "His nose speaks him things that will not come to my eyes."

"Oh, Tan," she said, "there's more to it than that. I've seen you work with him." She made a slight gesture with her finger the way she had seen Tan do. The vark hesitated for an instant and then rose uncomfortably and came stiffly to her side. Another movement caused the animal to seat himself, and she began scratching his ribs the way Tan would have done.

Tan was staring at her incredulously, and she could see the struggle that was going on inside him. His curiosity was battling with his fear of her, and there was a twinge of jealousy. He wanted to ask her how she had come to know the proper commands, but he was afraid she would be angry.

"He seems nervous, Tan," she said, "did I do something wrong?" Now what had she done? He was defensive again.

A trap, he thought. *The dame would have me name a wrongness in her, that she may have my ass for it another time.*

"There is no wrongness, dame. It is only that…"

"That he's not used to women?"

Tan shook his head. "He knows a manyness of dames, but his playing with them has differentness." He did a beautiful job of keeping the resentment out of his voice.

I suppose there's a stigma attached to masculine behavior in 'dames'. Why can't I get anything right?

"I'm sorry, Tan," she said, "I didn't mean to confuse your friend. I saw how you made him come, and I did the same thing you did. I never intended to make both of you uncomfortable. Will you try to remember that I'm a stranger when I make mistakes like that?"

Again, she sorrows of her doings. It is of ease to remember her strangeness.

"It needed a muchness of time to bring the vark to his knowing of commands, dame, but it was ever one of the Hunters who did the teaching. You have given me gladness to see that he makes obedience, also, to a dame."

Oh, look! See the pretty lie? Let's frame it and hang it on the wall. She had demonstrated knowledge of one of his trade secrets, declared herself an uninvited initiate.

"Tan, I really admire the way you work with your vark. I'd like to know more about it."

"You wish me to speak moreness on our huntings together, dame?" Karel nodded.

"I will speak, then, since you have wish to hear."

He did a great deal more than speak of hunting. Karel had read poetry from a hundred planets, written by scholars who were masters of their art, but when this man began to speak of his forest, she listened in awe. He spoke of the vastness and the silence, and the loneliness that came over him whenever he intruded on the place. He spoke of the birds and the trees and the animals, and it was as if he could have called each one by its individual name. One by one he climbed inside each of the things he talked about and told her where it lived, how it moved, what it did, how it grew, what it was.

Without moving from his seat, he took her by the hand and led her into a world, his world, where she was a complete stranger, and taught her how to live there. Kept her with him while she was learning to crawl, to walk, and to run. When she was ready, he released her.

They struck a trail, she followed it with him, and felt the thrill of the chase. She saw the quarry, quivering and beautiful, as it stood frozen with fear in the midst of a clearing. She heard the singing of the bowstring and the whistling of the arrow, and she saw the prey drop. Her hands were bathed in the bright, warm blood as the throat was cut, and she could feel every gram of its weight on her shoulder as they carried it home.

It was hunger that drove the Hunter, but there was pain and fear in the prey. He gave them both to her. In one instant she was fleeing in panic, her eyes wide with terror, her tongue hanging and her breath coming in gasps. A moment later she was stalking relentlessly and smiling to herself as she thought of the moment when she would make the kill. It was her hand that released the arrow, but it was also her body that screamed its agony and thrashed and died on the bloody ground.

They met a man in the forest, and they killed him and died with him. Karel had never known a real terror as great as the one she felt when Tan brought her face to face with a Raider and put a knife in her hand. She stood there tearing herself to pieces as her mind struggled to mend the rift between the part of her that wanted to run, and the part that knew she must stay and fight or be killed from behind. Then Tan put her into the mind of the Raider and showed her the same fear, the same courage that existed only because cowardice was fatal, and the same desire to be out of there.

He left her in both places as she leaped forward to kill. She felt the jar against her arm as the knife went home, but she felt, too, the agony of it as it drove into her. He let her hear the scream that was forced out of her as the knife left her body, and then he pulled her away from there.

He lifted her up out of the morass into which he had plunged her and brought her back into the light. When he had talked of pain, he had shown her pain. He had taken her into the pain. He had taken her into it, immersed her in it, and just when it had become too much to bear, he pulled her out of it again.

He showed her how the forest looked in the early dawn, with the darkness retreating into the tiny crevices where it hid until the time when it could once again envelope the world. But it was the light that he was giving her, so that she could see the flowers opening to greet it, hear the birds that woke and sang to it, the animals that danced beneath it like speckled whirlwinds.

He left her there in the sunlight, in a soft breeze that gently lifted her hair, among flowers that kissed her nose with delicate scents. He left here there and went to a place of his own, a secret place that he would not show her. It took her more than an hour to get back to the cave and realize she had never moved.

"Thank you, Tan," she said when she could bring herself to break the silence.

"Dame?"

She was sorry she had interrupted his thoughts. He had apparently been a lot farther away than she had. "I thank you for telling me about the things you love." *What have I done now?*

"Dame," his voice pleaded with her to believe him and not be angry, "it is a truth that a man can love a thing to which he goes and have no hating of the place he leaves."

"Have you been accused of that, too?" She could not keep her voice from showing the contempt she felt for whoever had made that stupid charge.

"It was in the saying of my once-wife the sixth," he began slowly, "that we who are of Hunters make our going to the forest that we may be free of the watching of dames. Of this, in her saying, we have sameness to Tervil."

"Did you come here often when you were married to her?" She could not really blame him for wanting to be "free of the watching" of someone like that.

"Oh, no, dame," he was horrified at the idea. "When I am in my Time, my staying is in the town and my doings are the doings of townmen."

But you can't bring yourself to say that you love it—only that you don't hate it. "Then you don't go hunting at all when you're married?"

"When a man is in his Time, dame, he must do no risking of his life in the doings of Hunters, there would be none to care for his once-wife's small ones."

His wife's, Karel noted, *What he has are nieces and nephews.* "Is that what townmen do, then? Take care of children?"

"When the small ones have much youngness, dame," he agreed, "their once-fathers care for them. When they have more years, he can also make working."

"What work do you do?"

"I, dame," he said proudly, "am a printer of books."

Well brutes of trueness are educated then. "And I suppose you read a lot, too." *Now what have I done?* He was terrified again.

"Dame, I have said that I know of printing. I have made no saying that I know of reading." He was literally shaking with fear.

"But," she protested, "you'd have to. I mean, how could you..."

"I know the shaping of the letters, dame," he explained insistently, "and their names. The Mistress of the Printshop gives me a paper on which she has made writing. I take the first of the letters from the case to put it in the page, then I make this doing with the second and the third...until it is ended."

"And you can't read it yourself?" *Of all the ridiculous...no, it's not.*

Mik had once remarked that the easiest way to control a populace was to keep it illiterate, and the Termans were a very tightly controlled populace. Mik had also remarked that the cheapest way to run a government was to shoot the opposition or, if you ran out of opposition, shoot anybody who was handy and claim they were opposition. Mik, apparently, had seen this happen on one of the worlds he had visited.

"Please, dame," Tan was still terrified, and she gave him a reassuring smile, "there was a time when my once-wife the sixth saw of me that I looked on one of her books. I speak only of looking, dame, for seeing of pictures, but it was the saying of my once-wife the sixth that a brute who would know the things of books would..."

Tan, I'm beginning to dislike your once-wife the sixth. "What did she say this time?"

"It was her saying, and no truth to it, that I would have this knowing so that I might become as Tervil."

"That's ridiculous," Karel said disgustedly. "Whatever Tervil was, it had nothing to do with his education. Where I come from everyone knows how to read—everyone."

"Truth, dame?"

She could see from his face that he had often dreamed of learning...then a new terror gripped him.

We'll settle this right now, she thought. I am not your once-wife the sixth.

"Tan, I will never, ever repeat anything we've talked about. What you say in this cave is yours and mine. I won't give it to anybody else."

"Truth, dame?"

"Tan, I will never lie to you, and I will never, knowingly, say anything to cause you trouble. I...*Tan, the Raiders are coming!*"

At the same instant the vark came to his feet and stood bristling at the mouth of the cave. If Tan had noticed that it was Karel who gave the warning first, he made no sign of it. He did do something that she would never have expected from him. For the first time in their association, he voluntarily touched her, forcefully. He shoved her behind him and crouched behind the vark.

The tracking party had finally come to the edge of the rocky shelf where, it was hoped, they would lose the trail. The telepaths were showing Karel a cluster of men milling about in confusion at the point where she and Tan had stepped onto the lava flow.

She eased forward and tapped Tan gently on the shoulder. He looked at her almost angrily, and she signed to him that there were three of the Raiders and pointed to where they were. She continued to keep him posted as the trackers fanned out across the shelf, searching for some sign of their quarry. After the initial shock, he accepted the information she was feeding him without questioning it.

The Raiders covered the rocky area from one end to the other. Their search took them back and forth across the shelf for nearly two hours. Finally, they realized they were not going to find any tracks on the barren ground. They gathered at the edge of the shelf and began a careful search of the perimeter. When they came to a stream which flowed down through the rocks and into the forest, they separated. One man took the left bank and the other two took the right, and they moved off downstream.

When they were far enough away, Karel heaved a sigh of relief. "They're gone, Tan."

"You spoke me this, dame," he said, "that the curls make warnings to you."

"Yes," she agreed.

"I sorrow that it comes in such lateness to my thinking," he went on, "but there is no need of waiting for the change of the wind. Our going could have been sooner if my stupidity was less."

"There's nothing stupid about you, Tan," she said. "I should have thought of it myself."

As a matter of fact, she had thought of it, but she had wanted the delay to prepare herself for what she would find in Term. She had managed to learn very little.

Tan went to the mouth of the cave and looked out, but he came back disappointed.

"There is too much lateness to the day, dame, our going must wait for morning."

25 CHAPTER 25

Term was built into the sides of a canyon. Many of the natural caves that honeycombed the walls had been reshaped into dwellings. An occasional wooden ladder rested against the wall, leading upward to a broad ledge that had been hewn out of the rock.

It was a fortified city. At both ends the entrances were narrow, and the ladders could be retracted in time of peril, leaving the population stranded, but beyond the reach of an enemy. The approaches to the city had been cleared to a distance of nearly half a kilometer, and the guards were watchful. No army could approach without being seen, and no individual could cross the barren stretch of land without being recognized long before his arrival.

The farmers who daily left the city in the early morning and returned shortly before sunset did so under the watchful eyes of skilled archers. The hunters who scouted the surrounding countryside in search of game, sent their varks ahead of them when they returned, and did not venture into the open until the animal had been recognized. No one else left the city or returned to it, and the guards knew the face of everyone who had the privilege.

Tan halted while they were still within the concealment of the trees.

"This is a place of safeness, dame," he said. "There is none among the Uglies who would come to such closeness. Yet it is best that I make a going to warn of your coming. Also…"

"Tan…" *Well, my goodness. Don't we sound motherly.* She tried again. "Look, there are going to be a lot of things I don't know about, and you're going to have to get over being afraid to tell me. I can make an awful lot of mistakes in there, Tan, as bad as the one I made before." She saw him wince and went on quickly. "Do you believe me when I say I'm sorry?"

She of Strangeness

Be it of truth or of lies, his answer must be that he believed her. He gave thought to her question, to know if his answer be of the one or of the other.

"Yes, dame," this was truth, "I believe it of you."

"Please promise to tell me, ahead of time, if you see me about to make a mistake."

"This is not of mistakes, dame," he said cautiously, "you have escaped from the Uglies. Your nakedness is a thing of *their* vileness, but I must go to my once-wife the ninth and ask a lending of clothing. Else you would come to shame as we enter the city."

"All this time, and you never said anything." She had been naked for so long, she no longer noticed it.

"Nothing could have been done about it until now, dame."

"Tan," another thought occurred to her, "should I keep the knife or get rid of it?"

"Dame?"

"Would it look strange for me to be wearing this knife when we arrive? I could leave it here."

"The wearing of knives," he joyed that she had thought of this, as he had not, "is a thing of Archers and of Hunters. No other has need of such."

"All right," she said, "then let's find a place to hide it. You can come out and pick it up later, without mentioning where it came from."

He regarded her solemnly for a time, then he nodded. "There is a thing," he said, "that was ever needful of doing, but it places my life in your mouth."

For the first time in their association, he had not called her 'dame'. It was almost as if she had to reestablish her right to the title.

"My mouth," she said, "has held a lot of lives lately."

"The life of an Ugly," it needed much courage to speak as he did now, "is less easily taken. If this, that you will see me do, were known, I would sit in the cells of the Archers until my dying came with more hardness than that of this Torn you have spoken me."

I had no idea it was that bad! No wonder he's afraid of me.

"I...I can't promise not to make mistakes, Tan," she said, "I can only promise that I will never knowingly cause trouble for you."

So? None could make a better promising. There were few, among dames, who would make this one, but he believed her.

He led her to a tree some distance away, dug underneath it, and extracted something.

"In the city, dame, a vark must be collared. In the forest," he shrugged, "he is my friend."

She took off her belt and handed it to him. He placed it in the hollow and carefully covered it.

They went back to the place where she was to wait for him and, after sending the vark out ahead of him, Tan set off toward the city. Karel began to prepare herself for the forthcoming contact.

By the time she arrived, Tan would have laid the groundwork, and there would be some sort of reception committee. The manner in which she dealt with that reception committee would set the tone for her stay in Term.

I'm tired of being pushed around.

There was more to it than that. She was going to try to persuade these people to help her construct a landing marker. When the rescue mission finally came after her, she wanted it to come to where she was. She did *not* want them to land near the stockade.

In dealing with an authoritarian society, Karel and Mik had a long-standing agreement that one or the other of them would assume command for the duration of the contact. Which of the partners played the role of superior would be determined by their best guess as to whether it would be Karel's height or Mik's age that would impress the people they were dealing with. In Term Karel would have wound up with the job, even if Mik had not been…

"I sorrow," Tan was back already, holding out a one-piece garment that she could only assume was what Terman women typically wore. "that my staying was so long, dame. There was meeting of my friend Dorn, and he is a man of much talking, I…"

"Listen, Tan," she was putting on the garment as she spoke, "when we go into the city, I'm going to act differently."

"Dame?"

"I was a prisoner for a long time, now I'm free. I intend to be my own person, do what I choose."

"You are of dames," he said, "this is as it should be."

"Tan, no matter what I do," she said insistently, "no matter how different I may seem, I want you to remember what I say right now."

"Yes, dame."

"I'll keep my promise, Tan. What you said in the cave, is yours and mine. *I won't tell anybody.*"

"I had made believing of it, dame, else I had not..."

"I want you to stay as close to me as you can, Tan," she went on. "I'm a stranger here, and there'll be a lot of times that I'll need your advice."

"Mine, dame?" In the forest, this was logic, but in the city...

"Yours," she said emphatically. "I don't have anybody else I can trust, and...what's the matter?"

"At the meeting of my friend Dorn, dame, I spoke that I would make caring this night for the small ones of his wife, who is also my sister.

Uncles, she remembered. He was so obviously disappointed that her heart went out to him.

"You love children, don't you?"

"They are the greatest of goodnesses, dame." *With small Myrn gone, only Sare and Gido were left to him.*

"In that case, Tan," she said. "I'll try to get away somewhere by myself tonight. Someplace where I can't make any mistakes, and you can babysit for your friend."

"There is much kindness in you, dame," he said sincerely, "of sameness to my once-wife the ninth."

Which is probably more of a compliment than I'll ever understand. He had gone to his ninth once-wife when he needed a favor.

"Just remember that you can always trust me," she emphasized. "If I seem to have changed, it's only a pretending."

They worked out a signal that he could give, a gesture that would warn her when she was heading into a blunder. Then she took the lead and started off across the clearing.

Her prediction had been accurate. A crowd had gathered about the gate. Curiosity seekers for the most part, but there was one woman who stood apart from the rest, rather the rest stood back from her. Karel assumed her to be at least an officer, but...

Captains, she thought, *do not come themselves, they send flunkies.* Hopefully this captain had sent a junior flunky.

"The Captain will have your seeing," the girl said as Karel arrived at the gate. "You will come with me."

She spun around, and the crowd scattered in front of her. Karel stood her ground.

"You!" The woman froze in her tracks, then turned to find herself staring into Karel's accusing finger. "I want your name and rank."

The woman marched stiffly back to where Karel was waiting. She drew herself up to her full height, placed her hands on her hips, and glared indignantly at Karel.

"I have said," she repeated coldly, "that the Captain will have your seeing."

You want a showdown, lady? Watch me win.

"I have every intention of seeing your Captain," Karel said with disarming smoothness, and just enough of a pause to allow the other to begin to think she was giving ground. "The very first thing I'm going to speak to her about is how you address your superiors. Name and rank!"

The Terman had dropped her guard just enough, and Karel's ringing command knocked it down the rest of the way.

"Dia," she said as she snapped to attention, "lieutenant. Orderly to the Captain of Term."

"That's better," Karel said. "I am Karel. Commanding Officer of the Federation Scout Ship Dart." A lie. The ship's name was S723/A.

Karel received the salute, surprisingly similar to the one that was still used by the Survey Corps and returned it with the sloppiness of commanders.

"If you will form a suitable escort," she said quietly, "I would like to be taken to your Captain."

Dia saluted again and spun about to look over the crowd. Six women, probably petty officers, stepped forward. These were apparently the only ones present who were qualified to perform the required service. They, as well as everyone else, knew it. They arranged themselves in two ranks, and Dia inspected them carefully before returning to Karel.

"There are only a few, dame," she said uncomfortably. "I can send for more, if…"

"It will do," Karel interrupted stiffly.

I'm beginning to enjoy this too much, she thought. *I'd better ease up on her.*

"Then, if the dame will have the kindness to make my following, I will take her to the Captain."

Karel gave a curt nod.

Dia led her to one of the ladders where they halted while half the escort bounded up and stood waiting while Dia and then Karel mounted the steps at a more sedate pace. When the escort had reformed, Dia led the way to one of the nearby dwellings where she halted again.

"Captain," Dia called, "is there room inside for a moreness?"

"You will enter," said a hard voice from inside. Dia stepped aside and allowed Karel to pass while the escort remained in place. Just as she was about to enter, Karel glanced up and noticed that Tan had followed them but was hanging back.

"I want you with me, Tan," she said quietly and then stepped through the door. Dia followed her and Tan brought up the rear.

Karel found herself in a cave, more spacious than the one in which she and Tan had hidden, and better furnished. She stopped just inside the entrance and pretended to take more time than necessary for her eyes to adjust. Directly opposite her in a high-backed chair sat a woman that Karel guessed was the Captain. She was perhaps twenty local years old, with steel gray hair and a sharply lined face. There was a hard strength in the eyes that bored out of that face and penetrated anything they touched.

Dia stepped forward and gave a sharp salute. "Captain, I have made bringing of a dame," she announced. "She speaks her name Karel, commanding officer of the Federation Scout Ship Dart."

The older woman's eyes narrowed, and she looked Karel up and down before she spoke. "So," she said finally, "you name yourself Captain, is it?"

"I do," Karel said calmly.

The Captain's eyes studied her for fully a minute, and Karel met them with something akin to defiance. She caught herself wishing she had something to do with her hands, but she stifled the thought. She had won the power struggle with Dia easily, but this was a different situation. She was dealing now with a woman who was not accustomed to having equals. Where Dia needed to be cautious until she learned what the Captain's reaction was going to be, the Captain was the one who would make the final decision.

"I would learn of this ship," the Captain said, "and this Federation you speak of."

"Well, it includes about fifteen thousand planets…"

The Captain held up her hand and Karel stopped.

"There are," the old woman said, "things that I wish for doing, and things I have need of doing. Your coming is at a time when there is a thing that needs doing. I must ask waiting, Captain Karel. I have agreed to hear the saying of one who would speak with me. You will, I hope, understand it of me if I postpone our speaking together until I have ended this unpleasantness."

Karel's claim had been accepted, at least tentatively. It was a good time to give a little. There was no good will to be gained by demanding immediate attention.

"Naturally, I have to make allowances for the fact that I arrived unexpectedly, Captain," she said. "Please don't let me upset your schedule any more than I already have."

"There is kindness in you," the Captain replied formally. "I have said that the thing will be an unpleasantness. Would it please you to make your waiting in a place of more comfort?"

Karel hesitated. Calling it 'an unpleasantness' might be a polite way of saying it was none of her business.

"I'm at your disposal, Captain," she said. "Which would be more convenient for you?"

"That you stay," the older woman said bluntly, "and waste none of my time in sending for you when this thing is ended."

Karel agreed to that readily. Whatever was about to happen would give her an insight into the Terman power structure. A chair was brought for her, and she seated herself.

"DeMyrn Tan," the Captain said suddenly. "It is long since the day I spoke to the Mistress of Printings that you are to have sight of your work as it comes from the press. This was done?"

"Oh, yes, dame. It is ever thus now." *And I sorrow that you remember me.*

"Your woodcuts?"

"They have betterness, dame."

"Your sister," the Captain went on, "is Myrn of the Archives?"

"My oldest sister, dame." His name, DeMyrn, should have told her that.

"How is it that you are here?"

"I made finding of this dame," he gestured toward Karel, "in the forest, Captain, and I have brought her to safeness."

"How is it that you are here," the Captain repeated.

"The dame wished it, Captain."

The Captain nodded. "We will speak, later, of this finding in the forest." She turned to Dia. "The brute who seeks divorcing—he is here?"

Dia nodded, and the Captain indicated with a gesture that he was to be brought in. Dia went to get him.

He entered with his shoulders stooped and his eyes on the floor. Karel hid a sudden start. He was acting the way Mari did when Sang was present.

"Your name?" The Captain rapped out a question that was more of an order.

"Clar DeTera Sin, dame," he replied barely audibly.

Tan had taken a position slightly behind Karel's chair, but he had carefully placed himself where she could see the signal they had agreed on if it was needed. She saw, from the corner of her eye that he flinched at the sound of the name. He had not recognized the man, he was reacting to the name.

"So, Sin," the Captain said with uncharacteristic gentleness, "it is not in you to continue living with your once-wife?"

"I cannot…remain in that house, dame, I…" he stifled a sob and fell silent, but there had been a world of suffering in his voice.

"Sin," the Captain said softly, "can it be that you speak of it?" The same woman who had been ready to climb all over Tan for being in her presence, was behaving sympathetically. "Is it a thing of beatings?"

"This is done betime, dame," he said, "but…it is things of her sayings…I…" They would never get him to repeat them, that was obvious.

"There is making of pain in the things of her saying?"

"Truth, dame," He was afraid of the Captain, he was incapable of looking at her, and barely able to speak, but, rather than go on living under the conditions his once-wife imposed on him, he had braved her presence. Karel had seen how easily, and how deeply Tan had been hurt by an accidental remark. What kind of things could be done to a man by someone who knew how to hurt him intentionally?

"Sin," the Captain must be feeling some of what Karel was picking up, "it is but two sort months to the Time of Changing. Can it not be that you make this waiting?"

"Please, dame," he was terrified, the tears had already started to flow.

In another moment he would be sobbing. "I can make no going back to that house. I...PLEASE, Captain."

"Sin," the Captain's voice now held a pain of its own, "it brings much sorrow to me to send a man of your beauty among the Unchosen." She drew a deep breath and went on, "I will ask, once again, for the changing of your mind."

"It is not in me, dame."

"Two months, Sin," she insisted, "a very short time."

"I have no doing of it, dame."

The Captain came to a decision. Her voice was firm when she spoke again. "Very well. You are released from your marriage. You may choose from among the homes that stand empty. She is no longer your once-wife."

"Thank you, Captain!" He kept his eyes on the floor in front of her, but he could not keep the relief out of his voice.

"Dismissed," the Captain announced brusquely and then turned to Dia. "The woman makes waiting?"

"Outside, dame," she started for the door, "I will..."

"You will let her wait," the Captain ordered sharply. "DeMyrn Tan!"

He nearly jumped out of his skin when she addressed him unexpectedly. "Your wish, Captain?"

"It was never mine," the Captain said slowly, "to make forgetting of the name of the bitch who wasted my time at your questioning. If you wish to pretend that you have made this forgetting, do so. How many are the Uglies of your killing?"

The question surprised him, but he recovered. "My own, dame, or I and my vark in togetherness?"

"Shit," the Captain grunted disgustedly. "A vark is a weapon. Of betterness, that it may be sent as an arrow is sent and need not be kept to the hand in the way of a knife, but the killings are yours. How many?"

"Twenty-sev...twenty-six, dame."

The old woman regarded him curiously. "You change the number?"

"The dame," meaning Karel, "spoke me the living of one I had counted as dead, dame."

"So?" The question was addressed to Karel.

"He was badly wounded," Karel explained. "They brought him in while I was there, but he didn't die." She did not mention her part in keeping him alive.

The Captain nodded. "Twenty-six, then. Term owes you much, DeMyrn Tan, and I am Captain of Term."

He said nothing. He could not meet the Captain's eye, but not the way Sin hadn't, he was embarrassed by the complement.

"Ordinarily," the Captain went on, "I would not have it that a brute be present at the punishing of a dame, but DeTera Sin spoke me the name of Clar as he asked to be rid of her. There is a writing in the files of the Archers to speak me the name of Clar, once-wife to DeMyrn Tan, who reported to us a thing of innocence, and wasted our time in the investigation of it." The old woman smiled coldly. "You will stay, DeMyrn Tan. Term owes you much."

Karel made a note to herself. Clar DeTera Sin had walked into the room and DeTera Sin had walked out. Tan had flinched at the sound of the name. The Captain must know Myrn of the Archives, at least well enough to guess from her age that she was Tan's sister, not his mother. So, men carried their mother's name permanently, added those of their once-wives, during the marriage, and dropped them again at the Changing Time. In Sin's case, the name was dropped as a result of divorce. It gave her a better understanding of the insult she had accidentally given Tan.

"Bring me the slut," the Captain ordered.

Dia went to the door and returned shortly with a woman whose attitude and posture were only slightly less deferential than Sin's had been.

"Clar," the Captain began icily, "your once-husband has been released from you."

"Thank you, Captain." It was a ritual response, required by protocol, not sincere.

"I am not yet finished," the Captain snarled and Clar stiffened. "It is a thing of your shame, and a shame on the house of your mother, that you have sent a man of such beauty among the Unchosen. I would come to more nearness of your forgiving were it that he was ugly, but this was a man to make turning of heads. I came, myself, to a tightening in the throat at his seeing. Are you blind?"

"No, dame, I…"

"Is it, then," the Captain interrupted, "that you have such a greatness of love for your mother that you would make your bedding only with those who have sameness to her?"

A tiny flicker of anger flashed across Clar's face, but she was too much afraid of the Captain to give vent to it. The insult must have been deadly, though, and Karel added a strong prohibition against female homosexuality to her list of Terman prejudices. *Logical in a society where women were scarce.*

"The brute had great beauty, you imbecile," the Captain continued. "It is criminal to send one like that among the Unchosen. A brute, known to have broken his marriage promisings, will be Unchosen for the allness of his living." The Captain paused, drew out a handkerchief, and calmly blew her nose before she looked up again. "His going will not be in loneliness. You are relieved of your other duties. You will be Mistress of Unchosen until the Time of Changing."

Karel guessed the severity of the punishment from the look of horror on Clar's face. "Dame, I…"

"You speak, bitch," the Captain bellowed, "and in your speaking I hear that a twoness of months is not enough. Be it, then, that you are Mistress of Unchosen not until this Time of Changing but to the one that follows. Is there more to your speaking?"

The last was a threat that hung over the room while Clar struggled valiantly against her desire to make another protest.

"Thank you, Captain," she said when she could manage it.

"Let it be known," the Captain ordered.

Dia opened a drawer, took out a knife and stepped forward. Clar stood with her head hanging and her shoulders drooping while Dia casually slit the shoulder straps that held up her garment and allowed it to fall to the floor. Clar was nearly in tears, but she knew better than to say anything. All she could do was wait to be dismissed, and the old woman seemed in no hurry to let her go.

Indeed, the Captain seemed to be enjoying the younger woman's discomfort. Finally, however, the Captain remembered that she had other things to deal with.

"Leave this place," she snapped, and Clar stumbled through the door. They heard her break into a run as soon as she was out of their sight. The Captain turned her attention to Karel.

"This had more hardness," she said, "than I might have given it, but we were without a Mistress of Unchosen. The brutes must have a place to take their rutting, eh?"

"I…I'm not sure I understand the nature of the punishment."

"We have brought her to nakedness," the Captain smiled, "a thing of great shame. Of this it is known that she is Mistress of Unchosen, that she must bed with any brute, no matter his ugliness, who speaks to her of his need."

And you needed somebody for that job, anyway.

"I…uh…I owe DeMyrn Tan a great deal myself." He had, after all, been allowed to stay and watch his ex-wife being humiliated—payment for killing people.

The Captain chuckled her approval of Karel's remark. "Yours is a great youngness to have come to a captaincy, but you have wisdom. May it be that I have speaking firstly with this Hunter, that we may dismiss him and have our own talking in privateness?" When Karel nodded her assent, the Captain turned to Tan. "Make me your telling."

While Tan was describing everything he cared to tell about his meeting with Karel, and her safe delivery to Term, Karel was making a mental list of the things he chose *not* to mention. He gave the impression that they had sat in the cave, without talking, until the wind had changed. He was careful to omit any reference to Karel's telepathic contact with the curls. She had planned to include it in her own story, but she respected his judgment and decided to withhold it.

When he had finished his recital, the Captain dismissed him. After a moment's thought, she turned to Karel. "A Federation," she prompted, "of fifteen thousand worlds…"

"Approximately."

"This may be truth," the Captain said. "In a time of short pastness there was seeing of a light that flashed in the sky. You would name this the coming of your ship?"

"Probably."

"There is another thinking that comes to me," the Captain said. "Never has it been that a spy of Raider sending has come among us, but such a sending would be of a dame."

Karel smiled ironically. "I understand your suspicions, Captain. I'm willing and, I think, able to answer any questions you care to put to me."

26 CHAPTER 26

"It is not of my softness," the old woman said at last, "that I came to be Captain of Term. It is not the way of Captains to be soft. In beforeness to my captaincy, I was Mistress of Archers. You have heard of our Plotters?"

"One or two references," Karel shrugged, "pretty vague."

"Harmless," the Captain grunted. "Convenient, betime, to hang one or two, but they are harmless. When I was Mistress of Archers, I made questioning of many of them, and the screaming of brutes is truth when it seeks to stop the touch of a knife. There is no dangerousness in any brute of Term, except…"

The Captain paused and gathered her thoughts. "Betime," she continued, "I made marriage with one of the Hunters. A foolishness, they called it, that an officer make such a marrying, but I had youngness, and he was beautiful." She shook off what was apparently a very pleasant memory. "I learned from him a thing of usefulness. I sorrow that my learning of it cost him his beauty."

Karel did not want to interrupt. The Captain hesitated, apparently considering whether or not to say what she was thinking, then she shrugged and went on.

"Betime there is taking of prisoners," she said. "Not often, most fighting is ended in death.

"This one had taken a wounding that robbed him of consciousness. He was carried among us, allowed to heal so that he could speak, eh?"

Between screams! Karel managed not to shudder and thought about how nice it would be to go home to a place where people did not do things like that to each other.

"So!" The Captain's voice grew harsh. "I was Mistress of Archers, the work of making him speak was mine. With Raiders, Captain Karel, the touching of the knife must be *done*, not merely threatened as it is with our own brutes.

"I approached him to make this doing, and some shithead of an Archer had tied his hands in such looseness that he had come to freedom." She waved her hand disgustedly. "He took the knife from my hand, and he threw me against the wall. With that knife in his hand, Captain Karel, he faced six of my Archers. Six, and they ran.

"Archers! Not one man in Term can look on an Archer without shaking in fear, even if he be innocent of all plottings."

So, you run a police state and 'conveniently' hang the harmless occasionally. Lady, I'm beginning to like you not.

"I watched my sixness of Archers as they scrambled to the far corner of the room and struggled with each other. Every damn one of them trying to stand behind the others, and the Raider to make laughing at them." The Captain seemed torn between amusement and disgust at the memory of it.

"In my foolish youngness," she went on, "I had married a Hunter, and it was the greatest of goodnesses that he came at that moment to speak to me of…something."

"'Would you have it, dame,' my Hunter said as he stepped to the door and saw the thing that had come to be, 'that I make his killing, or again his taking?'"

Karel was beginning to see the point that was being presented. For all that he threw up after a fight, she could not imagine Tan cowering in a corner.

"The Raider turned," a statement which Karel had more or less anticipated, "turned his back on the six to face the one." The Captain held up a single finger to emphasize the number. "And his body changed. Before he had toyed with the Archers, laughed at them. Now he made readiness for fighting.

"There was a thing in the voice of my Hunter that spoke *ableness*. It was that sound that turned the Raider toward him."

"What," Karel was not really sure she wanted the answer, "happened?"

"He killed," the Captain answered gruffly. "The Ugly had too much skill at fighting, there was no retaking of him. My Hunter took a scar in the fighting. In the next of his Times he was Unchosen, and in the next of his Lonely Times he went to a far northness and failed to return." She shrugged.

"Had I been Captain, I would have hanged all six of the ever-fathers."

Karel managed to hide her amusement and consider the significance of the term. *Uncles,* she reminded herself. *Uncles are permanent—fathers don't count.*

"She who was then Captain would allow only the hanging of him who had tied the Ugly's hands in carelessness. Archers, she told me, are valuable."

There was a long pause and then… "Now it is I who am Captain, and I say that a Hunter is worth a hundred fuckin' Archers. But," she sighed heavily, "I wished to become Captain, and it was never again that I made the foolishness of marrying one."

Because you are judged, to some extent, according to the appearance and/or status of your once-husbands? The Captain had indicated, twice, that people had looked askance at the choice of once-husband that had saved her life. Karel had the feeling that she was going to have to learn, very quickly, exactly what constituted a suitable choice.

"Tunnels," the Captain remarked suddenly. "A spy of Raider sending had never spoken me tunnels."

"I…I'm acquitted, then?"

The Captain shook her head. "Plotters are harmless, war is *not.*"

I know, Dreena told me. Karel had, instinctively, watered down her conversation with Dreena.

"I have named one Hunter," the Captain said, "of more worth than a hundred Archers. I know it to be thus, Karel, but even our Hunters fear the Archers."

Quite understandably, Karel thought. *I gather that a visit to one of your little cubby holes is anything but pleasant.*

"Tunnels," the Captain mused again. "How is your knowing of the things of war?"

"Where I come from," Karel tried not to sound as sarcastic as she felt, "it's something of a lost art."

The Captain smiled. "I would hear more of this Federation, but in beforeness I must end a speaking of my own. To make war, Karel, there must be brutes who will fight. We have two hundred Hunters."

What was that word Sang would use to describe what you're getting ready to tell me? Oh, yes—BULLSHIT! The Termans would fight. They had been told there would be war if the Raiders' hiding place was found. For this, they would fight. And men would die, and women would become plentiful and...

"Are you asking me to...uh...hold the knowledge of these tunnels in my mouth?"

"You have wisdom," the Captain said. "I have understanding, now, that a dame of such youngness has come to a captaincy. Speak me this Federation."

For the first time since landing on the planet, Karel had been presented with an opportunity to function as an outsider representing a foreign government. She began to speak as she had been trained to speak, in the cautious, neutral terms that presented the Federation as objectively as possible. It was not a sales pitch, she was making no attempt to convince the Terman Captain that participation in the Federation was more desirable than her current situation, she was presenting the facts, as clearly and accurately as possible. The decision, one way or another, would be up to the Captain.

Karel did not, with a twinge of guilt over the omission, mention the telepaths who were the rightful owners of the planet. Her avoidance of the subject was based on the fact that Tan had withheld it. But when she started describing the landing marker that would guide the rescue mission to Term instead of allowing it to land near the stockade, she recognized the personal interest she had in the omission.

One does not say, 'Please help me get in touch with my people so they can kick you off your planet.'

"I will think on this thing," the Captain said. "We will speak of it again later. Meantime..." she regarded Karel with almost alarming gravity, "you are without once-husband, and we have many Unchosen."

Here I go again.

The trouble was that she had not the slightest idea...better ask Tan. He would tell her, honestly, who to pick and how to approach him, if she could just stall long enough to find him and ask.

"Will you give me a little time to make my choice?"

"Would," the Captain agreed, "five of days be enough?"

Alone in the room the Termans had assigned to her, Karel stared at the wall. She was stunned by the thing she had been asked to do, by the decision she was being asked to make.

She was pregnant.

The curls had discovered it and told her it would be a boy.

The curls had placed her mind in contact with one of *their* embryos, and the result had been a curl who was capable of communicating with her and interpreting for the others.

Now that she was pregnant, would she consider letting them do the same for her son?

I have no right to make that decision!

A child is not a possession. A child is a loan. A son is himself. A parent is a guardian. She had no right.

The offer was tempting, however. They guaranteed that it would not harm the child. They did it to their own children, and they considered those children improved as a result.

But it's an experiment. They're not sure how it will turn out. She had no right.

The child has a father. A decision this critical, this final, this irreversible, should not be made without consulting the other parent.

There is no way I can do that.

There was a remote possibility that, someday, she might see Sang again. After she had gone home, after she had reported, after the Federation had established itself on this planet, she might be ordered to revisit the place. She might see him then. Their son would be born before the rescue ship could arrive. No telling how old he would be when she came back, if she came back.

No, she told the curls. No, I can't do it.

They were disappointed, but they understood.

27 CHAPTER 27

DeBerta Zek stood on the edge of the crowd around the dame who was new to the city. From early this morning he had worked, with his friend Tan, to bring himself to beautifulness. There had been cutting of his hair and beard, and much brushing. There had been oiling of his body, and he had perfumed himself. There had been twisting of his hair about the stems of flowers until his head had more colorfulness than a birzekota bush in springtime. But there could be no covering of the scar, and because of this there was no hope in him.

Zek had come because he must, because he was Unchosen and there would be those to wonder if he did not come. But he had come, also, to learn of the dame, and he saw of her face that the speaking of Tan was truth. She spoke kindly to the Unchosen, with fairness. Never did she speak longer to one man, that the others might think she favored him. Never did she speak less to one man, that he might think she did not.

She would choose, she had said, but the Captain had given her five days for the making of this choice. She would take all of those days before choosing, before then she would not even hint.

In Zek there was nothing of hope, but there was no sadness in him. A Hunter must be a man of great beauty to make a good marrying, and Zek had been thus before he was scarred. He knew the ugliness of that scarring and the impossibility of its hiding. The dame would see, and her choosing would be another.

Such a gathering of men who courted, so many perfumes, such a muchness of flowers filling the air with a thing that was stink rather than goodness. In the eyes of the others, he could see hope, hungry, desperate, frightened hoping, and in their voices he could hear it. It brought him to memory of the first of his Times among the Unchosen. There had been hope in him then, and fear, and desperation, but he had not gone, as Garl had gone in a time of short pastness, to the far north to fight and fight again until he died.

Zek sorrowed that he had come to ugliness, done much crying, but he had gone to the forest with his sadness. There he had found a way of living with his ugliness.

The dame spoke him. She had learned his name, but no more quickly than she had learned the names of the others. She listened with politeness to his sayings, but her politeness had sameness when she listened to others. She smiled on him only as she smiled on the allness. She was fair.

She held his friend's life in her mouth, and Tan was sure she would not loose that hold. She had spoken tunnels, and tonight Tan would speak loudly of tunnels to the any who had wish to hear. There would be war.

There would be war, or there would be a hanging. Zek had offered to share in this speaking of tunnels, but Tan had asked that he keep silent. If there was war, Zek would fight, and he would help in the teaching townmen to fight. If there was hanging of Tan, Zek would live in afterness to his friend, speaking quietly, with much care, until there were enough believers. Then there would be war.

A small one stood in nearness to the men who crowded around the dame, and Zek had sight of the tears that were held, barely, behind the eyes of the child. There was a thing in the boy's hand, but Zek could not see what it was. He knew of it, though, that it was of things to bring tears to the eyes of a boy of youngness.

Zek went to him.

So! The uncle had such wish to catch the eyes of the dame that he had not turned to see the child of his sister. There was no blaming the man. The thing he did now was important, and the nephew would still be his after the dame had chosen. To take oneself from her seeing, now, was to hurt the chances of being chosen.

Zek went.

He was stealing, for a time, of another man's nephew, but it would be two months yet before Tan would marry and ask him, often, to sit with the small ones of his once-wife. Zek had a no nephews, no sisters to bear them. Were it not for Tan, he would have no seeing of small ones, no playing with them.

When he returned the dame asked of his going, but before he could speak there was another who made answer.

She of Strangeness

"A scar is the greatest of all uglinesses, dame. He had wish, perhaps, to end your sickening at the sight of it."

It had been thus, the allness of this day, that the Unchosen had spoken of each other. Things of hurt were said, and answered, and said again, each hoping that his own ugliness would seem less did he speak on that of the others. Zek had not entered into this foolishness. He would not enter into it now.

He walked from them.

In a time long past, he had ended his hoping. Often had he seen the disgust in the eyes of a dame who looked on him, and he had taken to going from the city that they would have no seeing of him. Now he would go, again, to the forest and end the sickening of a dame at the sight of him.

"Zek!" She had come after him. She had sent the others from her to run to an easing of hurt. Tan had spoken truly of the kindness in this dame. "Zek, I'm...not going to apologize for...what somebody else said." She had run quickly, her breathing had hardness. "Who was the little boy? Your nephew?"

He shook his head. "A friend, only, dame."

Karel was angry with herself. Sending the others away and running after this one was almost an announcement of her decision, and that was a mistake.

I was going to be so mercenary about this, she thought, *so cold-blooded.*

A Terman once-husband was an ornament, his beauty enhanced his once-wife's status. The Captain would be watching carefully to see if Karel made a tasteful selection, allowing for the fact those who were left were everyone else's rejects. A bad choice now would reduce the Captain's respect for her when she talked about the Federation.

And I have been specifically warned away from Hunters. The man wore a knife, a weapon restricted to Hunters and Archers, but she doubted that an Archer would be Unchosen.

"Why was he so unhappy, Zek?"

"His doll had broken, dame."

Terman boys played with dolls, then, and Terman men, whose value was measured in terms of their looks, gave up their chance of being chosen to go see why little boys cried. At least this one did.

"Did you fix it?"

"No, dame," he smiled. "There was no fixing of it. I made a doll of newness."

None of the others would have dared to be out of her sight for nearly an hour. The competition for her attention had been so fierce, and so frequently vicious to each other, that it would have been funny if it had not been for its pathetic desperation.

Zek had been the only one who had never once tried to undermine the chances of his competitors, never bragged about himself, never pointed out their shortcomings.

But he's a Hunter!

It might be true that a scar was 'the greatest of all uglinesses'. Baldness was common among the Unchosen, and there were other things she had guessed, or been told, were considered ugly, but she had no idea which was worse than what. Beauty is comparison, this to that, and learning which is preferable begins in early childhood. Karel was an adult who had been dumped into the middle of a society where male beauty was extremely important, and she was ignorant.

"Zek, do you know DeMyrn Tan?"

She had not seen Tan today. She wondered why, but not critically. He had promised to stay close to her, to keep her from blundering if he could, and now he was not around. There had to be a reason for his absence, and she trusted him enough to assume it was a good reason. *But I need his advice!*

"Yes, dame," Zek answered. "He shares my vark."

"Your vark? I thought it was his vark."

"When he is in his Time, dame, and has no need of a vark, it is I who make hunting with it. Now it is I who am in my time, and Tan has the vark."

"Oh, then you're friends."

"Good friends, dame."

"Has…has he told you anything about me?"

He hesitated long enough for her to be sure he was carefully selecting which of the things Tan had mentioned were safe to reveal.

"He has spoken of you, dame."

Good! Then you know you can trust me. Oh, my God!

She had promised the Captain that she would not reveal the existence of the tunnels. The Captain did not want a war, and Karel did not want it on her conscience that she had been instrumental in starting one. Karel had promised—Tan had not. He had to be warned.

"I need to talk to him, Zek. Right away, I…"

Excuse. Excuse. Come up with an excuse. If Tan had already told Zek, then Tan could untell him—once he had been warned. But if Tan had not told Zek, Karel must not.

"Zek…uh…were you beautiful…before the fight?" His incredulous, almost shocked expression caused her to snap, "I don't know. Didn't Tan tell you I sometimes ask questions that sound stupid because I really don't know."

"There were some, dame," he said modestly, "who thought me thus."

It's not fair, she thought, *to get his hopes up and then…*

"Zek, I won't promise you anything," she said carefully. "I have five days, and I'll take all five days. I'll talk to Tan, and if he…"

Hold it, stupid. You don't tell a man you'll marry him if his best friend thinks you can get away with it. I was too late.

"Zek, I…I didn't mean to hurt you!"

He heard the pain in the dame's voice. It was even as Tan had said. She feared the giving of hurt, shamed of it, and sorrowed afterward. This, that she had nearly spoken him was because that there was a thing of otherness to her mind, a thing that had brought her to much excitedness.

"I am of Hunters, dame."

"I know."

"You are…of officers?"

"I suppose so," she sighed.

"It is of unusualness that an officer and a Hunter…"

"I know," she said heavily, "and that's why I can't promise anything, but…oh, Zek, find Tan for me, please. I've got to talk to him."

"DeTera Sin," he said quietly.

"What?"

"Did you speak with Tan, dame, he would name DeTera Sin the best of choosings. The Captain has seen him, she has, I am told, spoken well of him. She would have admiration of your wisdom."

"Zek, do you realize what you just said?"

"My hoping was ended, dame," his finger traced the scar that ran across his chest and abdomen, "in a time long past."

Kind enough to place a child with a broken toy above his own feelings, proud enough to be hurt by one of the vicious things the Unchosen said to each other, but too proud to retaliate—and now courage. He had given her honest advice knowing that if she took it he would remain Unchosen—with all that meant to a Terman.

The situation was stupid! Even if she did marry him, two months would hardly be enough time for her to woo him away from the forest he loved more than any woman, and she would be foolish to try. The Terman women had the right idea. Pick a pretty one, hang him on your arm for a while, and then see if you can get one just as good next time. *But, for God's sake, don't like him. It'll hurt too much when he leaves.*

"I still think I'd better talk to Tan," she said, "but...even if it's somebody else, Zek, I...I'll wish it was you."

That, for now, was the most she could give him.

28 CHAPTER 28

The two-leg is being hurt!

The Interpreter dived into her mind the instant her torture began. Straight to the interception point his mind flashed, caught, and held.

The People took the pain.

Not all of it this time, the two-leg kept her share, as was only fitting. She was almost one of them now, one with the Interpreter, close to the rest. Her pain was theirs, and they shared in it automatically. Neither dutifully nor gladly—reflexively, like breathing.

The baby! Protect the baby!

She had not yet agreed. She had, in fact, refused, but her refusal had been inconclusive—she was still tempted.

The healers were called.

Two very large, very strong two-leg females were harming the two-leg, striking her repeatedly, rhythmically, with practiced efficiency—often in the stomach. Two dozen healers leaped into the two-leg's mind. Some of them went immediately to the area around the womb to stiffen protective muscles and hold them in more tension than the two-leg could manage alone. The others raced back and forth along the nerve paths, guiding the healing force and adding to it with the power of as many minds as were needed. The two-leg was fully recovered from the beating almost before it had ceased.

The baby was safe.

"Enough," declared one of the Archers. "The Captain wishes seeing of this one, there must be no marking of her."

"Ah," replied the other, "but in afterness to her seeing by the Captain…"

The jubilant threat as allowed to hang in the air, and Karel smiled inwardly at it. Everything that was being done or said was calculated to terrify. It was a softening process preparatory to her interview with the Captain. She was supposed to be thoroughly cowed when she got to that interview.

If it wasn't for the curls, I would be.

She had no illusions about her courage. She knew what she was capable of facing, and she knew when something was too much for her. Without the intervention of the little telepaths, the idea of falling into the hands of the Terman secret police, of being subjected to the treatment they routinely gave prisoners, would have reduced her to panic. With the aid the curls had already given her, and their promise of similar aid in the future, she could face whatever came next.

Her captors fell into place on either side of her, and she was half-dragged, half-carried out of the apartment. When they reached the door of the Captain's quarters, the guards stopped, and one of them announced the arrival of the prisoner.

Tan was already there.

His beating had been much worse than Karel's, and he had taken it without help from the curls. The sight of him made her angry.

A brief glimpse was all she got, however, before she was thrown on her face at the Captain's feet. She lay there seething. The Captain was not going to like what Karel would have to say when she got the chance.

"We have come to a deciding, spy," the old woman's voice had turned nasty.

So now I'm a spy, am I? Karel wondered what had happened. Two days earlier the Captain had seemed willing enough to accept her story.

"You came near to my fooling," the Captain went on, "had made it, even, were it not for a thing of your own foolishness. My suspecting began at your naming of my own daughter in you lyings."

Your daughter? When did I...oh, yes. Mari had said, once, that her mother was next in line for the Captaincy.

"Did you think me of such softness that this naming would bring more ease to my believing of your bullshit? Eh?"

Karel refused to answer. In the first place, she was still lying at the Captain's feet. She was not about to mumble her reply into the floor. In the second place, she had no answer. The thing had already been decided, and not in her favor.

"Tunnels," the old woman shrieked derisively. "If there be such, their making was a thing of trapping my brutes as they came blinking from the darkness into the light of the sun, eh? And the mouths of these tunnels to be of such smallness that each must come singly to his dying?"

So that was it.

Either Zek had not been able to locate Tan yesterday or, having been found, Tan had decided that Karel as not that badly in need of his advice. She had not seen him, and she had not warned him. He had talked.

The blunder had probably cost both of them their lives.

Some sort of signal must have been given, because Karel was yanked roughly to her feet where she met the old woman's blazing eyes with an air of calm disdain.

"This bastard," the Captain was pointing to Tan, "made your bringing among us. It is he who has spoken to my brutes the words from this lie of your inventing, brought them to this sharpening of knives, this testing of bowstrings, this preparing for war. Your choosing of him was a foolishness, bitch. We have long known of his plottings against us."

Be careful what you say, Captain, Karel thought, *he might learn of yours against him.*

"If I'm the spy," she said, "then his only crime is believing what I told him. Why don't you hang me and leave him out of it?"

"So?" The old woman chuckled, "and how of his claim that his vark made finding of these tunnels in beforeness to your telling of them, eh?"

Karel shot a questioning glance at Tan and felt reassured by what she saw in his face. If he had believed she was what the Captain accused her of being, he would never have been able to hide his dismay at the betrayal. His face was sullen, resigned, but it showed that he understood the real reason behind what was happening.

"Tan, I'm sorry I got you into this," she said seriously.

"Confession!" The Captain shouted the word, primarily, for the benefit of the Archers. "You hear her admission that is she who leads in these Plottings?"

"Captain, I feel sorry for you, I really do."

"For me, bitch?" Smug complacency, too secure in its position to even feel indignant. "You should keep your sorrowing for yourself."

"I mentioned my friend," Karl said quietly, "I didn't know she was your daughter. I told you what had happened to me, but Mari was involved in much of it, and now you know what's happened to her. That makes you the unluckiest mother in Term.

"The others can comfort themselves with the hope that their daughters are dead," Karel went on, "or they can take a sort of morbid pride in the belief that their daughters are miserable. There's no disloyalty in being miserable, no softness. But Mari isn't dead, Captain, and she's not miserable. She's one of a very few who like it there, and she would hate you for starting this war you're so anxious to avoid and killing the man she married."

Go on, stupid, say it. Consider the old bag's feelings? Why? She's going to kill you.

"She loves him, Captain."

There was a murderous silence in the room. The Captain as struggling against the fact that it would be undignified for her to snatch a weapon from one of the Archers and slaughter Karel then and there. Until now this had only been a political maneuver, an attempt to discredit Tan's story by declaring him subversive, a rational and calculated reaction to something that threatened the Terman power structure. Karel had changed it into something personal, or she had looked beneath the surface and pinpointed the reason it was personal. No matter, the Captain hated her now, wanted her dead, and...

"Don't do it, Captain," Karel said sarcastically. "You've planned a big, very public ceremony for my hanging. You've probably written a speech for the occasion. Much as you'd like to do it with your very own hands, mustn't spoil the show."

The Captain glared at her balefully, and then threw back her head and laughed.

"Your saying has rightness, bitch, but one small wrongness. The brute will hang. You will be Mistress of Unchosen for the allness of your days."

Oh, really? The rest of my life? How long will that be?

"Your living will be short, dame," Tan was trying to reassure her. "Men are executed, dames have accidents."

Well, well, Mistress of Unchosen, a fate worse than death. I wonder if that applies when death is the result of several days in a cubby hole with the Captain and a meat grinder.

"Thank you, Tan," she said sincerely, "I guessed that, but thank you for telling me."

"And," he added significantly, "the marks on the body must be only those of the fall.

My God! What did I do to deserve that kind of loyalty. He was going to die, soon, and he was doing what he could to comfort her.

"You forget, brute, that a spy must be questioned."

Well, nice try, Tan. Korl, I'm sorry, I won't be able to wait nineteen years.

"Enough of this bullshit," the Captain snorted. "The gallows has readiness, the people have been called to watch. Would you make speaking with The Mother before your dying, brute?"

Tan smiled threateningly. "My saying will be made when I am come into Her presence." He did not, Karel noticed, add the word 'dame', and his conversation with The Mother would not be favorable to the Captain.

With a jerk of her head the Captain ordered the prisoners taken outside. The Archers were anything but gentle about it.

When they reached the top of the ladder that was to take them down to the floor of the canyon where a crowd had already gathered, the guards suddenly halted and drew back. A vark, Tan's vark, was stationed at the foot of the ladder. The animal was relaxed, simply waiting for its master, but the guards turned fearfully to their Captain for instructions.

"End the animal," she ordered curtly.

With a sadistic grin on his face, one of Tan's captors stepped forward, unslung his bow and sent a shaft through the unsuspecting vark's throat. There was a yelp of pain from the vark, and Karel half expected a cry of anguish to be wrung from Tan, but he took it as calmly as he had everything else.

"Ever-father," he commented softly when the guard returned to his side, "the braveness of your doing speaks me that you have made growing of a set of balls. Loose my hands that I may cut them from you and return you to normalness."

The answer was a fist in the face. Tan laughed.

Negotiating the ladder with their hands tied behind them would have been awkward, if it had been attempted, but two of the guards went below and waited while one and then the other of the captives was shoved off the ledge. No effort was made to catch them, but they both landed lightly enough. As soon as the party was reassembled, they began the trip across the canyon floor to Tan's place of execution.

They had taken only four steps, however, when a scream of rage caused them to whirl around. There stood Zek with a knife in one hand and the arrow he had pulled from the body of the vark in the other. He was advancing grimly, with a look on his face that left no doubt as to what he planned to do when he arrived.

Half of the Archers bolted at the sight of him. It was the two women who stood their ground. Karel wondered if, perhaps, they relied on a belief that no Terman male was capable of harming a woman. If they were, it was immediately disproved. Tan, having been freed by the desertion of his captors, slammed into one of Karel's with a force that sent the woman sprawling. A moment later Zek arrived and laid the other out with his fist.

Two swift flicks of the knife freed Tan and then Karel from their bonds, and the three of them fled toward the gate with Tan in the lead, Zek following and Karel between. The guards on the gate were as terror-stricken as the others had been, and the fugitives passed without interference.

It would take only a moment for the Archers to realize that an arrow kills at a safe distance. As soon as they were past the gate, Tan dropped back, allowing Karel to pass him, and he and Zek closed up shoulder-to-shoulder, protecting Karel with their bodies. Still Terman, both of them, they could hit an Archer, but they would die before they let anything happen to Karel.

Halfway across the open field Zek screamed and pitched forward with an arrow in his back. Karel would have stopped, gone back to him, but Tan grabbed her arm and forced her to keep moving. She ran, however, looking back over her shoulder. Zek was alive, he was moving. Then she saw what he was doing and screamed.

She was nearly hysterical when they reached the cover of the trees and Tan allowed her to stop.

"Zek," she gasped frantically, "he...he killed himself, Tan, he took his knife and..."

"Better his own," Tan snapped, "than those of the Archers."

He reached out and grasped one of her shoulders firmly in each of his hands, forcing her to face him if not look at him. Eventually, she did look at him and he jerked his head back toward the city where, no doubt, pursuit was already being organized.

She of Strangeness

This is not, Karel realized, *a time of thinking.*

They went straight to the hollow tree where they had hidden Karel's knife. Tan offered it to her, but she shook her head.

"I...I hope it won't come to fighting," she told him, "but if it does, you'll have to do it."

"There will be no fighting," he told her. "We will lose them in the forest as, betime, we lost the Uglies, eh?"

"But...won't they be able to track us?"

"I am of Hunters," he said, "and Zek was of Hunters. Even did they trust the others of Hunters to search for us, they would make no finding."

He was right.

29 CHAPTER 29

Karel was bringing home a prize.

Only a pisone, a tiny thing, hardly a meal for one of them, but she had killed it herself.

In the six weeks that had passed since their escape from Term, Tan had managed to teach her a great deal. Even without human enemies, from which they now felt completely safe, the planet offered plenty of danger, and Tan was afraid that his own death or injury would leave Karel helpless and unable to provide for herself.

Helpless she had been when they first arrived at the clearing where they built her hut and then Tan's. Clumsy she still was, but improving, and today she was bringing in a kill of her own.

She wanted to hurry. She wanted to run to him, present him with her prize, and dance around him like a three-year-old while he solemnly skinned her treasure. But she mustn't forget the lessons he had given her.

He had taught her to approach the camp with caution, to glide from one tree to another, never revealing herself until she had seen that everything was as it should be. He always heard her coming, often saw her before she saw him. When she arrived he would explain what she had done wrong.

It had become a game with them to see how close she could get before he noticed her, and she was looking forward to the day when she would be able to surprise him. Perhaps this would be the time, a double victory, and she slipped cautiously through the trees, moving closer to the camp.

Oh, my God! No!

The men faced each other in the middle of the clearing, knives drawn, eyes narrowed to tiny slits. They circled warily, feeling for an opening.

Each was tense, each was afraid, each was determined to kill the other.

"Sang! Tan! Stop it!"

Sang's jaw dropped, and his head turned mechanically toward the familiar voice. Were it not for Tan's habit of obedience to women, Sang would have been killed the instant his eyes left his enemy, but Tan stepped back a couple paces and drove his knife into the earth in this world's signal for a truce. Sang's weapon fell from his hand without conscious effort on his part.

"You," he said incredulously. "You entered the water!"

"It...it never occurred to you that I could swim?"

His amazement turned to disgust, and then to anger.

"At our first meeting," he declared, "I asked thrice if you were a she of sameness to any other. You lied!"

"Not intentionally."

"Not once, he shouted, "in the allness of my knowings of you, not once have you done a thing that was of shes."

"I thought there was once."

Shit! Your son-making has more differentness than all your other doings. This answer was not, however, of things to be shouted across a clearing before others. He crossed to the place where she waited him.

"Tan!" He had already grabbed his knife and was rushing to what he must have imagined was Karel's defense. "The truce is for both of us."

"Yes, dame," he said reluctantly and retired.

"Yes, dame," Sang mimicked, favoring the Terman with a contemptuous sneer. "This is the way of rightness because it is his?"

"You know the answer to that, Sang-ser," she said.

He looked at her then, studied her, considered her, fought with himself, weighed, balanced, sorted through a series of conflicting emotions, decided.

"I have yet" he announced, "no wanting of you."

It was true, barely. He was, exactly where Karel had been the day she had decided to leave him. He did not love her, he did not want her, but he knew that, given time, he would.

"What are you doing here, Sang-ser," she asked quietly.

He had not come looking for her, that was certain. He had thought she was dead.

"You are not the first," he explained, "of shes to enter the water, but ever before it was a thing of self-killing.

Suicide! I thought you knew me better than that.

"The Elders have named it of sameness to wife-killing that a man drive his she to such a doing, eh?"

In other words, what I did almost got you killed, leaving Mari and the baby to starve.

"I didn't know that, Sang-ser, I really didn't." There was no need to add that she would have stayed if she had known.

"I waited only the coming of the sun," he went on, "and then I took my son and the other of my shes to a son-making from which we have not returned."

Oh, thank God! Then they're safe.

"What are you going to do now?"

"In the way that has rightness because it is mine," he jerked his head toward where Tan sat waiting to resume hostilities, "I would end this she-whipped bastard and take you again to myself."

"I'll go with you, Sang-ser," she told him, "there's no need to fight."

He smiled at that. "You would sorrow of his dying, eh?" Not jealousy, understanding.

"Or yours," she said. "No matter how it came out, I'd lose."

I will not, he thought, *kill a second of her friends.*

"There is another of knowings that I have kept from you." It took him a moment to decide how to begin. "Betime, if a man find that a she of his taking has great goodness, he asks of the Elders that she be belted, naming his reason for wishing it."

"And the belt that I stole was…"

"I had named your help in my healings a great goodness," he agreed, "but the meeting was ended by the news of a she who had entered the water, and the belting had not yet been agreed."

"Why," she asked, "did you ask them to do that?" Not her nursing ability, surely.

"At the dying of a healer, instruments, not only those that were his, but the allness, are shared equally among those yet living. This is done because, in the thinking of those who began it, the differentness between healer must be only in the skill of the hands, not in the things taken to those hands."

"That's a very wise custom, Sang-ser." Considering the breakage she had seen in Sang's instruments, the redistribution made sense.

"Had there been no dying, I would have requested a special time of such sharing that the instruments of..." it cost him a great deal, but he said it anyway, "of your giving...be shared. But..." he looked at her significantly, "I feared their seeing of those instruments, and their asking of how I had come to their having. It would give them to think on othernesses that might be in your ship, things of usefulness for warring with Termans. Their thinking could be that in your ship there are weapons of powerfulness."

Guns! She would never have permitted it, but she saw his point, "Sang-ser, you know I would never have let them..."

"A belt," he interrupted, "be it that she was born to us or made, may not be tortured into a giving she has no wish to make."

She understood, then, fully, and she thanked him with her eyes. "It's too late, now, isn't it?"

"They are not stupid," he told her. "Betime they would have guessed the reason of my doing, but a belt, once given, cannot be taken again. Your running has ended my arguing for its giving."

She considered it for a moment. She was afraid, yes, but her sense of fairness won out over the fear, and the curls would be helping her, after all.

"I...I'll still go back with you, Sang-ser. I...I think I can hold out."

He was staring at the pisone, which had fallen from her hand, and been forgotten.

"You have made this killing," he asked, "in loneliness? With no helping of the hair-face?"

"Yes, I..." then she saw what he was driving at. "Oh, no! No, Sang-ser! No! It's too small. It's what Tami...it's an *insult*!"

"Insult," he replied, "must be first in the mind of the giver of insult." He looked at her closely. "I see none."

"Please, Sang-ser," she pleaded. "Let me get something else. I...I'll get you a gezel."

He stood there insistently, hand outstretched, waiting for her to pick it up and hand it to him. She saw, after a few more inarticulate and futile protests, that he was not to be moved.

"At least," she said, "let me skin it for you."

She was clumsy, and the task was made all the more difficult by the tears that kept getting in the way, but she managed it eventually and carried her pitiful offering over to the fire he had built while he was waiting.

She handed it to him with an air of finality. He accepted it solemnly, spitted it, roasted it, and ate it slowly, chewing every last scrap of meat from the tiny bones, then cracking each one and sucking out the marrow. When he was finished he looked up, but not at Karel.

"Ho, Mari," he called loudly, "I have need of your mouth."

She came out of the brush with the baby in her arms. Apparently she had seen and understood everything that had happened, and the smile of greeting she gave Karel was warm and genuine.

"There is a she who is in your knowing," Sang told her. "You will ask of her if it may be that I have her seeing, her speaking and, if it be needful, her touching."

The request was something Karel should have anticipated, but she had not. It brought home to her, more forcefully than the act itself, that his acceptance of the pisone had been the only way he knew of granting a divorce. Sadly, he had needed to make a man of her to do it.

"Certainly," she told Mari, "and ask him if I may have the same privileges."

Sang looked at her then and invited her silently to sit with him across the fire that had separated them. Somewhere along the line, Tan had come to the conclusion that there would be no fight, but he had a desire to stay close to Karel in case she needed him. He came over and sat beside her. Sang ignored him but raised no objection to his presence.

"I am Sang," he said, as if re-introduction were necessary. When Karel thought about it, she realized that it was.

"I am..." she hesitated, glancing at Tan and then shook her head. "My name is my own. Among the Termans, Sang-ser, only a husband has the right to use it."

"Or a brother," Mari confirmed.

"Did I give her a name of my own inventing," he was asking Mari, "for using in place of the true one, is there harm in this, also?"

"I have never heard of such a doing," Mari said, "but I see no wrongness in it."

"Sky-stone, then," he chuckled. "How has it been with you?"

Briefly, without omission, she gave him the details of her escape, her meeting with Tan, the visit to Term, and their escape from there. He listened attentively, nodding occasionally, not speaking until she had finished.

"To my thinking," he said when she was done, "the pisone is enough. But you have spoken a wish to make greater payment. This is yet so?"

"If you'll let me."

"There is a thing," he jerked his head in the direction from which he had come, "needful of my doing. Be it that I make no returning, your paying can be made to my son, and you," as if the baby could understand the order, "will share of it with your mother."

"No!" this, desperately, from Mari. "We must keep to our running!"

"Forever?" The question was sarcastic. "It is also that their following of me will lead them to this place. I will not have it, and you know the reason of this, that Sky-stone fall again into their hands."

"Who is it," Tan spoke for the first time, "that makes your following?"

"Death-trackers."

"This name," Tan admitted, "is not in my knowing."

Helplessly Sang turned to Mari for a translation?

"Speak him," she said, "their sameness to Archers."

"That I made no returning," Sang was explaining to Karel, "my name will have been given to the Death-trackers. It is a thing of pride with them that, when they have taken a man's trail, they will find its ending place or die in the trying. But it is *my* name they were given. If they make my finding, they will look no further."

In other words, though you're too proud to say it, you want me to take care of your family after you get yourself killed protecting me.

Without a word Tan glided to his feet, collected his own knife and the one Sang had left lying where it fell. The latter was tossed casually to its owner, and the Terman began a quick survey of his other weapons.

"She-whipped," Sang said belligerently, "the fight is mine."

"Half of it," Tan agreed, "but the killing of Archers, be they yours and not mine, is of things not easily taken from me."

"I will have no debt," sang said coldly, "to a fuckin' she's ass-kisser."

"My niece was taken," Tan remarked casually, "in the last of the raidings."

Sang shrugged indifferently.

"How was the naming," Tan inquired, "of her that you healed of her cuttings?"

"There was need for a healing," Sang was fuming with indignation. "I asked no names."

"Then she may have been small Myrn," Tan replied courteously, "and I take debt from her healing. You would steal from me the right to make payment?"

Put in those terms, Sang could no longer reject the help that was being offered. He turned to Karel.

"This mind-speaking with curls," he asked, "can name you the closeness to which they have come behind us?"

She asked the question, and the answer was frightening.

"There are two of them, Sang-ser," she told him, "and they're very close. They could be here in less than an hour."

"Only two," he was insulted, "four were sent to the taking of Torn. The place?"

She pointed and, without further discussion, the men were gone.

It had been, except in this one isolated pocket of humanity, centuries since there had been the kind of fear that was now in Mari and Karel. They refused to look at each other. If they had tried to speak it would have ended with them screaming at each other. They were *afraid*, anxiety was too weak a word.

Karel had an immediate, powerful, and very personal understanding of the day the women of Earth had risen in a body and screamed, 'NO!' No more. Never again would their sons, husbands, brothers, friends be sent out to be maimed, mutilated and killed in wars. Never having understood, or been taught any necessity for war, Karel had not been able to understand the significance of that day or the motives behind it—until now.

Now, when the waiting was as bad, if not worse than the fighting, she understood. Two men, men she cared about, loved, perhaps unequally, and in different ways, had gone out deliberately seeking other men who would do their best to kill both of them. If Sang or Tan were so much as hurt, Karel knew, she would be devastated. She dared not even think about what Mari must be feeling.

Time passed, and Karel was not even aware of sitting with her eyes closed until Mari sprang to her feet with a cry of joy and ran to embrace her husband. Karel looked up, then, but remained where she was and watched with some embarrassment as they greeted each other. It was quite some time before Sang happened to glance over and see the look on her face.

He shook his head and pointed backward over his shoulder.

"When I thought to make fighting of him," he said, "there would have been more fear in me had I known he is the Puker. I did not think he would wish my watching of the thing that names him."

Tan arrived a few minutes later with his face and beard still wet from washing. "Ho, Ugly one," he said boisterously, "we work well together, not?"

"Oh, stop bragging," Karel told him disgustedly, "the two of you have just created four brand new widows." *Who will be allowed to starve to death.*

"Is not," Sang protested indignantly. "Death-trackers do no marrying, they have each other." But he turned to Tan and added quietly, "I have no wish for a moreness of such work."

"The dame speaks," Tan replied seriously, "that in the place of her coming such things are not done."

Sang's face took on a pensive expression and he walked over to where Karel was sitting.

"I have returned," he said.

"And you're welcome to stay, Sang-ser, you know that."

He did, and that was not his point. "You have yet wish to make a paying of more than the pisone?"

"Sang-ser, I owe you more now than I did before."

"In the place of your coming," he said, "a man calls a she 'friend', and feels no shame at the saying?"

"That's right."

"I," he tapped his chest several times to emphasize it, "would choke on this word." He stopped, and considered something, then began shaking his head. "I had a thought, but it can not be done."

"What can't, Sang-ser?"

"In afterness to a raiding," he answered, "there is ever a time of quietness, the allness to keep to their homes until it has been that the Termans have gone. Your mind-speaking with curls could name the time of the next raiding to us. Did we travel with much swiftness, we could come to your ship in during that time of quietness."

"Sang-ser, you're brilliant," she said excitedly, "I…"

"You," he interrupted, "will be late in your pregnancy at a time needing swiftness of walking."

That was true, and her face fell, but only for a moment.

"There's another way," and she explained the rescue mission that would come for her and the landing marker they could build to bring it here.

"Your paying, then, can be thus," he said. "I would have it that my son come to manhood in a place where a man names a she 'friend' and does not choke on the word."

30 CHAPTER 30

Mari moved in with Karel temporarily but Sang insisted on sleeping in the open while he was building a house for himself and his family. He selected a tree of appropriate thickness and set to work, burning and scraping and burning again, from the first hint of daylight until it was too dark to continue, breaking only, and that reluctantly, for brief hunting excursions with Tan.

The others sensed an urgency in him, a need to complete the task, that could not be accounted for by the occasional drenching he received at night. Nor was his pride, powerful though it might be, a satisfactory explanation. If he had been ashamed of placing his family under someone else's care, he would have thrown together a hut to house them until the project was finished.

It was the house. This house. He wanted it built immediately because it represented something extremely important to him, and when, two weeks after he had begun working on it, he finally came to collect his family and install them in it, it was as if a tremendous burden had been lifted from him.

He slept late the next morning, but Mari emerged glowing with a kind of happiness that Karel assumed was none of her business. Tan joined the women for breakfast and then disappeared for most of the morning. When he reappeared it was with hair that had been recently cut and carefully arranged. The extent to which he had perfumed himself was apparent from across the clearing and reinforced by a layer of floral decoration.

"Mari, get to Sang," Karel said urgently under her breath, "explain this to him and ask him, please, not to laugh."

"Truth," Mari giggled, "he would laugh, were it not explained, but I think it a betterness that you make the explaining, Karel. DeMyrn Tan," the last was called sweetly, almost flirtatiously, "will you help in the bathing of my small one?"

"A pleasure, dame," he was always delighted to have anything to do with the baby.

Mari carried the baby over and handed it to him. A moment later, he had the child laughing delightedly. Just as they turned away and started for the nearby stream, Mari swung back.

"Karel," she called as if it were an afterthought, "you must see the innerness of our house. There is a thing there that you must see for yourself."

Well, that was settled. Tan would be out of sight for a while, Karel was stuck with the job of explaining his behavior to Sang, and Mari would have an opportunity to play at courtship. That was how Karel read it, based on the way Mari was acting.

It is also true, Karel thought, *that this will not be the easiest idea anybody ever tried to get across to Sang. Mari tends to duck the tricky ones.*

There was no sense in putting it off, however, and there was something she had to talk to Sang about, anyway. Now more than ever.

Karel got up, walked to the door, and called politely for permission to enter, hoping to find him awake. He was, and he invited her in with unmistakable excitement in his voice. She stepped through the doorway and halted in surprise.

She could not move. She had to stand there, staring stupidly at the center of the floor. She was that stunned, that awed by what she saw.

So that's it. That's why he worked so long and so hard. Was so desperate to finish.

It was a statement, a declaration. It was meant, perhaps, for Mari, but it certainly included Karel. A multitude of meanings had gone into it.

In the center of the room, matching exactly the size, shape and position of the legs of the chair, were four stumps. It was not, definitely not, as if the chair had never existed. No, this was the place where the chair had been, before it was chopped down, thrown out, burned or destroyed some other way.

When Karel finally managed to raise her eyes, look at him, she was trembling, biting her lip, very close to tears. He sat, as she might have expected, in the corner of the room with his back to one wall, waiting patiently for her to join him. He was watching her, understanding her reaction, and assessing it as would an artist observing the impact of his work. If he had anything to say about it, however, it would be indirectly, and based on his knowledge that she already understood.

Karel walked over and sat down. She wanted to reach out, touch him, but the contact was not 'needful'.

So, she sat, experiencing as she had twice before with Korl, the silent communication that sometimes said more than words. As with Korl, she felt a sense of purpose radiating from him, but this lacked the finality that had been in the old man. There was something he wanted to do, needed to do, felt obligated to do, but afterword he would do other things.

"Saying of Korl," he began at last, "spoken at the time of his dying..." he saw her face and changed what he had been about to say, "I spoke of a healer who had come to his dying."

"Yes, but I didn't know you meant..."

She covered her face with her hands and grieved. Sang waited patiently giving her all the time she needed to recover from the shock and pain of the loss. His grieving had been done earlier.

"What did he say, Sang-ser?" She asked finally.

"He wished to know the way of my payment for the learning I would take from you."

That explained it. He apparently felt, believed, that he had learned something from her. The thing that was driving him now was a sense of indebtedness.

"Sky-stone," he went on, "you know the reason I give you this naming?"

"I understand part of it, I think."

"Your understanding is of falling from the sky, and of hardness, eh?"

She nodded.

"That is enough," he said, "the rest comes of a speaking that was mine and Korl's long before your coming. He has not spoken that I may give of this."

Then, of course, I won't ask.

"There was a need in me," he went on, "in afterness to the time of thinking. You took of your having and gave into that need, that it be ended."

"I needed it, too," she said honestly.

He knew that. "Of this, a small one makes growing in you. His making was a thing of friendship?"

"Yes," she said, "it was…at least that."

"At least! I am come…" he shot a glance at the legs of the non-existent chair, "this far, woman, speak me no fuckin' morenesses."

With that attitude, she thought, *you're going to need more than the nineteen years Korl asked for.* But he was right, it was no time to push.

He reached in his pouch and drew out the stone that Korl had given him, placed it on the floor and sat waiting for her to take it.

"An apprentice," he said, "pays for his teaching."

Karel looked at the stone, but she made no move to pick it up. "I don't believe I really taught you anything, Sang-ser, I think it's…" she sent her own glance at the empty space where the chair would have been, "the way you always were."

"I was brought to the knowing," he replied firmly, "by a son-making that was given."

Given, she thought sadly, *when you, and everyone you know, have always had to take.*

"All right," she picked up the stone and slid it into the pouch on her own belt. "Now we're even."

His relief was immediately evident. The thing had, apparently, been eating at him for a long time, more seriously than she had ever guessed.

"Now," she said quietly, "there's something I have to talk to you about."

Quickly she explained what the curls had asked her, what they wanted to do to the child she was carrying, and her own misgivings about it. When she had finished, she sat half expecting him to announce that the child was hers, that his authority, if not his responsibility, had ended with their marriage. But he thought about it too long and too seriously for her to retain that impression.

"My mother was Terman," he said at last. "My second-mother, Polyan."

"Your…second-mother?"

"A thing of naming she who was wife to my father but did not my birth-giving."

Yes, of course, they would have to have a name for that.

"It is seldom," he went on, "that there is raiding of Poly. The place has farness, and we must pass the Termans to come to it. There is more danger in such a taking. One raiding in ten, perhaps, is made on them, and even these, betime, are unsuccessful. My brother was killed in a try for such a doing."

In other words, captured Polyan women are scarce.

"My second-mother," he added emphatically, "was more to me than she who did my birthing. I grieved her dying as it was never in me to grieve even the dying of my brother.

"Of Korl, also, of Jamshi and of Chars," he continued, "it is truth that in their smallness there was a Polyan she to the house of the father."

Karel was beginning to see his point.

"A manyness," he smiled, "the times of my second-mother standing in beforeness to me when my father was come to anger, taking pain to herself that it be kept from me, when the punishing was of my deserving."

While your first-mother sat back and did nothing.

"I am come to think on this," he said, "taking of hurt to the self that it be kept from a small one as a thing of a mother."

Or a father, but I'll speak you no "fuckin' morenesses".

"Only when they're little," she said, "sooner or later they have to learn to deal with it themselves."

"Ah," he said, "and teaching the bearing of hurt without flinching is the thing of a father, not?"

"Only one of them," she said, "there are a lot of other things a father..."

"This," he interrupted, "that the curls would do to my son, it would bring him to differentness?"

"It would change him, yes."

"He would have *differentness*," he was insistent, "to all other men."

"I know," she said, "that bothers me, too."

"Differentness is a hardness," he said. "I know the wearing of differentness without flinching, Sky-stone, I can teach it." A thought struck him, and he leaned forward. "It is yet that we are...friends?"

It was hard for him to understand the concept, let alone confess it. He had, as he had said he would, choked on the word.

"Yes, we are, Sang-ser."

"And I will have seeing of my son," he insisted, "when we are in the place of your coming?"

That hurt. The idea that she would even consider depriving him of his son was insulting. He took all this from her face and did not bother waiting for an answer.

"Your deciding," he said quietly, "must be made in the knowing that you have the strength for the years of pain-taking that must be done before he comes to readiness for my teaching."

Years? Yes, he was right, it would be years. But she could also arrange it so that it would be years before the child came back to this planet, and his differentness was brought home to him.

"The curls think," she told him, "that he'll also be able to communicate with me. He'd have that, too."

"This thing," he said, "needs a moreness of thinking. We must come, you and I, in togetherness, to its deciding."

"All right," she said, "we'll talk about it again later."

"So," he said in an entirely different tone, "today marks the beginning of the Time of Changing, eh?"

Karel started. The explanation she had prepared so carefully, and worried over so anxiously had become unnecessary. Sang smiled at her surprise.

"We have spoken muchly on this thing," he said, "and on your saying that his ways have rightness because they are his, and my ways have rightness because they are mine."

"When did you have time to…"

He laughed. "It is you who takes the allness of a day for hunting," he said. "We spoke at the skinning of a kill and in afterness to it. We have learned many things of each other. We have disagreed muchly, but we have tried to think always on the rightness of each other's ways.

"I am not," he went on, "come to any understanding of this everness of changing wives, but he has no understanding that Mari is mine and will not be changed."

The last was stated vehemently.

"But I am come to know this," he said. "To be this that he calls Unchosen in a time when there is but one to make choosing and one to be chosen would have sameness to falling from the plank at a Dancing."

I came here to explain what I'm going to do, and he's trying to talk me into doing it.

"I made helping," he said, "with the cutting of his hair. It needed much explaining for me to understand how it must be done, but I am good with my hands. He is pleased with his 'beautifulness'?"

She nodded.

"When there was a need in me," he said, "you took of your having and gave into the need."

It was both an argument in favor of what he had done and an attempt to convince her that she should…

"He won't be Unchosen, Sang-ser, I'll see to that."

"Soon," he said insistently, "there is much fear in him."

"Today," she agreed, "Right now."

She got up and started to leave, but she stopped in the doorway and turned back to him.

"Do…do you wish it had been different?"

"Only," he said, "that I have yet to learn of living in a house that has no chair, and my teacher goes from me."

"I do," she said, "I wish…"

"The stone is yours," he cut in harshly. "Lend it but take it ever again to yourself."

The stone is mine, she thought, *and I am the stone. Give of myself, you say, but always be myself.* She could do that. Had done it.

"I…I'm going to name the baby Korl."

With that she fled. Not in tears, not even close to them. It was finished, ended, and she had no regrets. She was going to find Tan, lend him the Sky-stone, and someday that, too would be finished.

At least, she thought, this time he won't cry.

###

ABOUT THE AUTHOR

J. Sheldon Jones lives in Colorado Springs. When he is not writing, he spends his time in the mountains with a camera.

www.ingramcontent.com/pod-product-compliance
Lightning Source LLC
LaVergne TN
LVHW051037070526
838201LV00010B/232